Shanta Gokhale was born in Dahanu and brought up in Mumbai. She has worked as a lecturer in English at Elphinstone College and H.R. College of Commerce, as a sub-editor with *Femina*, as a P.R. Executive with Glaxo Laboratories and as arts editor with the *Times of India*. Gokhale has written two novels in Marathi, *Rita Welinkar* and *Tya Varshi*. Both won the Maharashtra State Award for the best novel of the year and have been translated by her into English. She has translated *Smritichitre: The Memoirs of a Spirited Wife* by Lakshmibai Tilak and the novel *Kautik on Embers* (*Dhag*) by Uddhav J. Shelke. Apart from these she has also translated plays by Vijay Tendulkar, Mahesh Elkunchwar, Satish Alekar, G.P. Deshpande, Premanand Gajvi and Makarand Sathe. She has also translated from English into Marathi the play *Mister Behram* by Gieve Patel and the novel *Em and the Big Hoom* by Jerry Pinto. She is the author of *Playwright at the Centre: Marathi Drama from 1843 to the Present;* and the editor of *The Scenes We Made: An Oral History of Experimental Theatre in Mumbai, Satyadev Dubey: A Fifty-Year Journey Through Theatre* and *The Theatre of Veenapani Chawla: Theory, Practice and Performance*. She has been a culture columnist with *The Independent*, *The Sunday Times of India*, *Mid-Day* and *Mumbai Mirror*.

In 2016, she received the Sangeet Natak Akademi Award for her overall contribution to the performing arts. She has also received lifetime achievement awards from Thespo, Ooty Literary Festival and Tata Literature Live!

One Foot *on the* Ground

A Life Told Through the Body

SHANTA GOKHALE

SPEAKING TIGER

Speaking Tiger Books LLP
125 A, Ground Floor Shahpur Jat, Near Asiad Village
New Delhi 110049, India

First published by Speaking Tiger in paperback 2019

ISBN:978-93-88874-85-4
eISBN: 978-93-88874-86-1

10 9 8 7 6 5 4

Typeset in Adobe Garamond Pro by SÜRYA, New Delhi
Printed at Sapra Brother, Noida

For Nirmal

and

In memory of our parents

Contents

0. Why? 1

1. Early Memories 7

2. Tonsils and Adenoids 16

3. Lessons in Anatomy 22

4. Menstruation 28

5. Breasts, Buttocks and a Lisp 38

6. Hair 45

7. Athletics and Dance 49

8. Badminton 60

9. Food 68

10. Home 78

11. The Nose 85

12. Teeth 94

13. Dance Again 98

14. Rag Day Shivers 103

15. Dark-skinned in Gothenburg 110

16. Adipose Tissue and the Mating Game 116
17. The Babies Are Born and How! 128
18. Back to Bombay 144
19. Divorce and Marriage No. 2 161
20. Hair and Heart 170
21. Mother 179
22. Menopause, Eyes, Fibroids and the Arts 182
23. The Body Politic Fractured 195
24. Glaucoma and a Fracture 198
25. Horse Fall 203
26. Full-blown Cancer 208
27. Cataracts 222
28. Time, Space, Work 226
29. And Now the Brain 231
30. Today 242
31. Boots for My Bunions 248

0. Why?

In *Angela's Ashes: A Memoir of a Childhood*, Frank McCourt says in the second paragraph of the first chapter, 'It was of course a miserable childhood: the happy childhood is hardly worth your while.' Leo Tolstoy gets there even before him. He dismisses happy families in the first line of *Anna Karenina*. 'Happy families are all alike,' he writes. 'Every unhappy family is unhappy in its own way.' The line has lived on in people's memories as one of the most striking first lines in a novel. Altogether, there seems to be no getting away from the fact that happy people are uninteresting, possibly even stupid. Despite which I must confess that my childhood was not just happy; it was extraordinarily happy. I am therefore a subject that makes neither a worthwhile memoir nor a great novel. So why am I writing this?

However peremptorily Tolstoy may dismiss the idea, the fact is happy families are not alike at all. One happy story is very different from another. No outsider can decide which is happy and which is not. A woman of my acquaintance has chosen to remain single. She is one of the happiest people I know, hard-working, generous, full of beans and complete in herself. Yet her neighbours see her as someone who has been left on the shelf and is putting on a brave face. When I was working as a sub-editor in the women's magazine, *Femina*, a gentleman came to see me for advice on what career his daughter should choose. Why he came to me is a mystery. Perhaps he was under the impression that a magazine that dished out various kinds of advice to readers in its columns, was likely to be staffed by experts on all aspects of life. A brood of agony aunts in fact going, 'I'd like to assure you first that your problem is not uncommon…' In the course of describing his daughter's qualifications, the gentleman mentioned a quality of her personality that he was proud of and which he thought would impress me too. 'She is so modest that she has never raised her eyes to look at a man,' he said. 'Poor unhappy creature,' I thought. But who was I to think that? Perhaps her happiness lay in making her father happy. I asked around the office for reliable career counsellors' phone numbers and handed him the list. It struck me then that twenty years before this girl was even born, we sisters, Nirmal and I, had been going around town with eyes boldly raised, looking at everything there was to see, including men if they came into sight. Ours was an unusual kind of happiness in a culture where women who looked only at the road beneath their feet when they walked were most valued. In the great Indian battle between tradition and modernity that was playing out then, modernity had the upper hand as an aspirational value. Today the battle has continued with tradition, or what's constructed as tradition, inching ahead. When tradition rules, women's lives are more radically affected than men's. Happily for Nirmal and me, our parents had positioned themselves firmly on the side of modernity. Which meant we respected all human beings and rejected every barrier to equality, whether of religion, caste or gender. We were also brought up to understand and respect our bodies as much as our minds. We had to eat a balanced diet and play games. Even during examinations, Father would order us out in the evening. 'No sitting at home cramming. Fresh air, fresh body, fresh mind.'

Last year I came upon something interesting in Siddhartha Mukherjee's *The Gene*. It appears Queen Victoria, once Empress of half the world, was a carrier of the gene that caused Haemophilia B. Women were carriers of the gene and male descendants the victims. Victoria passed the gene on to her daughter Alice, Alice in turn to Alexandra the tsarina of Russia, and she to her son Alexei who became a victim of haemophilia. The sickly child was just shy of fourteen when the entire family was assassinated by the Bolsheviks. A gene that had crossed continents was fascinating enough. But what held my attention even more was the irony, as the author put it, of 'the disjunction between the prince's all-too-human genetic condition and his all-too-exalted political inheritance.' Our all-too-human condition is the gift of the body we inherit. Hamlet realizes that the court jester Yorick and the great emperors Alexander and Caesar are all undifferentiated dust. However high the flights of the mind or of ambition, it is ultimately the body that allows or disallows them. Athletes have a proper sense of this. After his eighth Wimbledon win, Roger Federer said, 'Again and again I am grateful my body has cooperated.' He was thirty-six, which is supposedly ancient for tennis. It is vital then to accept the body in all its beauty, mystery and power; to know that the images we build of ourselves might one day be rudely shattered by its exigencies.

Post cancer surgery, my mother was being fed through a tube. Two things mortified her deeply. One, that the doctor kept noting whether or not she was passing gas. This was a bodily function that she, like everybody else in polite society, was used to pretending did not happen. To have it so blatantly brought to public notice—the public being the group of students who always accompanied the doctor—was an unforgiveable breach of social behaviour. Two, she was taken in a wheelchair for tests with the feeding tube still attached. 'Why don't they remove this nose ornament when they take me out,' she fumed. It hurt her sense of personal dignity to leave her room with that ludicrous object hanging from her nose. Mother believed in mind over matter. The body does what you train it to do. The body cannot be permitted independent decision-making. Nor was it to be mollycoddled. When she napped in the afternoon, she called it resting her back. She never admitted even to herself that a human body that was up from the crack of dawn, stretching itself to the maximum to look after home and family while simultaneously trying to fulfil personal ambitions, needed a short rest in the middle of the day. Similarly, she never fully accepted the fact that she had cancer. All those who ask 'Why me', suffer from the delusion that they are endowed with specially blessed bodies unlike other people's. Tolstoy writes in *The Death of Ivan Ilyich*: '...the mere death of a near acquaintance aroused, as usual, in all who heard of it, the complacent feeling that it is he who is dead and not I.'

Father had a more robust sense of the body. Lying in hospital after a massive heart attack that finally took him, he did not say 'Why me?' Instead, every time a train arrived at the nearby station heralded by a clanging bell, he would say, 'The bell tolls for me.' The question is, how do you come to a rational view of the body that allows you not to be afraid of it while being aware that its workings are ultimately beyond your control.

One day, when I was surfing the net, I came across Thanissaro Bhikkhu's *Contemplation of the Body*. Thanissaro Bhikkhu, I discovered, was an American Buddhist monk. I read through his advice aimed at those who aspired to escape from the sufferings of samsara—the worldly coil. I have never been spiritually inclined. So I had no such aspirations. But reading what the bhikkhu had to say, I realized here was an idea I could use to tell my story. I was being told to look at the body organ by organ, accepting it for what it was. The end to which this was meant to lead was not the end I was interested in. I did not want to contemplate the body in order to detach myself from it. I would never want to do that. I loved my body too much for what it had given me and for what it had not. However, the idea of looking at the body and its life not as incidental to mine but central to it, excited me.

Thanissaro Bhikkhu is perhaps the most recent of the stimuli that have gathered and cohered in my mind to give form to my story. I have never looked at myself through the prism of my body. To look at it now, one organ at a time, remembering the circumstances that forced it upon my attention in the course of my seventy-eight-year-old life, promises to be a heuristic exercise leading to another kind of self-knowledge than the one we normally aspire to. In the process of putting my body out there in plain view, I will also be keeping faith with my belief in transparency. We do not talk openly about our sexual organs. We are horrified by nudity. Disease is to be kept a dark secret. The poet Jayadeva wrote lyrically about Radha's voluptuous breasts. But then he was a poet. Akka Mahadevi is said to have gone unclothed in search of Lord Shiva. But then she was a saint. Saints never fell ill. When they died it was not of disease but of choice.

Their death was called samadhi, a metaphor. Susan Sontag says in 'Illness as Metaphor' that 'the most truthful way of regarding illness...is one most purified of, most resistant to, metaphoric thinking.' The body is the ultimate truth. You can falsify your thoughts, your feelings, your knowledge. But your body, however surgically falsified its appearance may be today, is still prone to disease.

There is also a purely writerly reason for telling my story through the events of the body. It gives me a readymade structure, a spine around which to build the narrative. I am not going to be stumped by that dreaded question, where do I begin. I will begin at the beginning. Birth!

1. Early Memories

It was the afternoon of 13 August 1939 when Indira Gokhale, born Yamuna Behere, aged twenty-six—seen in family photographs as dark and thin with long silky black hair—was taken in a tonga to Cottage Hospital, Dahanu, to have her first baby. Her husband, Gopal Gundo Gokhale, was in Patna, finding his feet as a journalist. Dahanu was then an almost-town, two-and-a-half hours by train from Bombay, touching the border of what was later to become Gujarat State but was still part of Bombay Presidency. It was a seaside place of chiku orchards owned by Iranis and a long, wide pristine beach backed by a stand of casuarina trees known locally as suru. I have no idea who took Indira to the hospital. It must have been one of her uncles who lived with their wives and children under the benevolent gaze of her father, Narayan (Nana) Gangadhar Behere, the eldest brother. Nana was only a matriculate, but endowed with an innovative brain. He was a Gandhian and manufactured rice mills.

Indira was a tough woman. She had grown up without the protective love of a mother. Hers had died in the great influenza epidemic of 1918, when Indira was five and her brother Ghanashyam two-and-a-half. Her father's mother took care of the children. Later Nana married Lakshmi Ghanekar who was only thirteen at the time. Known as Mothi Kaku (eldest aunt), she gave Nana thirteen children in quick succession, two of whom died. I do not know how painful Indira's journey by tonga from home to hospital was. It is not one of the many stories she was to tell me about her life in later years. What she did tell me was that the labour was hard and seemingly never-ending. I came on a Sunday morning. Dr Nikki, the American missionary at Cottage Hospital, had just returned from church. By then Mother had spent twelve hours trying to eject me. She was exhausted. There was just about one last push left in her. The good doctor knelt by her bed and prayed. I popped out. Whoever was responsible for that emergence, whether divine agency or a woman's determination, Mother could not stop laughing in gratitude. The doctor said it was a girl. Mother said, 'Does she have all ten fingers and toes?' The good doctor counted them off. All ten present. The doctor said, 'She's going to be a philosopher.' Mother asked weakly, 'Why?' The doctor said, 'She has put her hand to her forehead and is refusing to bawl.' The doctor turned me upside down and slapped my bottom. Philosophy fled. A lusty bawl filled the air. I had arrived.

But about the toes and fingers. There was, and probably still is, a superstition that says a pregnant woman who is outdoors during an eclipse will produce a deformed child. Mother, like her father and mine, was a rationalist. There was an eclipse during her last trimester. She had come down to Dahanu from Patna where Father was working as a sub-editor on the staff of a newspaper owned by the Maharaja of Darbhanga, *The Indian Nation*. She happened to have washed her hair that day and was sitting out in the yard to dry it, when half-a-dozen aunts descended on her to shoo her in. The eclipse, they cried. Go in. Mother said, so what if it's an eclipse, and stayed put till her hair had dried. But somewhere in the remote recesses of her mind lurked a smidgeon of doubt. It was all very well to stubbornly refuse to follow Pascal's ultimate play-safe wager. But even then, what if…? With my emergence, fully fingered and toed, she was relieved that rationalism had won.

I was a healthy baby and Mother had plenty of milk to nurse me. As a matter of fact she had so much, she even nursed my aunt who had arrived seventeen days before me. This was Nana's eleventh surviving child. Relationships got pretty muddled in joint families those days with everybody who could breed, breeding. Whatever age a child, certain relationships demanded respect. The eldest son's wife had to refer to his baby sister respectfully as Vansa. She might then be heard exclaiming, 'Agabai Vansa mutlya' (Oh my! Respected sister-in-law has peed). There is a picture in the family album of me carrying an uncle on my hip.

Father was an enthusiastic picture-taker. I call him that rather than photographer because he was not into finding the right light to frame and compose a moment. He just liked taking pictures. So there are pictures in the family album which are underlit and there are those that are overlit. But there are also some which are perfectly lit. There's a picture of me in which I am sitting on the floor, head drooping from a thin neck grown too weak to hold up its weight. This was when my first tooth was coming out. I had lost the urge to eat. All I did was shit; and all Mother did was wash. Her comrade-in-arms was Unilever's 501 bar soap. In those 'Glaxo builds bonny babies' days, I had been bonny on Mother's abundant milk. But my first tooth had reduced me to a boney baby.

Teeth were to play a big part in the story of my body. My milk teeth had begun to shake. The girls and boys I played street games with were shedding theirs without a fuss. My bête noire Ravi Deshmukh from across the street, who would turn up his eyelids to scare me, scared me even more once by giving his shaking tooth a hefty tug and laying the discard on the palm of his hand under my nose. My teeth shook but stayed put. One lower molar in particular was so recalcitrant that the permanent tooth lost patience and emerged to double park itself behind it. Dr Vitthal Palekar, a family friend and a Licentiate of the College of Physicians and Surgeons (LCPS), was assigned the job of pulling out the molar. The operation was traumatic, as much for me as for the doctor and Father who had taken me to his clinic. The doctor sat me on the examination table, sprayed my forearm with topical anaesthesia to demonstrate how it numbed the part and prevented pain, dabbed it on my gum and approached me with an injection. I created mayhem. I have no memory (I have probably erased it) of how Dr Palekar and Father managed between them to put that injection into me and pull that molar out. But when I examined the gap later, I realized the permanent tooth was lying half supine behind it at a 45-degree angle. It was not going to be much use in the chewing and grinding business. We might as well have let its predecessor fall in its own time.

I made no fuss with small-pox inoculations administered by middle-aged men who sat between our house and the next on chairs provided by the residents. They came with boxes full of vials and little knives. They lined up the neighbourhood children in an orderly queue. The children held out their forearms. The men dabbed three dots of vaccine on them, made three quick deep nicks with a knife and that was that.

An injection was different. You watched with a thudding heart as the needle went into the rubber top of the vial, as the vial was held up to the light, as the plunger sucked up the liquid and as the syringe advanced towards you. Naturally you ran. Imagination does make cowards of us all.

I have another injection story. The chief protagonist of this story is Dr Jaywant. His clinic stood at the corner of the street we lived on, then called Bhandarwada Road. Later, when its demographic changed from toddy-tapping Bhandaris to bank-employed file-pushers, it was renamed S.H. Parelkar Marg. I had a fever, a common occurence which called for nothing more than a bottle of the sickly aniseed smelling syrup that the doctor's compounder concocted for you. Perhaps my temperature had risen to a degree that made Mother fearful and she had called Dr Jaywant in. Just to take a look, she told me. But you could never be sure with him. I had experienced his treatment once before. He did not have gentle hands. Someone had thrown a stone through the window of the train we were travelling on from Neral after a fun visit to Matheran. Sitting at the window, it had caught me just above the left eyebrow. The blood streamed freely despite the handkerchief with which Mother had attempted to staunch the flow. We rushed from the station to Dr Jaywant's. He dabbed some iodine on the wound, stuck a strip of plaster over it and said gruffly, 'Come back next week.' When I returned, he pulled the plaster off in one violent move, taking with it, as I thought then, much of my skin. I still retain a memory of the sound it made as it came off: Phrrrsh. But the skin was intact. The wound soon healed, leaving behind a small scar that came in handy years later when I was applying for my first passport and had to fill a column that said identification mark. Scar over left eyebrow, I wrote. Somewhere down the line the scar faded and passport requirements changed. In my next passport my identification was a photograph in which I looked like I had just seen a ghost.

To return to my fever, Dr Jaywant looked at me, looked at my tongue, felt my pulse, stethoscoped my chest and said I needed an injection. I said nothing. But the moment he turned away to fill his syringe, I leapt out of bed and ran. Dr Jaywant ran behind me followed by Mother shouting, 'Nothing will happen, just a pinch, like an ant bite.'

Our flat is on the first floor of Lalit Estate. It has more doors and windows than walls. The master bedroom, a misnomer, because it is the only bedroom in the flat, but which I call the master bedroom because it is spacious and my parents slept there, has three doors. One door gives on the kitchen-cum-dining room, one on the living room and one on the verandah. The living room out of which Father later carved out a bedroom-cum-study for Nirmal and me with the aid of a floor-to-ceiling wall of bookshelves, also has three doors. One leads to the kitchen and the remaining two—don't ask me why two—lead to the verandah. When Father turned the larger part of the living room into our bedroom-study, he converted the verandah into a living room, covering its front with plywood shutters that could be opened and closed. The kitchen has another door besides the two that connect it to the master bedroom and the living room. This one gives on the bathroom. The toilet which has three doors lies off the living room. One door gives on the landing from where the sweeper is supposed to enter to clean the toilet. This convenience is for flat owners who do not wish to have sweepers enter the living room. In our house this door is kept locked. Our sweeper enters the toilet through the living room door. Between this door and the one that opens on the toilet itself, lies a space measuring 4 feet by 4 feet. This is made for sweepers to step in from the landing. But with our landing door locked, it serves no real purpose.

Given this general design of the house, it was possible for me to dodge around through the kitchen into the verandah into the living room into the verandah into the bedroom into...but you get the picture. Now put into this picture Dr Jaywant who was chasing me. He stood about 5 feet 6 inches tall in his bare feet, and measured roughly the same in girth. The bush shirts he wore failed to make it all the way round him so he did not attempt to force their last buttons into their corresponding buttonholes. His trousers too didn't make it round him. They curved under his belly leaving a triangular gap of hairy skin showing between the trouser belt and the open end of the shirt. Dr Jaywant was light-skinned. Running behind little girls with a syringe brought him out in a red-hot flush that began at the bottom of his throat and rose upwards over his three jiggling chins onto his face which ultimately took on the appearance of a beetroot.

I, on the other hand, was dark and thin with spindly legs and a single chin. On the morning of the great injection chase, I was also a little weak with the fever. While the two of us, patient and doctor, went round the house thus, a nasty possibility occurred to me. Might Dr Jaywant not, at some point, halt in his tracks while my frenzy drove me round a corner straight into his syringe-holding hand? It happened in Laurel and Hardy films where the duo used the strategy to hoodwink cops. Like me, Dr Jaywant too would have drawn life's lessons from those films. Doing some quick thinking, I stopped zipping around the house and zipped straight into the bathroom instead, bolting the door firmly from inside.

Dr Jaywant came to a halt outside, huffing and puffing. I pictured him as the big bad wolf who would finally go away. I pricked my ears for his goodbyes. Instead, there was silence. And then the scrape of a chair. And then Mother asking, 'Shall I make you some tea, Doctor?' And he saying, 'Yes. Make it strong. And tell your daughter I'm not moving till I put what's in this syringe into her.'

I admitted defeat. Hoping tea would have put Dr Jaywant in a mellow mood, I came out of the bathroom sheepish and full of dread. He yanked me forward and plunged the needle into my arm. I felt every drop of that liquid course through my veins. The following morning my fever had come down. Mother thought it was the effect of the injection. But it could have been the sheer fear of a repeat performance.

I stopped fussing over injections after Sadhana Moghe died. Sadhana and I became close friends when we were about eight. For two years we sat together on the same bench, shared our tiffin lunches and visited each other's homes. Sadhana lived on the other side of Shivaji Park from us with her brother Ashok who was a couple of years senior to us at school, and her warm, friendly parents. Sadhana was dark and thin, very much like me, but shorter. Her hair, which she wore in two tight braids, was wavy and she had a mole on her upper lip. When she spoke and laughed, her voice tinkled like a bell and her large, liquid black eyes glinted with mischief.

One day Sadhana stopped coming to school. I walked over to her house to find out why. Sadhana's mother said she had a touch of fever but she would soon be back. A fortnight went by and the promised soon did not come. I went over to find out why. Sadhana was sitting up in bed, looking weak but still asking brightly about school. This time her mother did not say she would be back soon. In fact, her mother said nothing. Only smiled wanly. I saw Sadhana take an injection without a sound.

After that I felt I had to go and see her as often as I could. Each time I went, Sadhana looked weaker. Her skin had darkened and her stomach was distended. One evening I found her lying in bed, eyes closed. Her arms were like sticks. Her stomach had swollen to an enormous size. Seeing the shock on my face, her mother took me aside and said, she had water in her stomach and she would be fine after the doctor removed it. How would he remove it? He would drain it out with a needle. Wouldn't it pain? Sadhana's mother smiled and said Sadhana is a brave girl.

A few days later Sadhana died. Mother gave me the news in a soft, sad voice. 'But only old people die,' I protested. I do not remember crying at Sadhana's death. Death was a state I could not comprehend. I understood it only as a dear friend never coming back to school again.

2. Tonsils and Adenoids

Tonsils are two small masses of lymphoid tissue in the throat, one on each side of the root of the tongue. They are fixed appendages. If you open your mouth wide enough before a mirror, you will see them—two pink bulges flanking the uvula. You might consider calling the uvula your throat dangler or your throat thingy if you don't want to call it vulva by mistake. Just a suggestion. Because whenever I need to talk about the uvula, I have to stop myself from saying vulva. My grandsons, Shouryaman and Satyendra, used to call it lalala. Shanti, the big-eyed little girl who lures Mowgli away to the Man Village in an animated version of *Jungle Book* which they loved watching when they were five and seven, sings a song, at one point in which she opens her mouth wide and trills lalala. That's when her uvula shows. The first time the boys saw it, they asked what is that? We said uvula. Naturally the boys called it lalala.

Adenoids, also known as pharyngeal tonsils or nasopharyngeal tonsils, are masses of lymphatic tissue located behind the nasal cavity where the nose leads into the throat. There is one adenoid to two tonsils per person. Unlike tonsils, however, as wide as you might open your mouth before a mirror, you will not see an adenoid. To believe in the existence of adenoids thus becomes a matter of faith, just as you believe in other vestigial parts of the anatomy like appendices and tailbones which serve no apparent function but still exist.

I was six (or was it seven?), when I heard my parents discussing my tonsils. I was not so possessive of my body then as to demand to be included in the discussion. But when it was decided that my tonsils would have to come out, I was agitated. There would be injections and I was damned if I was going to allow any needle in a syringe to get within pricking distance of me. There will be no injections I was told soothingly. I would be put to sleep gently and feel nothing thereafter. And when everything was over, I would be given ice cream. That sounded like a good deal. Two globules of flesh out. Two scoops of ice cream in. But I was nervous all the same.

I'd been reading *Alice's Adventures in Wonderland*. It had scared the knickers off me. I couldn't stomach the idea of a girl drinking something and growing into a giantess and drinking or eating something else and being reduced to a dwarf. I particularly couldn't stomach the Queen of Hearts who had 'only one way of settling all difficulties, great or small. "Off with his head!" she said, without even looking round.' John Tenniel's picture of the queen in my copy of Alice, which I still cherish, showed her exactly as I would have imagined her—bulldog face and a crown on the head, surely a cover-up for horns. Somewhere at the back of my mind I visualized the tonsils surgeon as her male counterpart, his only way of settling all difficulties being: 'Off with her tonsils'. In my worst moments before the surgery I saw him coming at me with an axe. To myself I said, I won't allow it. I also made covert inquiries amongst my friends about their tonsils. One friend declared proudly that she had already had hers out. Other friends looked envious.

Tonsils were not the only bits of tissue that were frequently discussed at our dining table in those days. Adenoids also put in an appearance. The dining table was the only place where the family foregathered at the end of day and thus the only place where serious issues about tissues could be discussed. Certain subjects were forbidden from being mentioned at the dining table. They were to do with human outpourings which often formed part of the jokes we told. But apparently it was okay to speak of violence planned against sundry body parts. The plan, as far as I could make out, was for me to have my tonsils out, and my sister Nirmal to have her adenoid out. This was presumably in order to keep a fair balance between us, so neither thought the other was being favoured. Getting children's tonsils and adenoids out seemed to have been considered a vital part of parental duties in those days. Why do we have them at all was a natural question to ask if they are to be carved out later. To prevent infections we were told. So will we get infections when they are taken out, we asked. No, was the answer. So they don't prevent infections? They do. So we'll get infections when...

That was my first time on an operating table. The table was high and, I am sure, covered in brown rexine. I was to wonder later if someone somewhere had a patent on these tables, unless only the ones I was regularly anaesthetized on were covered in brown rexine while other people got to go senseless on primrose yellow or rose pink. I am prepared to admit of course that believing every operation table I lay on was covered in brown rexine was just my way of expressing resentment against the procedures themselves. Or I might go even further and admit that it could be a symptom of a mild persecution complex. Anyway, there I was on this brown rexine-covered table and, without much warning, a mask was clamped on my nose and I was ordered to count. I went one, two, three, ffourr, fiiii and pouf, I was out for the count. This was the first and last time I was chloroformed. Later I only saw chloroform as the mugger's weapon of choice in films. Man walks up to victim from behind, covers her nose with a handkerchief soaked in the stuff and pouf! she's out, leaving her handbag and all else to the man's ministrations. Not everybody in cinema halls could have shared a real-life body memory with the happenings on screen. I used to feel pretty special to KNOW the smell the victim was smelling and the pouf moment which she would soon experience.

When I came to, I found myself on a white-sheeted bed in a tiny resting room, feeling a stretched pain in the throat and the semblance of a viscous gargle gurgling around in it when I swallowed. The gargle tasted of iron; so it must have been blood. Whatever it was, it would neither come up to be spat out nor go down to be digested. It just stayed put, rolling around in the throat. I have a very strong body memory of that. A while later my tonsils were brought out in a white enamel kidney tray rimmed in ultramarine. I guess my journalist father had to see everything with his own eyes before believing it. He was thrilled with the sight. 'See? They're out. It was nothing,' he said, holding the tray before me. There they were, two bloodied blobs of pink, once attached to me, now lying detached in the tray as though we had never been together. I felt no emotional pain at the severance, just the raw physical pain in the throat and the annoying gargle. I stared at the tonsils dispassionately, their power to do harm now neutralized. But meanwhile I wondered when the talk would turn to ice cream.

Finally, Father said, as he returned the kidney tray to the hovering nurse, 'So what will you have?'

'One scoop of vanilla and one of rose.'

The ice cream was good. But it was not a patch on the vanilla and rose at Azad Ice-Cream House on Ranade Road where all our treats happened. It was not so much the quality of the ice cream as the manner of serving it that made the difference. This ice cream was a square slab that came on a plate. When you think ice cream you think scoops. At Azad, the vanilla and rose came in scoops in a wide-bodied glass goblet and was eaten with a shallow, square-bowled steel spoon. You could not eat rice or curry with that spoon. It was meant exclusively for ice creams and added enormously to the unique aesthetics of the experience. The sensuous experiences of childhood remain most vividly alive in later life, causing you to say things like, 'Ice cream isn't as creamy or mangoes are not as sweet or the mogra doesn't smell as heady as back then.' I know that I have never eaten potato wafers as crisp and delicious as the ones we got in Kohinoor Cinema located on the third lap of Ranade Road just before you got to Dadar station. One went to the cinema not only to see *Tanaji Malusare* or *Ramshastri*. One went for the interval when thin young men came around popping the marbles stopping the necks of lemonade bottles, and crackling square packets of wafers before you. We were given money for wafers, not for lemonade. Reason? Adult prejudices. But we did not complain. Those wafers were small and crisp and full of real potato flavour. They also left you with salty, oily fingers that you could lick through the rest of the film.

Minus tonsils I did not get more infections than I had done with them in. So I suppose their usefulness was not critical. But for some reason Nirmal's adenoid stayed. Perhaps because there was some danger, going by such statistics as were available, that its removal would cause her to speak nasally. That's not something you want to do to your child. So there it was. You lost your tonsils, you got ice cream. You got to keep your adenoid, you didn't get ice cream. Life is basically pretty fair.

3. Lessons in Anatomy

When I was eight, Govind Ramji Chavan of Chiplun, Ratnagiri district, an excellent live-in domestic and otherwise a good and responsible young man, held me close to him and rubbed himself on my behind. I knew this wasn't a game because I wasn't being asked to participate, and it ended within a minute of beginning. Govind Ramji Chavan trotted off, back to his work. I was about to trot off to the book I was reading, when I saw a blob on the tiled floor of the room. 'Govind,' I called out. 'See what you dropped.' Govind hastened to the room, took a look at the blob, said, 'Oh that? It's nothing,' wiped it with a rag and threw the rag away.

A year later, we hired a cook called Sathe to help Mother during her college Intermediate exams. Sathe was in his sixties. He was bald except for a monk's fringe around the back of his head. He wore a dhoti that had once been white. He squatted on top of the cooking counter when he cooked, looking for all the world like an aged, displaced monkey. Throughout the few months he was with us, his white stubble neither grew nor disappeared. I often wondered how it stayed the same, defeating natural processes.

Once he had cooked and eaten his own lunch, he snoozed in the corner of the verandah. That day, I had come back from school at four. Mother was to return from college a little later.

Nirmal had had a quick glass of milk and run off to play. What happened then needs to be contextualized.

I was addicted to stories. My uncles in Dahanu told stories that were so long we fell asleep before they reached their middles. Vasu Mama told a hilarious tale about the ogress Hidimba, made up with a cast of extra characters. In Bombay there was nobody to tell me stories. Mother was too busy. But there was a man who came around selling date ice-candies. She had been fascinated by his street call and his choice of fruit for candies. She visited the place where he made them, found it was sparkling clean, also found that he boiled the water for the candies and so engaged him to deliver one candy a week for me and one for my friend Chamraj (official name Beliappa) who lived across the street. He had tasted mine once and liked it. Mother also discovered that the candy-seller could tell a good story: he had kept her engaged one delivery day with a long-drawn-out tale about the man from whom he had learned ice-candy making. She asked him if he could tell a story along with selling his candy. He thought it was a fun way of making extra money. Those were wonderful days when he sat on the doorstep and told me stories. I remember one about a man whose wife threw him out of the house for not earning a paisa, giving him a bundle of stale rice to carry. Some tree fairies ate up his stale rice while he slept and gave him four empty bowls in exchange. The bowls produced food on demand served by a bevy of beautiful women. I remember the story particularly because of how long the ice-candy man took to describe the women's beauty. I don't remember much else except that a greedy king also slept under the same tree and got in return for his rich food four bowls which produced wrestlers instead of beautiful women.

One day the ice-candy man disappeared. There were no more candies and no more stories.

Many months later when Sathe had been sacked and Kaku came to cook, she told me nostalgic stories about her village Gulsunde, located somewhere in Panvel taluka in Raigarh district on the banks of a pretty stream. Her husband had thrown her out of her home after practically breaking her back with a stick. She had no children. Was this the reason? The beating had left her with a permanently bent back, a deeply furrowed brow and a mouth that turned down. She sang to us a song that she herself had composed in which her grief over being forced out of her home was mixed with the pleasure of being able to sing about it. I remember only the first line of the song. 'Gulsunde gav amuche kharokhara nandanvana shobhale' (Our village of Gulsunde is truly a divine garden of pleasure on earth).

One Sunday afternoon—perhaps she had eaten too much lunch—she made the mistake of starting a story before her siesta and fell asleep halfway through. I waited for a few minutes to see if she would wake up and continue. Then I called her loudly. Then I shook her hard. Then I pulled her hair. She screamed, her eyes flew open and stayed open till she had completed the story. I have to say here in self-defence that I was not normally given to violence. In fact, violence disturbed me deeply. But people had to be responsible towards the stories they told. This feeling was obviously so deeply embedded in my gut that a half-told story turned me into a creature of pure instinct.

That afternoon Sathe said from his corner in the verandah, 'Come here girl, I'll tell you a story.' I ran to his corner at once and sat down beside him. He began telling me a story which

I thought was quite stupid. He was no storyteller. He wasn't attending to the finer details of people, places and events. That upset me. He was bald so I had no means of protesting. But meanwhile his fingers were snaking into my knickers and hurting me. 'Govind,' I called out, getting up. 'Shush shush,' said Sathe. 'Govind, Sathe is hurting me.' Govind rushed to the verandah, realized what had happened and called my mother at the college. As a journalist, Father had a phone. Ours was the only house on the street that had one. It served the communication needs of the entire neighbourhood, including the singer Mukesh's beautiful wife who often came to call, her alabaster skin glowing, her thick light brown hair swinging in a braid down her back. When a call came for people across the road, we would clap and they would come. It was easy then for Govind to call the college office and ask to talk to Mother. Govind told her what had happened. Mother took the first train home from Marine Lines where her college, Shreemati Nathibai Damodar Thackersey University for women, was located. Practically running home from Dadar station, she asked me what had happened; then told Govind to pick up every scrap of Sathe's belongings and throw them out with him. Sathe went away crying and pleading, 'I didn't do anything.' Mother said, 'That's why we don't need you.'

It was probably in the same year a few months later when an uncle (not to be named), who had been transferred to Bombay, came to stay with us. One day I pushed open the door of the toilet thinking it was unoccupied, and discovered him squatting over the pot, his face puckered with excessive straining. But it wasn't the face I was looking at. It was the thing dangling underneath. Even as he shouted, 'Shut the door idiot' (Me idiot? *You* didn't bolt the door properly, right?), I had got an eyeful of his wrinkled appendage. I shut the door quickly and pondered over what I had seen. Nirmal and I didn't have a brother. So the male anatomy was a dark continent for us. It now turned out to be a weird continent.

A couple of years later, I saw a sadhu in a saffron kurta and lungi leaning against a wall behind the bus stop where I was waiting for the 'F' route bus to take me to Scottish Orphanage Society's High School, Mahim. I was probably in Standard Seven then. The bus stop was right outside the lane that led to Mr Bal Thackeray's house. Balasaheb was nowhere on the political scene then. He was a cartoonist with the *Free Press Journal.* His father Prabodhankar Thackeray, so named after the fortnightly magazine *Prabodhan* which he edited, often stood at the mouth of the lane, looking around with what I thought was a bitter expression. He wasn't there that morning. But leaning casually against a wall beside the lane, was this sadhu smoking something and grinning from ear to ear. The grin annoyed me because I didn't think there was anything to grin about, especially since my bus was late. So I was giving him a dirty look when, just before I turned away, he parted his lungi, popped out his appendage and proceeded to wave it at me. You might wonder why I watched long enough for me to be able to report it now. I did not WATCH. It happened in such a flash—perhaps that's why it's called flashing—that I took time to collect my wits. In those brief seconds I noticed that his appendage looked aggressive whereas my uncle's had seemed harmless, just something he had, not a prize to be waved about.

By then I had also discovered that these appendages were sources of mysterious pleasures. Coming downstairs one evening to go out to play hopscotch with the girls, I had heard murmurs from the bottom of the stairs. Halting mid-step I had peeped over the banister and seen a neighbour (not to be named) with an unknown boy, both fiddling with each other's appendages. Something about their expressions made me sit down on the step, quiet as a mouse, till their noises stopped and I heard footsteps running out. Then I got up and went out to play.

When I was twelve, I read the unabridged *Arabian Nights* from Father's library. It was full of those mysterious pleasures between men and women. Two years later I read James Baldwin's *Giovanni's Room* and discovered that men and men shared similar pleasures. But before that, came age eleven. Age eleven was when I started my periods.

4. Menstruation

Mother had been taken out of school in the fifth standard to look after her siblings who had come at the rate of one a year till there were finally eleven living. Two had died. Through it all, she had cherished a burning desire for education. Married to a man who did not think women should be confined to cooking and child-bearing, she sat for her matriculation examination externally after marriage and passed. She then joined the Bombay college of Maharshi Karve's Shreemati Nathibai Damodar Thackersey University for women and graduated with a degree known as GA. GA stood for Gruhitagama. I looked up the word in the dictionary and what I got was a near tautology. GA was defined as a 'degree awarded by a women's university equal to a BA'. The university was soon to rid itself of this strange sounding degree, modifying its curriculum to allow its graduate degree to be accepted as the regular Bachelor of Arts. Of the many liberal arts courses offered at this university, some were aimed at making women efficient home managers and well-informed child raisers. If Mother was an exemplar of what GA did for women, then I owe SNDT college many thanks.

Menstruation happens to every girl, but is not always treated as a natural part of a woman's life, to be understood for its function and dealt with without a fuss. Girls hide the fact that they bleed every month. In the old days and in some communities even now, they had to undergo the Ritushuddhi ritual which told the community that one more woman was now ready to bear children. Mother took the rational path. One day in the spring of 1950, when I was ten-and-a-half, she sat me down in the verandah. The coconut trees in the wadi across the road swayed in the balmy breeze that blew every afternoon from the sea barely ten minutes away from the house. She drew a diagram on a notepad and said that was the female reproductive system. 'Every month, tissue builds up to line this bag called the uterus. The lining is meant to feed an embryo. The embryo is formed by a male sperm meeting a female egg. The sperm is like a little tadpole. Don't ask me right now how it gets to the egg. It does. The egg comes out of this thing here called the ovary. The eggs keep coming regularly. But when there is no sperm around, no embryo is formed. So the tissue that lines the womb is shed and comes out of this passage called the vagina, as blood.' Handing the diagram over to me for further perusal, she said, 'If you see a spot of blood on your panties, tell me, and I'll show you how to deal with it.' Mother also warned me not to blabber to the other girls at school about this because their mothers might not want them to know just yet. But which ten-and-a-half-year-old was going to resist using the power of knowledge over her classmates? I not only told my closest friends at school the very next day, but also showed them Mother's diagram. Some had known through hints that a major change was about to happen to them. But none of them had diagrams to show for it.

Later that year the reproductive system appeared in our hygiene and physiology textbook. When the teacher passed over it in haste, we exchanged secret smiles. The diagram of the digestive system, which appeared in the next lesson, showed the mouth, throat, oesophagus, stomach, small intestine, large intestine and a small triangular bit at the end of it which was unlabelled. One of the boys helpfully filled in the gap. A note was passed around the class in which an arrow beside the tapering end said 'asshole'. Years later I was to become painfully aware of the entire digestive system, every muscle of it, when a glass of obviously polluted water that I had drunk produced the expected result. The family had driven out to see a fig orchard on the Pune–Solapur road. We had stopped off at an eatery on the way back where we were served the dubious-looking water. Mother said wisely, don't drink. Father said, my stomach is lined with iron. Nothing will happen. I said rashly, mine too. Both of us drank the water. Father was fine. I was not. Every inch of my 20-feet long small intestine, and 5-feet long large intestine leading all the way to its unmentionable end, was in spasms. This was a lesson that required no repeating. After the agonizing days that followed, I have been deeply respectful of my digestive system, never allowing my ego to spoil relations between it and me.

In the January of 1951, a drop of blood duly appeared on my panties and Mother gave me a wad of cloth and a jock-strap arrangement to contain what would follow. It wasn't the most comfortable way to spend six days of the month. But there was no alternative till Mother heard of Kotex pads and introduced me to them. Apparently, during World War I, when cotton was in short supply, the American corporation Kimberly-Clark introduced cellulose wadding to replace it in hospitals and first-aid stations for dressing wounds. Army nurses in Britain, thinking as only women can of women's comfort, adapted the wadding for menstrual protection. In 1920, the cellulose wads became sanitary napkins, Kimberly-Clark's first consumer product. From those early days to today's no leaking, no wetness, extra long, extra absorbent, extra all sorts of things, sanitary napkins is a history I would dearly love to follow one of these days. But at the moment I was grateful to British army nurses whose concern had made my leak days so much more comfortable. What did poor women do I wondered, because cellulose was expensive.

'What do poor women do?' I asked Mother.

'I wish I knew,' she said with a sigh.

'And Granny? Does she wear pads?'

Granny wore nine-yard saris with copious pleats in front which were parted to allow the central lot to be yanked up between the legs and tucked tightly into the waist at the back. I couldn't figure out how a belt and napkin could be accommodated in that arrangement.

'Must you know?' Mother asked.

I looked at her. 'Does Granny wear napkins is all I want to know.'

Mother sighed. 'No she does not. There's a lot of cloth that goes between the legs in a nine-yard sari. That's Granny's napkin.'

I felt sorry for Granny. She'd have to sort out all those soiled layers of cloth and wash them every day. No wonder she took so long in the bath some days.

'And Pili Maushi?' I asked. Mother had had enough.

Pili Maushi, mother's fourth sibling, had been struck by polio as a baby. That's how she came to be called Pili instead of her real name Varanasi. We were often told that she had been the best looking of the children. Now she sat on a flat wooden seat in the passage between the kitchen and the store-room, near the steps leading to the bathrooms in the New

House in Dahanu. She wore front-buttoned printed dresses that came down to her calves and read aloud from pothis the whole day, her dribbling mouth twisting over every word. She even told us stories, dragging her words out in an effort to say more than she could. During our summer holidays in Dahanu when everything else was fun and games, her slurred, halting speech, her inability to walk out into the sun and her swaying, bent-kneed gait caused me extreme pain. Then there were days during the month when we were told not to touch her. After I started my periods, I knew what that meant. It meant that, although she was never going to have a baby, tissue lined her womb unfailingly each month and each month ran out of her as blood. For that reason she became 'unclean' and could not be touched. What nonsense. If I could go to school during those days and do everything else I would normally do, why did Pili Maushi become suddenly untouchable? Once I deliberately touched her. She told me off. I touched her again. She called out to Granny. Granny said, 'It's okay. She's from Bombay.' Set apart as an alien being from another planet, I could hug her any day of the month.

All the girls in my class were now leaking regularly. You knew who had her 'chum' (oh cruel euphemism!) when a girl got up from her chair and the one behind looked surreptitiously at the back of her tunic. A lift of the eyebrows meant an immediate visit to the loo. A nod meant all was well.

Those days Sindhu Maushi, my mother's sixth sibling, born a few minutes before her twin brother Sudhakar, was staying with us for her college education. She was slim, built straight from shoulders to feet with no curves in between. The only curve in her body was in the nose. The story went that she had once fallen on her face and broken her nose. It had never healed properly, leaving her with a bump on the bridge that made her look like Julius Caesar in profile. The other notable thing about her nose was that she could touch its tip with the tip of her tongue. Her twin brother Sudhakar, not being identical, couldn't do the tongue-to-nose trick; but he could wiggle his ears without moving any other muscle in the vicinity.

Sindhu Maushi had a temper. She came to Bombay from Dahanu, bag and baggage, after a quarrel with Ghanashyam Narayan Behere or Anna Mama, to whom Nana, King Lear-like, had handed over the running of his rice-mill manufacturing plant lock, stock and barrel. Sindhu Maushi was running a high temperature on the day she arrived. Anna Mama later informed Mother in a long letter, written in his beautiful handwriting, that he would henceforth have nothing to do with Sindhu Maushi. So she was now the exclusive responsibility of Gopal Gundo and Indira Gokhale of Lalit Estate, Bhandarwada Road, Shivaji Park, Dadar. But being their responsibility didn't stop her from losing her temper with them. Father, who delighted in pulling people's legs, once bent curiously over a piece of embroidery she was working on and said, 'Those look like horns, so that must be a bull.' He was referring to the antennae of a purple butterfly she was embroidering in satin stitch on a pink poplin table-cloth for which Mrs Purohit, her embroidery teacher, had congratulated her. Sindhu Maushi's nostrils flared and she didn't speak to Father for a fortnight.

Sindhu Maushi went to SNDT college, following in the footsteps of her older sister Naloo Maushi, who had also stayed with us during her college years, and my mother. I became Sindhu Maushi's tail. I followed her everywhere like Mary's lamb and grew to know and get fond of all her friends, a jolly group of girls no more than a few years older than me. She even took me to her college a couple of times where she introduced me to the canteen manager Ramaswamy who made the world's freshest, crispest sev-puri.

Sindhu Maushi played a competent game of table tennis or ping-pong as she called it. She also played a vigorous game of 'Ring', known semi-formally as ring tennis and formally as tennequoits. Vanita Samaj, of which she became a table tennis member, was a brisk ten-minute walk away from our house towards Dadar beach. In those days it comprised one big hall under a tiled roof surrounded by a verandah with a kitchen attached, where the ever-smiling, gruff-voiced Leelatai Limaye supervised the making of foodstuffs that rendered two sets of social service simultaneously. It gave employment to women who needed it; and it supplied quality-guaranteed flours and eats to the club's middle-class members who did not have time to make them. Years later Vanita Samaj added an indoor badminton court behind the main building and, a few more years later, an auditorium with bad acoustics on the side. The auditorium soon became the desired wedding venue for upwardly mobile Marathi families. On Friday afternoons, Vanita Samaj members were entertained to talks, music, dance, drama, mimicry and magic shows arranged by the club's entertainment committee. On all other evenings, a table-tennis table was set up in the middle of the hall. This is where I went with Sindhu Maushi and learned to play my first indoor game. While I picked up the game pretty quickly, what I most looked forward to was watching the club's champions Ms Angre and Ms More play each other. Their forehand and backhand smashes set the goals I wanted to reach. I played the game with much love and dedication and even reached a point where I could do the Angre-More smashes. But then I discovered badminton which was to become the love of my life. Nirmal took to table-tennis later and, as with every game she played, excelled in it, reaching University and State competition level.

The one thing Sindhu Maushi failed to teach me was mounting a bicycle. Sudhakar Mama, who had joined the Victoria Jubilee Technical Institute for a diploma in automobile engineering, lived in its hostel and spent many Sundays at our house, also tried and failed. I desperately wanted to learn and he could hardly refuse to teach me with Mother's excellent lunch as reward. So he would push the bicycle we hired from Babu Cyclewala's corner shop to Shivaji Park, put me on and watch me go. 'Now try and get on yourself. I'm not going to help,' he would say. I was all eagerness. But the attempt always ended with the cycle and me on the ground. Sudhakar Mama couldn't figure out what my problem was. The problem was that mounting a cycle involved the briefest moment of being ungrounded. You ran beside the machine with your left foot on the nearside pedal; and even before you were sure it was secure, you threw your right leg over the seat to catch the rotating pedal on the other side. So for a fraction of a second, both your feet were ungrounded and you were wobbling. That sent me into a panic. Mother called it my one-foot-on-the-ground syndrome. One foot had to be grounded before I would lift the other. Mother had once dreamt of flying. A dream like that would have been my nightmare.

The month my periods began, Sindhu Maushi and her friends had organized a picnic to Vihar Lake. I was invited. Vihar Lake, created by damming the Mithi river, was the city's first piped water supply scheme and a very popular picnic spot. Powai and Tansa Lakes came later. The Vihar Lake picnic happened to be on the eleventh day of my period. Mother said don't go. I said but I'm not leaking. Just spotting. It's so little, I'm not even wearing my harness. Mother sighed and said, then go. So off I went with Sindhu Maushi and Shashi Gangal and Kala Kolhatkar and the rest of the group. They were all in saris. I went menstrually unprotected in a pair of cheerful red dungarees and a yellow T-shirt. Mother had made the dungarees and I was very proud of them. By the time we sat down to our picnic lunch, I had begun to feel strangely sticky down there. I whispered my suspicion to Sindhu Maushi. She walked me to a cramped enclosure of corrugated tin sheets and a hole in the ground that served as an improvised toilet for picnickers and asked me to check out the state of things. The state of things was bad. Sindhu Maushi told me to stay put in the 'toilet'. Since there was no roof to the shelter I could peer over the top, which I did. One of Sindhu Maushi's friends whipped out a towel from her copious bag. She was one of those people who carried pills and plasters, cotton thread and needles, clips and pins, empty bottles and boxes even to picnics—'just in case'. Sindhu Maushi handed me the towel over the top of the toilet. I shed my dungarees and undies and wrapped myself in the towel. My dungarees and undies vanished over the top. Another friend carried them to a trickle of water, source unknown, to wash. Meanwhile, other friends of Maushi's made a jock-strap out of handkerchiefs tied together. More handkerchiefs were gathered into a wad. My harness was ready. 'Get into that and come out,' Sindhu Maushi said with a sigh. She was kindness itself. Her friends too behaved as if fitting out young girls with an improvised sanitary harness was routine.

Stepping out of the toilet in my towel and T-shirt, I felt a little like our local narielwala. The only thing missing was the basket of coconuts from which I could pick one out, shake it at my ear to make sure it was full of water, put it on my thigh, shave off the top with a slicing knife, and hand the open fruit with a flourish to eagerly waiting hands. How often had I watched this refined performance with awe. And now I was in the right costume but with no props to make it meaningful.

We didn't do much picnicking after that. My dungarees lay drying on a rock and were ready to wear only when we were ready to leave. Meanwhile Sindhu Maushi and one of her friends sat with me playing paanch-teen-don. I lost as I always did and still do at card games. The others had wandered away to have a good time. We could hear them singing and shouting and laughing. Tricked out in a towel and T-shirt, playing a losing game of paanch-teen-don, I remember thinking it was no fun being a girl. But the takeaway from the picnic was my first precious experience of sisterhood.

5. Breasts, Buttocks and a Lisp

The seventh standard at school was unnerving. I had topped the class till the fifth; so Father decided I needed more competition. He suggested that the school allow me to leapfrog over the sixth and go straight to the seventh. This was known as double promotion. Schools encouraged the practice. Nirmal was also double-promoted from the fourth to the sixth. There were children in Shivaji Park who had been double promoted even twice over and appeared for their matriculation exams at thirteen and fourteen years old. In our school, the sixth standard was where Arithmetic turned into a monster called Maths. Two horns, Algebra and Geometry, were added to a creature that already had a forked tail. I had missed out on the basics of the two new subjects and scrambled to cope. In the struggle, my rank slipped from one to two. A series of tutors came to help me over the hill, failed, and left. None had the skill to hold my attention and to undo the knots in my brain. Finally, one Mr Nagarkar came. He pronounced plus and minus as 'plush' and 'minush' but managed to untie the knots. After that, Algebra and Geometry became friends and Arithmetic lost its sting. Meanwhile I was getting progressively better in English. I discovered I was a natural at parsing and analyzing sentences, writing precis, letters and essays. After prize-distribution days, it was gratifying to come home with books—*Middlemarch*, *Great Expectations*, *Far from the Madding Crowd*—which opened up new worlds to me.

Meanwhile our bodies were blooming in diverse ways. By the time we were halfway through the seventh, all the girls had burgeoning breasts. The glory of those twin globes was compensation for the six red-letter days that besmirched every month of our calendars. It seemed like a mean trick then, that some girls were heavily endowed while others were left with nothing to show. One girl, let's call her LK, belonged to the deprived group. The cheekiest Anglo-Indian boy in class, Clarence Crawford, who wore his hair in a classic quiff, and who later travelled the world to settle down finally in Walthamstow, UK, as a Victorian style portrait painter, had cruelly nicknamed her Manchester.

I regarded myself critically in the bathroom mirror to assess my standing in the breasts race. I was, I told myself brutally, amongst the stragglers. Despite which I persuaded Mother that I needed a bra. Sindhu Maushi was detailed to get me one. In those days of restricted nutrition for girls (not us), any lingerie company that wanted to stay in the bras business had to start at size 28. That was the size Sindhu Maushi decided my first Bridal Form bra should be. Later I graduated to a more respectable almost-32 in Maidenform. This was the brand that advertised itself bizarrely with women confessing to strange dreams. 'I dreamed I was a butterfly in my Maidenform bra,' said one. 'I dreamed I danced the Charleston in my Maidenform bra,' claimed another. And, most presumptuously, a third said, 'I dreamed I had the world on a string in my Maidenform bra.' I dreamed no such dreams in mine. I merely thought very practically of stuffing my larger-than-me Maidenform bra with cottonwool to compensate for lack of natural glandular and fatty tissue. The exercise lasted for a few days of trials in the bathroom. But the idea was finally crushed, quashed and pushed into the wastepaper bin as dishonest and too much bother anyway. Instead, I came to friendly terms with being small.

Being small was infinitely better than being large as I discovered each time I walked from school to the Park Club lane with my friend Mahrukh Irani who lived there. Invariably, a neighbourly neighbour with a newly-broken voice would call out from behind the curtains of an upstairs window, 'Hey bouncing balls.' This was followed by multiple guffaws indicating that the caller was not alone. I'd say, 'Ignore them.' Most times Mahrukh did. But once, her Irani blood boiling, she looked up and shouted, 'Never mind mine. Hope yours are bouncing.'

As against this, all I had to contend with when I walked down to the badminton club, were acne-ridden teens standing at the traffic island at the end of the street calling out 'chakleee' in high falsettos meant to disguise their natural croaks. I need to go back some twelve years to contextualize this. As a two-and-a-half-year-old in nursery school I had insisted on carrying chaklis in my tiffin box every day. Word of my single-minded devotion to the spicy snack had got around and stayed around in the neighbourhood for years afterwards. Back then Shivaji Park was a tight community where everybody knew everybody else, and almost everybody sent their children to Balmohan Vidya Mandir where I sat in the nursery class with my chaklis. During break the nursery class teacher would ask us what we had brought in our tiffin boxes. My answer was always chakli. The hulks who hung around the traffic island and hooted 'chakleeee' as I passed by were my classmates from then. Later one of them added another spicy tidbit to chakli. Bundi. My badminton racquet struck him like the large ladle with which the bundi maker lifts the besan pearls out the boiling oil in his fryer.

Actually, at two-and-a-half, I had no business being in school at all, with or without chaklis. I was admitted to Balmohan's nursery class as a favour. The story goes that I would stand in the verandah weeping silently every day because other children were going to school and I wasn't. There were no playschools in those days and I was too young for the nursery class. Fed up with my tears, Mother finally approached Shivram Dattatray Rege, fondly and respectfully known as Dada Rege, the idealist founder-principal of Balmohan Vidya Mandir and pleaded with him to let me sit in the nursery class as a visiting student. She offered to pay full fees for the favour. Dada Rege loved the idea of a child crying to go to school. He loved children anyway. So he took me in without the fees Mother had offered. I have only one memory of those years at Balmohan. The music teacher, Jogalekar Master, would put me on the teacher's table where he kept his harmonium to sing the songs he taught us. He told Mother I sang tunefully, albeit with a lisp. The 'r' was beyond me. It got converted into 'l' somewhere between the concept and the execution.

At age five, I was taken out of Balmohan and put into Bombay Scottish Orphanage Society's High School, Mahim. A huge debate was on in those days over sending children to English-medium schools. English had an edge over Marathi in the job market. It still does. The medium of instruction at Balmohan was Marathi. So I went to Scottish Orphanage. After Independence, when the Anglo-Indian orphans who had boarded at the school had migrated to the white countries of their choice, the school was renamed Bombay Scottish School.

I was still lisping when I was transferred to the new school. Father had taught us sisters Sanskrit slokas to acquaint us with our culture, but also in the belief that Sanskrit sharpened dull tongues. The time to recite them was in the morning, directly after teeth were brushed and milk was drunk. For me 'Lokabhiramam ranarangadhiram rajeevanetram raghuvansha natham' with its preponderence of 'r's was a source of daily despair, while Nirmal, eighteen months younger, rolled her 'r's with breezy nonchalance.

On my first day at school, Mother requested the teacher, Miss Lely of the enormous behind (glandular trouble I was to discover later), to make sure I wasn't teased for my lisp. I wasn't. Not because my fellows were especially kind, but because I didn't open my mouth throughout lessons. During breaks when we played catch-catch or hide-and-seek, nobody noticed that I was l-ing instead of r-ing.

There is a story about my lisp that Madhav Patwardhan, or Madhav Mama as we called him, told Nirmal and me roughly forty years after it had happened. His sister, the beautiful Sharayu Vahini, was marrying my first cousin, the handsome Vinayak Anant Gokhale or Baban Bhau. I was probably five and Nirmal three when we attended the wedding. Madhav Mama said I was sitting on his lap telling him a long-winded story about a warrior king, in which a sword was flashed at one point. The 'tarwar' naturally became 'talwal' in my story. Nirmal, impatient with the aural offence it caused her, interrupted to correct me. 'Tai, it's not talwal. It's tarwar.'

'I didn't say talwal. I said talwal,' I pointed out.

'Tarrrwarrrr,' Nirmal emphasized.

'Talllwalll,' I shot back. Madhav Mama said this could have gone on forever had he not intervened and said 'tarwar' on my behalf and allowed me to proceed. I overcame my problem at six. But even now, my 'r's do not roll quite as robustly as Nirmal's do.

To return to my anatomy at age twelve, if breasts put me amongst the stragglers in the race, buttocks put me way ahead. Indeed, I was not so much in the lead as running a one-girl race. I was the only girl in class whose pleated tunic stopped falling in neat pleats all the way down because they needed to part at the hips to accommodate me. Mother was an excellent dressmaker. She was famous amongst my classmates for creating dresses that blew their minds. I had a blouse whose sleeves were cascades of frills; a pink satin dress with a posy embroidered on the left side of the chest, but turned inside out to hide the sheen of the satin which Mother disliked; a deep green linen double-flared skirt that swung out straight when I twirled; and of course the ill-treated red dungarees that I wore to Sindhu Maushi's picnic. Yet, with all her inventiveness at the cutting table and sewing machine, Mother failed to find a way to cover the disparity between my 22-inch waist and 36-inch hips when she made my pleated shorts for badminton. As for my tunic, if I tied the girdle around my waist, the pleats parted. If I tied it loosely below the waist to keep the pleats together, I looked like a sack.

Father consoled me with the word, sinhakati, lion waist. That was what Indian beauty was all about he said and quoted me Kalidasa's *Meghadootam* to prove it.

'Tanvi shyama shikhari dashana / Pakwabimbadharoshthi,' he intoned. 'That means dusky of skin with pointed teeth and lips the colour of ripe bimba fruit.'

'Never,' I said. 'Mine? Crooked as they come. And lips? Brown yam.'

'Madhye kshama chakitaharinineprekshana nimnanabhi,' Father persisted, more because he loved the sound of Sanskrit than because he thought he was convincing me. 'That means, thin of waist (well okay), deep of navel (hunh?), with the eyes of a frightened female deer (nonsense).'

'Shronibharat alasagamana stoknamra stanabhya,' he wound up. 'That means one who walks slowly because of her heavy hips, bending forward slightly with the weight of her breasts.' I laughed out loud. 'Heavy hips, yes. But the other thing?' To which he retorted, 'You can't have it all.' That, more than the Sanskrit verse, was worth remembering. You can't have it all.

6. Hair

Father was not indulgent towards women's need to adorn and beautify themselves. Face powder was forbidden. It clogged the pores of the skin. Ornaments were barbaric baubles. We used none. But around fourteen years of age, I had begun to take an unconscionably long time over my hair. Although mine was not as long and thick as my best friend Usha's, it was not as inflexibly straight as hers either. In those days, natural curls or waves were the things to be born with. Both could be turned into ringlets, otherwise known as corkscrew curls. If your hair was not naturally curly, perms were available at fancy hairdressers. Usha's father's sister, Akka Naoroji, used to have her hair waved and tinted blue at the Taj. The non-fancy hairdressers in our neighbourhood only cut hair. Belinda Fernandes down the street had the most perfect corkscrews imaginable. At the other end of the street, the Chitre girls, poet Dilip Chitre's cousins, flaunted bouncy waves. Viju, who married Dilip, had the curliest of the lot. My cousin Vimal Tai, Baban Bhau's sister, who stayed with us for her final year at college, would wash her hair on Sundays and put bobby pins down both sides of the parting to induce waves. Some girls plaited their hair into thin braids at night, expecting to see a perfect perm when they were undone in the morning. What they saw instead was a frizz. Those who could not do any of the above, screwed the tufts at the ends of their pigtails into tight balls securing them with rubber bands. When undone the following morning, they were supposed to spring into ringlets. Usha's came out as straight as a horse's tail. Mine didn't require the screw-up treatment. I only needed to wet and twist the end tufts around my forefinger to create fairly credible corkscrews.

The Pereiras downstairs, aware of my obsession with curls, had given me a Toni home permanent set as a birthday present. 'Which twin has the Toni?' was its tantalizing copyline. However hard you looked at the chubby-cheeked, smiling English twins in the picture, you could not make out whose hair was naturally wavy and whose had been set with Toni. Of course, either both had natural waves or both had had perms, not necessarily with Toni. But it was a beguiling advertisement all the same. For me, the home perm box, with its blue plastic bone-shaped rollers and rubber bands, held the promise of hair that would at least match if not outcurl the Toni twins' locks. But the box lay firmly at the bottom of a small cabinet in my parents' bedroom, only to be looked at and covetously handled but strictly not to be used. The set wasn't just rollers and rubber bands. It was also a bottle of chemical, about which Mother had serious doubts. Suppose I came out in a green frizz or, worse still, went bald?

But the dream of wavy hair persisted and I spent rather longer before the dressing-table mirror trying to coax my hair into waves than Father thought was necessary or good. Watching my hairdressing with growing impatience, he decided one day to take action. He gave orders for the mirror to be covered with a bedsheet morning and evening when I was getting ready to go to school or to Park Club to play table tennis. Govind Ramji Chavan did the needful in his stolid mine-is-not-to-question-why manner. But there were others who questioned the idea. Rohini Patkar, who was the third part of my best friend trio at school, did so rather loudly. 'Gosh,' she screamed in astonishment when she saw the covered mirror. 'Why do you people cover your mirror?' Father overheard her from the verandah and responded equally loudly, 'Because we are idiots.'

Thwarted in my efforts to bring my hair into line with fashion, I finally gave up. My hair was okay. Long and fairly thick. I could do lots of things with it even as it was. At school it had to be braided, hung up like hooks behind the ears with red ribbon bows like identical butterflies (Mother: Shall I get you a tape measure? Maybe one wing is a little longer than the other?); or slung like a hammock above the nape of the neck. On days out, it could be crossed over the top of my head like a tiara. Sindhu Maushi's friend, Shashi Gangal, called it my Ajanta style. At university, I went into saris and my hair into a variety of chignons and buns and French rolls. Nirmal, majoring in Biology at the Indian Institute of Science, called one of my creations—a loose spiral pinned halfway up the back of my head—my foraminifera shell.

In those days brides didn't go to salons to have their hair done. My havan-bound friends turned to me instead. I created complex chignons for them, setting off the coils with flowers and hair ornaments. I responded to hair as a potter might to clay. The length, texture, thickness and weight of it dictated the sculpted forms I created. I will confess here to something I have never admitted even to my closest friends. After my Senior Cambridge exam, in which I got a First (with distinction in Maths!), Father asked me which subject I'd like to read at University. I would have dearly loved to say, 'Actually Daddy, I don't want to go to college. I want to train as a hairdresser.' Instead I chickened out and said, 'I'd love to do History or English Literature.' And English Literature it was.

7. Athletics and Dance

Thirteen was a crucial age for me. I was shooting up. In the next two years I was to achieve my full height of five feet three. It was awkward being suddenly taller than several boys in class who had still not started their growth spurt. I took to stooping and Father took to warning, 'Mind your hunch.' Today, when my stoop is the natural result of age, I still hear his voice and instinctively straighten up.

At thirteen I discovered Wordsworth, courtesy of 'The Solitary Reaper' which figured in our reader along with old gems like Longfellow's 'A Psalm of Life', Tennyson's 'The Charge of the Light Brigade' and Cowper's 'The Solitude of Alexander Selkirk'. I began to look upon every poor, half-naked child as a subject first of attention and sympathy, and then of verse. During a summer vacation at Holiday Home resort in Kodaikanal, I spent afternoons sitting by a stream that gushed past the back of our cottage, filling my notebook with mournful stanzas, all meticulously rhymed, about the poor and the dispossessed. My emotions were genuine. My verses were not. Sensing this, I let myself gently into self-knowledge. I was not to be India's Wordsworth. So I put down my notebook and picked up my table-tennis bat to join the youngsters playing in the resort's recreation section. There I made friends with the cousins A.V. Bharath and Jaykumar and the handsome siblings Gopi and Janaki Menon. One day Gopi fished Nirmal out of the lake. We had gone rowing that afternoon. Back at the jetty, Nirmal decided to leap out before the boat was properly secured and fell into the water between the bobbing boat and the jetty. Gopi, who had jumped off first to help us out, hoisted her up with a boat hook. We lost contact with Gopi after many years of being in touch; but Bharath was to become an important part of my life later.

For the next sixteen years, during which I abandoned table tennis to settle permanently with badminton, I stayed off verse, rhymed or blank. But it returned all of a sudden when I was living in Vishakhapatnam and my marriage was beginning to come apart. It was a time of great emotional stress. I was thirty, and doing again what I had done at thirteen: versifying my feelings. When it comes to feelings, we are not objective. We are too much in them and of them to have a critical perspective. The critic in me had gone temporarily AWOL. I desperately needed someone to tell me to stop navel-gazing and get on with life. Who better for the job than Nissim Ezekiel? Nissim had been our MA Part II lecturer. He had been keen for me to join Jhunjhunwala College where he was head of the English department after my Masters. Instead, I had married Lieutenant-Commander Vijay Kumar Mohan Shahane and disappeared from sight. I knew Nissim always had time for writers who sought his advice. I sent him my poems.

His reply which came by return of post was gentle. He advised me to give up on poetry. It really wasn't up to the mark. But my long covering letter had told him I was a good prose writer. Why not concentrate on that? And why not write in Marathi?

Why indeed. Marathi was my mother tongue. I had read a

lot of literature in it. I spoke it well. Perhaps I could write in it too. Nissim had produced an unlooked for but tantalizing fork in my linguistic road. With him as catalyst, an unexpected creative reaction took place. Ideas for short fiction that I had not known I was incubating, began hatching into life in Marathi. The time was right. The temperature was right. I began writing almost without thinking. Words and phrases that I didn't know I possessed, dropped fluidly from my pen. I had come into possession of a creative language besides English which was just as supple and just as rich. More importantly, it allowed me to say things that I could not say quite as expressively or 'truthfully' in English. The stories I wrote were published in two leading literary magazines.

But I have jumped the gun. Back to chronology, back to school and the discoveries of the body. In the eighth standard, at age fourteen, I won the long jump and the 200 metres sprint in the annual sports day heats, qualifying for the finals for the first time in my school life. I had always watched the finals from the sidelines. Now I was going to be at the centre. I trembled with excitement. I arrived at the long jump pit with a spring in my stride. I made my three regulation jumps. On the starting run before each leap, my eyes would focus on the spot in the distance where I aimed to land. But I landed short each time. My best jump wasn't long enough to put me even on the lowest step of the victory stand. It had measured, I remember clearly, 11 feet and 7 inches. Out of curiosity and also to put myself retrospectively in my place, I checked the Indian women's long jump record a few days ago. On 27 August 2004, Anju Bobby George had jumped 6.83 metres in the Olympics at Athens. That was almost double the length I had jumped and she stood fifth. Renee Thornbur of Yellow

House, endowed with muscular calves, stood at the top of the victory stand that evening. Anyone with even half an eye could have seen she was a winner. She put Yellow House in the lead. Green House, mine, was struggling to be third.

Carrying my heavy heart from the long jump pit to the tracks, I got ready to run the 200 metres sprint. This was the last chance Green House had to save its honour. My fellow Greens sat along the track to cheer me on. The tension at the starting line made me sick in the stomach. I was sure I was going to miss the word 'Go'. The PT teacher Arvind Damle's voice went, 'On your marks, get set, go.' Miraculously, I went. With chest stuck out bravely against the wind and my braids flying, I ran for all I was worth. Halfway through I discovered I was leading the field. It was a moment of sheer exhilaration. Hey, you louts back there. What did you have for breakfast? But the moment soon passed. The louts came thundering behind me and streaked past one by one, the Reds, the Yellows, the Blues. 'Come on. Buck up,' shouted my fellow Greens as though they would blow the air of their lungs into my bellows to move me on. But it was not to be. My calf muscles were turning to wood, my feet to lead. There were just two stragglers behind me now. The rest were within reach of the tape. The stragglers lumbered by as I hobbled painfully to the tape.

I came off the track gasping for breath and laughing at my ridiculous performance, but overjoyed to have run at all. It was not a sentiment shared by my fellow Greens. I had let them down; done them out of the only chance they would have had to shout 'Yellow Yellow, dirty fellow' to the inevitable winners. Not only had I failed Green House; I had shown the supreme idiocy of laughing at my shame. You ran a race to win. Not to have fun.

Usha asked me later what came over me suddenly. She was Yellow House, trying her best not to gloat but to remember that I was her best friend.

'As usual. My stamina and my metatarsals,' I shrugged.

'You mean metacarpals. The bones in your feet.'

'I mean metatarsals. The bones in my feet.'

'Shall we compromise and call them metacarsals?' She was being funny.

'No. They are metatarsals,' I insisted humourlessly. Having lost the race, I wanted to win the argument.

A couple of years later, Nirmal, who had never had problems with either her metatarsals or her stamina, jumped and sprinted her way to the school's Senior Championship.

The limits of my body on the field had announced themselves pretty clearly. If it could not run and leap or even mount a bicycle, it had to be good at something if it was worth having at all. Fortunately for my self-esteem, a couple of years earlier, Mother and a few of her Shivaji Park friends had got together to start a dance class for their daughters. Maharashtra does not have its own classical dance, nor indeed any dance at all other than the lavani which is performed to raunchy songs by professional tamasha artists. So Marathi girls do not inherit dance, not even osmotically, as Tamil girls do. In those early post-Independence years, we had barely heard of classical dance forms like Kathak and Manipuri. Odissi was still taking shape in Orissa and although Bharatanatyam had crossed the Kaveri, it had leapt directly to Delhi without a stopover in Bombay, except for Shantha Rao who performed once and left.

The teacher—Mother and her friends found for our dance class—was one Bhairav Prasad who claimed to be a disciple four times removed of some great Kathak maharaj of the north. He did not say whether the maharaj was from Benares or Lucknow or somewhere else, and the mothers were too ill-informed to ask. But dance was dance. There were twelve of us in the class aged ten to fourteen. Bhairav Prasad would teach us a step, go around the class, correct hand and foot positions and then float back to his seat to see us do it. His delicate walk with the slightest hint of a swing in the hips was made for Usha to imitate and she did so with relish. For two years our ghungroos rang out from an empty classroom in Balmohan Vidya Mandir. Then one day they fell silent. Bhairav Prasad's hand and foot corrections had exceeded the acceptable limits of physical contact with one of the girls. He was summarily dismissed and the class dismantled. But those two years of Kathak had told me I had dance in my body. I had found it deeply fulfilling to let my body flow with the beat; to use my eyes, eyebrows and neck to express emotion, and my limbs to create geometrical figures full of grace and precision. Dance was something I wanted to continue doing. I was in love with it.

After a few months of sadly unbelled ankles, Mother found us another teacher. The cherub-faced, ever-smiling Keshav Sahasrabuddhe was a relative of my great-grandmother's who lived for a few years with her son near Dadar beach. She was a tiny tiny woman with a tiny tiny bun tied tight at the back of her tiny tiny head. She was almost blind, but sat at the stove all day, her nine-yard sari tucked neatly and firmly round her compact body, cooking up simple, nourishing meals for the family. When we visited, which was almost every Sunday morning, she would break into a toothless grin of welcome and then shoo us out of the kitchen to go play with her grandsons. How someone related to this traditional woman could have chosen to make dance his profession and still be welcomed in the family was a mystery. But there he was, Keshav Sahasrabuddhe, fresh from Santiniketan, to teach us 'Manipuri'. The quotes around the word indicate my later suspicions. What we were taught as Manipuri was, I guessed, pure Rabindra nritya, an amalgam of Manipuri, local Santhali folk with a dash of Odissi that Gurudev Tagore had created for the students of Santiniketan. Why else would we have danced to a Bengali song which, the way we sang it, horrendously corruptedly no doubt, went, 'Debotal mandir angan talay, debdasi go ami pujarini?' Without putting too fine a point on purity of style, it must be said that Sahasrabuddhe kept our bodies moving gracefully to melody and beat. Good enough for us. Certainly for me. For a whole year on dance days, the Vanita Samaj hall was cleared of its table-tennis table. Then once again, dance ended. Sahasrabuddhe left for Ceylon (renamed Sri Lanka much later) to learn Kandyan dance. I wonder now if the inspiration came from Chitrasena the famous Kandyan dancer who had spent a year or two at Santiniketan in the forties. Perhaps Sahasrabuddhe was there when he visited and had cherished a dream ever since of joining his School of National Dance in Ceylon. Whatever be the case, his interest in Kandyan dance had put paid to my interest in 'Manipuri'.

I was fifteen by the time a 'real' dance teacher was found for me. Ravi Bellare taught Bharatanatyam one-on-one. I do not know even now which school of dance he belonged to; but he was rigorous in the hour-long sessions he put me through in my parents' bedroom, never speaking, only reciting the complex beats of the dance and using a stick to keep time. After Sahasrabuddhe left and before Bellare arrived, I had become passionately involved with badminton. I was playing for two hours every evening at the Municipal Employees' Club on Cadell Road as a guest member introduced by Father's school friend Dattaram Palekar, an engineer with the Bombay Municipal Corporation. My twice-a-week Bharatanatyam lessons meant no badminton on those evenings and that hurt. As I put on my ghungroos my heart yearned for the shuttlecock. The start of the dance lesson was always gloomy. But then the rhythm and the movement got into me. I forgot tossing and smashing. I wanted only to perfect the new adavu Bellare was teaching me. It was a cruel dilemma to have two loves vying for my body. The dilemma was solved, not entirely happily, at the end of the year. Bellare left for London. All he had managed to teach me in one year was an alaripu, a thillana and a jathiswaram.

In 1958 or thereabouts I passed Ravi Bellare on an escalator in London's underground. In the brief exchange we had as he went down and I went up, I gathered that he had joined Ram Gopal's troupe, then based in London. I did not have time to ask whether he had joined as a dancer or a percussionist for it could have been either. Bellare had been a student of the tabla maestro Pandit Taranath Rao. In the fifties, he and his brother Shashi had popularized their guru's pioneering concept of jugalbandi where two players performed in tandem.

Meanwhile, learning classical dance had told me where I stood in our Bollywood-obsessed culture. Classical dance, supposedly an expression of the finest culture of a proud new nation, occupied but a marginal space in the public heart. People had raved about Uday Shankar's dance in the 1948 film *Kalpana*. But that was an amalgam of Indian and Western, classical and folk. You did not need to be an informed rasika to appreciate it. The famous drum dance in S.S. Vasan's film *Chandralekha*, made in the same year, was more sensation than dance. I saw the film and knew how spectacular it was. Then there were the cousins Sayee and Subbulakshmi who bowled people over with their double act in the 1955 film *Azaad*. They danced in the Bharatanatyam style to 'Aplam chaplam', the hit song composed by C. Ramchandra and sung by Lata Mangeshkar. The dance was marked by speed, precise synchronization and swift pirouettes. The audience was awed. Classical dance did not aspire to sensation. Painful proof of the great divide between the classical and the popular was brought home to me during a school annual day programme. I was dancing my Bhairav Prasad todas and gats to a solitary sounding lehra played on the harmonium by his assistant. But I had a sensation up my sleeve. My last toda was going to end with twenty-seven chakkars executed in three sets of nine. Coming after a gentle gat about Radha going to the Yamuna to fill water in her pitcher, it was going to make an amazing finale. I threw myself into the toda, my satin ghagra whirling as I spun through the chakkars. The last nine done, I came to a dead halt without losing my balance in the graceful basic Kathak stance. I waited for the applause to break. What I heard was a polite clatter.

After me came Mohindra Batra doing the snake dance from *Nagin*. As the opening music of the popular song, 'Mana dole mera tana dole', began playing on the gramophone, the audience sat up, eyes glistening, smiles wreathing young faces. Mohindra entered swaying to the music, dressed in a body suit of black, shiny scales. His footwork was faulty but his extravagantly painted eyes were mesmerizing. If my chakkars had thrilled the audience only mildly, Mohindra's finale brought the house down. Swaying sinuously, he went slowly down on his knees and arched his back till his head touched the floor behind. The audience gasped, whistled and broke into wild applause. Standing forlornly in the wings I muttered, Kathak, go hide your face.

When Bhairav Prasad was dismissed, one person in Shivaji Park, essentially unconnected with him or with dance, expressed her great delight in colourful language. 'Good riddance to that chhakka,' she said, laughing raucously. This was my Mother's friend whom we shall call Queen G. Her house was located at a major crossroad, making her a natural recipient of gossip from both sides of the junction. All she had to do was stand in her ground-floor verandah, point the right ear towards one road, the left towards the other and collect the stories that flowed in. In Queen G's world there were only two genders, male and female. Both had to be true to the species. The in-betweens were all chhakkas. Eunuchs. She had no doubt at all that Bhairav Prasad had been one. No real man who wanted to be treated like one walked with mincing steps as he did. Queen G's taste in men went back to the denizens of ancient caves. I once heard her tell Mother that she had dreamt of marrying a lion of a man who would drag her to bed by the hair. Instead she had married a lamb. The romantic dreams of her girlhood rudely dashed, she took an exuberant interest in young love. As secretary of the Vanita Samaj badminton club, which also allowed membership to men, she had promoted several court romances with eager zeal. Marathi fiction of those times was full of young men and women falling in love on badminton and tennis courts. And here she was, living that life in full, albeit by proxy, watching glances being exchanged, hands brushing 'accidentally', unnecessarily slow walks home. Knowing how vigorously the girls' families would oppose such goings-on, she opened her house to the wooers and the wooed. If the badminton club secretary was inviting players over for tea, which family would object? Two such romances were flowering nicely under Queen G's patronage when a rival gossip spoiled the fun. She reported Queen G's activities to the mothers of the two girls. The girls' memberships of the badminton club were summarily terminated. Within a year both were married off to suitable boys, that is young men who had settled in America in lucrative jobs. The local boys whom the girls had unhappily dumped, spent their lives in Shivaji Park married to suitable girls, that is girls who had never stepped on a badminton court, but who cooked and cleaned for them and gave them two children apiece. Thus all four couples lived happily ever after.

8. Badminton

The game that had vied for a year with Bharatanatyam, finally won with Ravi Bellare's sudden and unexpected departure for London. The year was 1954 and every evening was badminton evening. By age fifteen I was being invited by sundry members of the Municipal Club to partner them in mixed doubles in open tournaments. We played at the P.J. Hindu Gymkhana at Marine Lines, Bhagini Samaj in Khetwadi and Vanita Samaj. We rarely progressed beyond round two; but it was exciting to share space with the greats of those times—the invincible Nandu Natekar, the debonair K.D. Seth, the powerful Sushila Kapadia and Tara Dandige. My lack of power was a handicap for singles. Fortunately, there was more to badminton in those days than that. One could play deceptive drop-shots and make deft net placements to bewilder and bug the opponents. These were skills that made the woman's role in a mixed doubles game valuable. Very few men allowed their women partners to cover the whole court anyway.

How happy I would have been to continue playing at the Municipal Club with the tubby Mr Franklin, the lanky Mr Kazi fondly called Chacha Chowdhary, the sprightly and deceptive Arvind Terdalkar, the hard-hitting Kusum Shirodkar, the nine-yard-sari-wearing Mrs Vaidya and her sister, my best badminton chum Sudha Patwardhan. But my academic performance at the Senior Cambridge exam did me in. I had gotten over my phobia for numbers with a little help from Mr Nagarkar. My newfound enthusiasm for Maths had fetched me a distinction in the final exams. A couple of boys in the class, who were brilliant at Maths and Science but not so brilliant at English, History and Geography, stood below me in the rankings. This prompted Father to go confidently ahead with his long-cherished plan—which many of his friends thought idiotic or just plain crazy—of sending me to England for my undergrad studies. He had been in correspondence with several schools in the UK and found one that suited him on all counts, location, reputation and an open attitude towards Third World students. St Paul's Girls School, Hammersmith, was the school I was going to be sent to for 'A' levels after which I was to try for a seat at a good university. Mother objected. She was not going to send me alone. Father solved the problem. You go with her. Mother objected. She was not going to leave Nirmal behind. Father solved the problem. Take her with you. Mother objected. You don't have that kind of money. Father solved the problem. Who says?

On 5 June 1956, two-and-a-half months short of my seventeenth birthday, we set sail for London on the P & O liner, *SS Arcadia*. A Mrs Godbole who lived in Clapham had offered us the use of her flat while we looked for accommodation. She was going to be away in India on a long holiday. At Tilbury, we received a letter from her saying she was calling off the offer. She had dropped her holiday plans. Sindhu Maushi's husband Chandrakant More, who was trying to settle in London before she joined him, turned up at Tilbury to receive us like an unbidden genie. He took us to a boarding and lodging place in 2, Parliament Hill, Hampstead, run by a jolly woman named Mrs Gulhane, generally known as Kaku. She was one of a whole clan of people from Yavatmal in the Vidarbha district of Maharashtra who had followed the legendary Ajibai Banarase into the lodging and boarding business. I shall not digress into Ajibai's story which calls for an independent book. Suffice it to say that her enterprise took her from being a penniless, ill-treated widow in London to ultimately owning twelve buildings and a fleet of cars. We were relieved to have a room in Kaku's lodgings, where we could stay while we went on our flat hunt. A month later, we were installed in 31, Coningham Road, Shepherd's Bush. This was a working-class neighbourhood, located a mere six-penny trolley ride away from St Paul's.

As soon as we had settled down, with a month still to go before school started, Nirmal took part in the sports day organized by India House, winning all the events in which she participated. Mrs Vijayalaxmi Pandit was to give away the prizes. But she could not make it. So Mr V.K. Krishna Menon, ex-High Commissioner to the UK, did the honours. Nirmal's prize was a thick, black cookbook and a trophy.

For the two-and-a-half years that I spent at St Paul's under the grey skies of a grey city, badminton became a memory. At school we played lacrosse in the winter and tennis in the summer, neither of which my body took to. I would serve well enough in tennis; but trained as I was in badminton, my returns were wristy, which made the ball drop dispiritedly to my feet instead of zooming over the net as intended. As for lacrosse, my arms simply refused to develop the skill required to catch the ball in the triangular net at the top of the crosse, cradle it as I ran across the field and toss it to the next player. If I managed to get the ball into the net at all, I would drop it as I ran, causing my team-mates to groan in mock despair. I ended up being a dispassionate spectator of the sport. The other girls played while I watched from a safe distance. This was in the best interests of all concerned. The girls were happy to play with an active ten while the non-performing eleventh stuck to her corner of the field, presuming neither to attack nor defend.

I was equally defeated by gymnastics which involved dangerous practices like getting up on your hands and walking on double bars. Or doing cartwheels. Come gym class and I would get as far as changing into the regulation pinky-beige gym slip and making it to the gym. But anything more than that? Nonsense. The gym teacher politely looked the other way when I attempted to do cartwheels, which in my case were quick tumbles with my legs barely leaving the ground before planting themselves firmly on the other side of the block. Mother was right. My life's philosophy was not to lift my second foot until the first had found a firm toehold. The gym, where the idea was to let go of all toeholds, militated against this philosophy. Having tumbled about a bit to show I was willing to try everything once, I would assume my regular position by the radiator where some of the cold that had got into my bones through the thin gym slip would get warmed out.

Soon after I joined St Paul's, I had made tentative inquiries with a classmate about badminton. 'Badminton?' she queried. 'Oh badminton,' she said off-handedly. 'I'm sure it's played somewhere, though I couldn't say where.' I was shocked. I mean utterly and thoroughly shocked. I was asking about a game that had originated in England for heaven's sake, not in the jungles of the Congo or the deserts of Rajasthan. It had a true-blue upper-crust history. It used to be played initially with a battledore and shuttlecock and without a net. British officers on India duty had developed it into the game of fine strokes and complex rules that I had discovered in Bombay. Those officers had come from the best British families and had thought the game fit enough to be carried back to England to become a sport for guests at Badminton, the Duke of Beaufort's stately home in Gloucestershire. Snooty St Paul's should have had a court of its own. That it did not was, in my disgusted opinion, a bad mark on its report card.

However, the school offered many compensations for my body being denied its highest pleasure, all to do with the mind. Before school term had begun, the high mistress Miss Osborne (not head mistress, as she would have been called in India) had detailed one of the English teachers, Miss Jenkinson, who was to be my friend, guide and counsellor, to check out what kind of English I had done in India where I claimed to have studied *Macbeth,* Wordsworth and Keats. Sitting out on a bench facing the tennis courts at the back of the school, I had rattled off a soliloquy from *Macbeth.* Miss Jenkinson had looked suitably impressed. Then she asked me why *Macbeth* was considered a tragedy. Glug. Was it? Of course it was, although the cover of my copy had only said *Macbeth*, edited by A.W. Verity. But Mrs Audrey Da Silva who had taught it to us, had not breathed a word about it being a tragedy. She would make us read it in voices and explain the meaning of difficult words. I was thinking hard and fast. The play could not be called a tragedy only because Duncan was murdered and the Macbeths along with a host of others died in various gory ways. The answer had to be something more subtle. Miss Jenkinson had been nodding encouragingly to help me break my silence, but soon gave up and moved on to the next question, fortunately not about *Macbeth*. Thus it was in that yard, facing the tennis courts, that my introduction to an education of the mind began. Mugging was fine. It helped you do well in exams. But asking questions was more important. It meant your mind was at work.

The seventh and eighth form classes turned out to be an exquisite pleasure. During English lessons we argued endlessly over the interpretation of plays, poems and essays, shredding the texts to pieces. Our discussions spilled over into the prefects' room and although my insights were nothing as sharp as Jane Thompson's (she was the genius of the class), they were personal discoveries, not borrowed ideas.

By the time I played Tybalt in the school's inter-form drama competition, in which I died a much-appreciated death, I had discovered loves that paralleled badminton. Shakespeare, all of him—tragedies, comedies, histories, sonnets. Christopher Marlowe's *Tamburlaine* and *Dr Faustus*. Chaucer's *Canterbury Tales*. Lastly but not leastly, the English language itself, through the books of the great language pundits of the time—Eric Partridge, Otto Jespersen and Ivor Brown, not to forget Nancy Mitford's *Noblesse Oblige* which vivisected the British aristocracy's usages and ways with a sharp, unerring scalpel. I was surrounded by girls who came from that kind of stock. Some of them were even preparing to come out as debutantes. They as insiders and I as a rank outsider chuckled over large sections of the Mitford book, particularly Alan Ross's essay on sociological linguistics titled 'U and Non-U' (upper class and non-upper class). One of the phrases I instantly dropped from my vocabulary as a result was 'studying for the exams'. We did not study for our exams. We worked for them.

There was a delicious irony in where we schooled and where

we lived. Although St Paul's was located in Hammersmith, a plebeian neighbourhood, the girls in their hats, coats and sensible shoes, were far from that. However, Father's strictly middle-class income together with the limits imposed by the Indian government on foreign exchange meant we did not live in the uppity neighbourhoods where most of them lived. Shepherd's Bush was a drab, grey, multi-cultural neighbourhood of poor whites and poorer blacks. Our flat was in an ancient terrace building owned by Mrs Newitt, a friendly, non-interfering widow who had lived her married life in South Africa. We had found it after several racially inspired rejections. Looking through 'to let' ads, I would dial a promising number and be asked to 'come and see the place dear'. When we arrived with our brown faces, the flat would have just been taken. 'So sorry dear.' One woman innocently told me I had sounded Welsh over the phone. So when I called Mrs Newitt, the first thing I did was to say we were Indian. She said oh how nice, come right over. We went right over, and the one room plus kitchen flat on the first floor with toilet and bathroom on the ground floor, was ours for a rent that Father could afford. Mrs Newitt lived on the ground floor with her son Peter. Above us on the second was Jean McIntyre, a pianist, and her flat-mate Russel, both from New Zealand. Russel was a tall, short-haired, laughter-filled woman who was out at work the whole day. Jean was square-built and friendly. She was an aspiring pianist who practised at home all day. Nirmal spent many hours with Jean asking her to play songs from the Dorothy Dandridge film *Carmen Jones* which we had been taken to see by our first cousin Bal Bhau, younger brother of Baban Bhau. Bal Bhau worked for De Havilland Aircraft Company at Edgware. He moved to America after it closed down in 1964.

When Mother returned to Bombay after a year, Nirmal and I moved into digs at 22, Bromyard Avenue, Acton. This too was a working-class area. But this time we were in a semi-detached with an unkempt garden at the back. Our landlord George Dean was a foreman in a factory. His wife Nellie was a homemaker who loved doing the can-can when she was feeling nostalgic. She regularly said non-U things like 'serviette' for 'table-napkin' and 'pardon me' for 'what?' The bay windows of her living room were draped in lace curtains which also announced her non-U status. Our days were thus spent swinging between U and non-U, getting to know London society vertically in the process.

9. Food

'Food glorious food / Hot sausage and mustard / While we're in the mood / Cold jelly and custard.' We were still four years short of the West End opening of the Lionel Bart musical *Oliver!* but these four lines musically expressed exactly the hunger pangs that drove us to the lunch room as soon as the bell went on our first day of school. However, one detail in those lusty lines was non-applicable to us. There were to be, or so we thought, no hot sausages in our lives. We were vegetarian. We were indeed that during the first four days of the first week, drearily chewing through bland boiled veggies and soggy salads, meagre fare that we bolstered with bread. Potatoes were always around to be had, but I was still pushing them away for reasons I must explain.

In one of the rounds of farewell dinners we had had before leaving Bombay, I had bitten into a green potato which, quite unknown to our overwhelmingly hospitable hostess, had made its way into a spicy preparation. Green potatoes have an indescribable metallic taste that makes you want to spit ten times, rinse your mouth ten times and repeat the cycle ten times. As a guest, I was not free to do that. Unsure what else to do with that disgusting mouthful, I held it between tongue and palate for so long before resignedly swallowing it that I gave the revolting taste time to penetrate right through my tastebuds and settle at the very root of my tongue. As I drank a whole glassful of water to chase it down, I knew I was never going to look at a potato again.

Sailing to London, I was brought to tears, not by the rocking and rolling of the ship—which, although minimal, destabilized many stomachs—but by the variety of potato preparations that came our way every lunch and dinner. Mashed potatoes, snow potatoes, chipped potatoes, roast potatoes, baked potatoes, duchess potatoes, potatoes Anglaise, potatoes Francaise and potatoes in their jackets. Urrrgh!

The school kitchen was more ascetic. No need to dress up a potato which, by any other name, was still a potato. Roast it or mash it was the rule. At most mix it with yesterday's cabbage and call it bubble-and-squeak and let the girls deal with it. But whatever the kitchen did with potatoes, they stayed off my plate. I managed as well as I could with what remained. But on the fifth day of the week, the dish that came to the vegetarian table was a fish pie. Pale fish at the bottom. Pale potato on top.

'But that's fish,' I wailed.

'So it is, dear. Friday is fish day.'

'But fish is non-vegetarian!'

'No it isn't, dear.'

'Oh? Then may we move to the non-vegetarian table from Monday please?'

I was not a strict vegetarian. Meat was not a religious taboo. I had occasionally had curried chicken and mutton back home in Bombay. Father liked meat once in a while and Mother, a strict vegetarian herself but a loving wife, would make it for him. He also liked fish which again she made. But to me fish was a totally different kettle of…well…fish. One knew its virtues backwards. Jeeves' brain had grown subtle with it. Bengali women's skin glowed with it. Kerala women's hair thrived on it. But I would rather have a dumb brain, drab skin and little hair to speak of than have fish. Or any seafood for that matter. One Sunday I was visiting Rohini Patkar in her home in Mahim. It might be recalled that she was my classmate and close friend along with Usha Paranjpe, who had screamed 'Why do you cover your mirrors' to which Father's answer had been 'Because we are idiots'. Her chore for the day I visited was to go to Gopi Tank Market on L.J. Road, Mahim, to buy fish for dinner. I said I'd stay home and talk to her cook. She said you'll do nothing of the kind; you'll go with me. I went, with her warning ringing in my ears. Don't you dare put your hanky to your nose. You'll hear cuss words you didn't know existed. So I held my breath instead. Bombay fisherwomen have a low tolerance level for offences against their profession, produce and persons. If men get fresh, they will raise their cleavers and hiss, 'Want it sliced?' I was happy not to have visited Rohini at dinner time. I always suspected fish-eaters of slipping some kind of seafood, prawns, shrimp, dried Bombay duck, into things that weren't normally meant to have them. Like rice and chapatis.

At the non-vegetarian table, I soon settled down to shepherd's pie, toad-in-the-hole, roast beef and Yorkshire pud, meat loaf and corned beef hash. Once in a while we were served Scotch eggs or fish. On those days I stuffed myself with bread. Why not Scotch eggs? That again is a sad tale. I had never had a problem with eggs, though I cannot say I leapt with joy at the sight of them. But they had ambushed me on the *SS Arcadia* where they began producing severe stomach cramps within moments of ingestion. Mother had always been allergic to them. Her tongue itched even if she had cake. That gene had intensified in me without warning out at sea, causing me unbearable agony. So I had restricted my breakfast to porridge with golden syrup, with second helpings to compensate for the absence of eggs.

There are people who believe that allergies are figments of the imagination. Dilip Adarkar with whom I spent occasional evenings discussing books, theatre and films, once treated me to a chocolate mousse in a wayside restaurant. Although I did not know that mousse was nothing but eggs and air, what came to the table looked highly suspicious to me. 'This looks like eggs, Dilip. I'm allergic to them.'

'Nonsense,' he said. 'No eggs. But I'll ask in the kitchen.' He went in and came back with a wide grin. 'As I thought. No eggs.' I walloped the mousse. He paid the bill. Within ten yards of the restaurant, I whipped around, rushed back and made a beeline for the washroom. 'What happened?' Dilip asked with genuine concern when I returned. 'The chef lied to you. The mousse was eggs.' He stood frozen, hitting his forehead with the palm of his hand. 'The chef didn't lie. I lied. He told me it was eggs. But I thought the allergy was all in your mind. I had planned to say to you when I dropped you home, "See? You just had a plateful of eggs and nothing happened."' At which point I ran back to the washroom.

Food at Mrs Deane's table presented its own problems. She did not serve second helpings and often covered her English food with Indian curry powder to make us feel at home. The result was so revolting that one evening, unable to take it, Nirmal packed her dinner and put it in the waste-paper basket in our room. Mrs Deane discovered it the following morning as she was bound to. She held up the neatly packed serving of curried mince and nearly wept with hurt. The upshot was that we got Father to agree to let us eat at an Indian restaurant on the way home from school. He was more than half inclined to agree because all the family friends who had visited us in London had gone back with reports of our waif-like appearance. But we could eat out only if Mrs Deane agreed to cut a commensurate amount from what we paid her for dinner. He wouldn't be able to afford the change otherwise. It was a delicate negotiation which I had to conduct with great tact. I finally convinced Mrs Deane that, however hard and sincerely she had tried to make us feel at home with curry powder, we missed the real thing and would be profoundly grateful if she excused us from her table. Dear Mrs Deane, not being a hard-nosed businesswoman, agreed instantly with much understanding and grace; and even before I got around to hinting at the cut in payment, she said it was only fair that she should not charge us for dinner! So from then on, it was parathas and kofta curry, the cheapest dish on the menu at the Taj Restaurant run by an East Pakistani who would be called a Bangladeshi fourteen years later. Occasionally we splurged on mutton do pyaza or rogan josh. Later, after Nirmal returned to Bombay, it was also bangers and mash for me at George's down the main road from 22, Bromyard Avenue.

When the time came to appear for my Oxford (St Hugh's) and Cambridge (Newnham) entrance exams for which girls like Jane Thompson were also sitting, I knew my chances of making it were at best slim and at worst non-existent. My self-knowledge was pretty acute. Oxford rejected me outright. Cambridge suggested I strengthen my Latin and sit for the entrance exam again the following year. Another winter in England? Never. Fortunately, of the several redbrick universities to which I had applied, Bristol was the first to call me for an interview. I was thrilled because the head of the English department there was the Shakespeare scholar, Professor L.C. Knights ('How Many Children Had Lady Macbeth?'). The poet Charles Tomlinson was assistant lecturer and the Russian and Spanish scholar Professor Henry Gifford was senior lecturer. At the interview, it was Mr Gifford who asked me most of the questions.

'And why may I ask did you not get into Oxford or Cambridge since you tried for them Miss Gokhaalay? Is that how you pronounce your name?'

'Actually it's Gokhlay, forget the intrusive "a" after "kh". That's just pedantry. I'm afraid my Latin wasn't up to scratch. I was asked to apply next year with better Latin, which of course I didn't want to do.'

'Quite right, Miss Gokhael. Have I got it right this time?'

'Sorry, no. But I don't mind being Miss Gokhael. Really.'

'Thank you Miss Gokhael. You know how the British are with foreign words. You were absolutely right about Latin though. What has Latin got to do with life? Your "A" level French grades are excellent and so of course are your English literature and language grades. We think that's quite adequate for an honours degree in English Language and Literature here. Would you accept a seat if we were to offer you one?'

'Wouldn't I just? Does that mean you are offering me one? I hope to take a six-month break in Bombay before term begins if I know I'm in.'

The two men and one woman—Susie Tucker, the Old and Middle English expert as I was to gather later—smiled, asked me to step out for a moment, then called me in and said, 'Yes. We are offering you a seat.'

Outwardly I said a sedate thank you, but inwardly I was

doing a jig. I was triumphant on two counts. I had got a seat. But almost equally importantly, I had got to the right room on the right floor of the right building for the interview. I am directionally challenged. Which means I turn left when I should turn right and right when I should turn left. It also means that I enter wrong rooms and exit through wrong doors. There were many ways to lose myself in Bristol University's main building, a Victorian pile that had rooms at ground level, and up a couple of storeys. But I had kept my wits about me all the way from the station to the University and managed to enter the right room through the right door at the right time. Now, with a seat in my pocket, I skipped down the stairs recklessly. Unknown to me, there was a basement lurking beneath where I had entered the building. I now found myself there, in a long passage, with no exit in sight. Optimistically trusting in the idea that if you walked long enough down any road or passage, you came out somewhere recognizable, I walked on. But the passage seemed interminable and no exit hove into view. I was on the point of admitting defeat when an angel in the form of a tall athletic man in a grey coat came striding down the passage from the opposite direction.

'Excuse me but could you tell me where the exit to Park Street is?'

He looked at me and knew instantly that I was directionally challenged. He smiled and said in accented English, 'Come. I'll show you the way.'

A couple of twists and turns and up one flight of stairs and we were in Park Street, breathing freely of the early spring air.

'Thank you er…'

'Otto. Otto Tokvam. And you?'

'Shanta Gokhale.'

He rolled the two names round his tongue and brought them out exactly correctly. Did you hear that Henry Gifford, did you hear?

Six months on, when I joined University, I ran into Otto in the Refectory. He hailed me by both names. We greeted each other and he said, 'Will you have coffee with me?' That's how our relationship began. It lasted all of the three years I was at Bristol and a little over.

I could devote a whole chapter and more to Otto. He was a lovely man, deeply respectful of my non-European culture, an expert skier with an irrepressible sense of a strange brand of humour that was occasionally embarrassing. At Joan Pick's birthday party, she dribbled a little as she cut her rosebud decorated cake, perhaps in anticipation of its chocolatey lightness in the mouth. Otto said, 'Don't water the flowers, Joan. They aren't real.' I was the only one who laughed.

At Bristol, as at any other university in Britain I guess, if you wanted to have a life besides the lectures you attended, the games you played and the plays you acted in, you had to have a boyfriend. If you didn't have one and you were invited to lunch or dinner, your hostess would find you a single male counterpart to maintain the gender balance. It's the old Noah's Ark syndrome I thought. Once when I was invited for dinner by an English couple who didn't know Otto, I was paired with an air force pilot called Buster. I had thought only Americans were called Buster. But here was a pure English Buster. He said he was charmed by my name. It sounded French to him. Like Chantal he said. I put it in sociological context for him. Shanta is the counterpart of Mabel, I said. Mabel had been a popular name in Britain circa the 1880s. That was also Shanta vintage. But do you know what Mabel means, he countered.

It means amiable, loving, lovable. Oh oh I thought, smiling warily. But he was just being gallant and charming. I never saw or heard from him again.

Girls without steady boyfriends at Goldney House, my Hall of Residence, casually haunted the kitchen which was next to the phone, hoping the Johns, Henries, Hughs or Peters they had met the day before or the previous week would call and make their weekends worthwhile. My friend Paula Kahn for whom the phone rang rarely, mainly I thought because her face was set in a permanently cynical expression, told me I should consider it my duty to introduce her to a handsome Indian man. As it happened Madhav Vaidya of the Indian Navy was to visit me. He was a friend of A.V. Bharath whose acquaintance it will be recalled I had made playing table tennis at Holiday Home in Kodaikanal. He had joined the navy even before we had left for London. We had met Madhav and Bharath's other friend Roy when they were docked in Bombay and we had been invited to the ship for dinner. The only other guests present, were two young women called Miss Barve and Miss Topiwala. Both were introduced to us as Madhav's cousins. Bharath had written to say Madhav was in England and would like to visit me. Since he liked having cousins, I was sure he would not mind having one in Bristol. So I told Paula her handsome Indian was on his way. 'He is tall, has a clean-cut face and his eyes twinkle when he smiles. Get ready to swoon.'

Madhav came. I had booked him in a bed-and-breakfast. Paula and I took him out to dinner. I told him I had a badminton match the following evening so I would not be able to see him; but Paula would show him the sights including the suspension bridge from where once a woman, disappointed in love, had thrown herself off; but instead of drowning as she had hoped, had been kept afloat by her crinoline till she was rescued. True or not, the story was always a great hit with tourists.

The plan was made. Paula was excited. Just she and Madhav. She was going to charm the pants off him. But the following morning I got a distress call from Madhav. The geyser in his room had exploded and nearly killed him. He was going to catch the next train back to London. Years later when I heard of Madhav's death in a road accident, a shiver ran down my spine. Paula was distraught. I wasn't playing a match that evening. I had lied. Otto and I took her out as consolation. She said morosely, glancing at Otto, 'How did you find this man? Why can't I find one?' To which I responded philosophically, 'You must first lose your way to find what you're looking for.' She rewarded me with a kick under the table for my wisdom.

Many of my class friends and Hall mates envied me for Otto in a good-natured kind of way. Otto's love for me was total. Mine for him, when it came to the crunch, was wanting. When we said our last goodbyes in July 1962 after my graduation, he proposed. I said it would not work. I wanted to live and work in my country. He offered to divide his time between Norway and India. He even made two trips to Bombay to see how he could work it out. It could not be and I was not willing to compromise. In the end, our long and lovely relationship ended in mutual pain. I knew I had hurt him badly but I also knew I would have hurt him worse had I married him.

10. Home

It had taken a lot to persuade Father that home was the best place for me to be during the five-month hiatus between being offered a place at Bristol and going up in August. I hated playing on the fact that it would be easier on his pocket to fly me home and keep me there instead of keeping me in London in wasteful digs doing nothing except eating up his money. While that was true, it was equally true that I was aching to be home. This was in no way to dismiss the enriching three years I had spent in London. I had loved its theatre and international cinema, its newspapers and bookshops, its flea markets from the inside and its Fortnum and Masons from the outside. I was grateful to my teachers at St Paul's, the brusque and affectionate Miss Jenkinson who took Nirmal and me to several plays, including *Salad Days*, the longest running musical in London before *Oliver!*; the tall and stately Miss Hurtley and even the short and chatty Miss Woods, my Latin tutor, who could not forgive the Germans for bombing London, and who once took me to Kew Gardens with a picnic lunch of ox tongue sandwiches, which my intestines revolted against violently. I valued the friendships I had made with several girls at school who had invited me into their homes over weekends and during Easter and Christmas breaks. I had spent many weekends with gentle-voiced Rosemary Devin and her loving

Plymouth Brethren family. I had gone camping in Cornwall with her too, learning to live in a tent, drink morning tea from a tin mug like a soldier and walk for miles over grass, rock and sand facing rain and sun which alternated within minutes of each other. I had spent a wonderful Easter break with Margaret Archer who had the rosy face of a Jane Austen heroine. Her father, W.G. Archer, an Indian Civil Service man, had spent over a decade in Bihar with his wife Mildred and authored several books on Indian miniatures, sculpture and culture. On their return to London, W.G. had been appointed keeper of the Indian section of the Victoria and Albert Museum. A few years later Mildred was working in the India Office Library, meticulously cataloguing its collection of Indian paintings. The Easter break with Margaret, her parents and brother Michael had been lovely. We had toasted crumpets over the fire for tea and had stimulating conversations while lathering them with butter and honey.

Myrna D'Souza had sailed on the *Arcadia* with us and had, by the greatest good luck, also joined St Paul's. It was in her company that I discovered for the first time that although two families might share the surname D'Souza, one might be brahmin and the other sudra. I had assumed that sudras had converted to egalitarian Christianity to get rid of their low-caste label. But, as the title of the brilliant play *Jaataa Naahi Jaat*, written by the dalit playwright Siddharth Tambe who died prematurely suggests, even when you lose all else in India, you do not lose your caste. Many were the weekends I spent with Myrna at her Earl's Court YWCA, playing table tennis and listening to jazz. Other friends took me to hear Duke Ellington and Ella Fitzgerald live (the melody and vocalization of 'Those Little White Lies' still haunts me), to see Shakespeare at the Old

Vic and Stratford. Most memorably I saw John Osborne's *Look Back in Anger* at the then unfashionable Royal Court Theatre. I loved its rawness and wondered at the reviews that dismissed it as loathsome. Yet Kenneth Tynan and Harold Hobson said it was a remarkable play. I was discovering that well-established critics could differ radically over a play. Some critics hung on to the comfort of the familiar; others like Tynan and Hobson were prepared to look at the new with new eyes. Indeed, they were positively excited by the new. The enigmatic, difficult to understand *Waiting for Godot*, directed by Peter Hall, had been wilting in its first week on the London stage. It was about to be taken off when Hobson in the *Sunday Times* and Tynan in *The Observer* told the world it was a breakthrough in theatre.

When I returned from my five months back home, I was going to leave this buzzing and beloved city to start a new life in Bristol. Fortunately my new home, located on the west coast of England on the banks of the river Avon, was home to the 250-year-old Bristol Old Vic, a branch of the London Old Vic, which promised to quench my thirst for theatre. Between London and Bristol lay Bombay, my family, my school friends Usha and Rohini, who were now at St Xavier's College, Amar Shroff who was at Jai Hind College and Kumar Palekar my table tennis pal who was now at Gordhandas Sunderdas Medical College.

'What do you want on your first day back?' Mother asked me in one of her last letters before I flew back from Heathrow. 'Birda for lunch,' I wrote, drooling; 'And bhelpuri for tea.' Birda is a curry made of dried field beans soaked overnight and sprouted. Into the curry goes a dry masala made from twenty-three spices, including red chillies, cloves, cinnamon and pepper; and a wet masala of coconut paste, tamarind and jaggery. Mother's birda was so hot your eyes and nose ran when you were having it, and speech became impossible.

Bhelpuri, the Bombay mix of crunchies, onions, coriander, raw-mango shavings mixed with hot and sour-sweet chutneys beckoned from the beaches of the city. Dadar beach was enticingly dotted with bhelpuriwalas. Their hands flew as they mixed the ingredients expertly in leaf cones, tossing the blend lightly in the final operation so that, when the cone was placed in your hands, the puffed rice was still puffed and the sev still crunchy. For us, bhelpuri and its cousin sev-puri spelt sheer seduction. But Mother, who watched the hands create what we thought was magic, wondered more about where they had been. She saw them as the Scylla and Charybdis of the beach, monsters who would grab and lay her daughters low with typhoid and worse. So, expert cook that she was, she figured out the secret ingredients that went into the bhelpuri chutneys, experimented endlessly at home and, after a few trials and errors, produced a rival to the beach bhelwala's product that was both droolworthy and hygienically guaranteed.

Mother's bhelpuri also turned out to be a sure-shot obstetrical tool. When I finally returned from England in July 1962, I found Usha big with her second baby. The first, Nitin, had come while I was in England. Usha's husband, Shantaram Jategaokar, had been sent to London by his employer, The Bank of India, for training. Nitin was six months old then. He was a toddler now with a tendency to walk into every compound we passed on our evening walks. Usha, weary with the weight of the second baby, would say, 'No Nitin, they haven't invited us for tea,' while I, unburdened, did the practical thing—led him out. One evening Usha asked my mother to make bhelpuri. She desperately needed cheering up. Usha and I hogged it in shameless quantities. The next morning Usha was in the hospital. Nandita had arrived.

Between the end of school term and finding a place at Bristol, I had not fed myself too well. I was down to 98 pounds from my normal 112. Back then, we weighed ourselves in pounds and measured ourselves in feet and inches. I am even now more comfortable with that than with the metric system that came into effect while I was away. Rohini took one look at me and said don't you dare come out with us until you begin to look human again. Right now you're a rattling skeleton. Mother got over her shock at my appearance and went into high gear action. She plastered my chapatis with obscene amounts of ghee, cooked up the richest sweets in her repertoire and got me back to 112 pounds within a month.

The body demanded attention in other areas too. Two of my molars needed filling. Father said go to Dr Ramakant Raut. So I went to Dr Ramakant Raut near Dadar station. I did not ask why I wasn't going to Dr H.V. Rau, our upstairs neighbour, whose clinic was also near Dadar station and whose children Chetan, Narendra, Ashutosh and Padmini had been our childhood playmates. Perhaps Father thought just in case one of Dr Rau's fillings were to fall out, something that was not likely to happen, it would create ripples of embarrassment in our otherwise warm relationship. There was also the other typically Indian problem of the professional getting mixed up with the personal. It was likely that Dr Rau would not charge a fee.

Dr Ramakant Raut filled my teeth so well, that I carried his cement in my mouth for thirty years before I needed to have it replaced. (The replacement too was done by a Raut, his son Pratap alias Kuka.) After the drilling and filling were over, Dr Raut said to me as he washed his hands, 'Your teeth are maloccluded.'

'Excuse me?'

'Mal-occlud-ed. That means misaligned. Maloccluded teeth give you a bad bite.'

'?'

'The grinders don't grind efficiently because they don't come together as they should.'

'Oh? Oh!'

'Yes. Since you're going to Bristol meet Nicol at the Dental Hospital. We worked together when I was in England. I think he'll recommend orthodontic treatment.'

'You mean plates on the teeth? Aren't I too old for that? I'm nineteen.'

'Just go,' he said brusquely. There were patients waiting outside. 'Let Nicol decide whether nineteen is old or young or not important.'

In August, having lived the good life in Bombay, and been seen off at the airport by parents, friends, aunts, cousins and Queen G, I went to Bristol, all 112 pounds of me, with a spring in my stride and good, solid cement in my teeth. There I met Otto in the Refectory, and discovered he was a dental student.

'Does that mean you go to the Dental Hospital for demonstrations or whatever?'

'Of course.'

'Do you know a Mr Nicol there?' I kind of hesitated at the Mr, remembering not to call him doctor. English dentists are plain misters, not doctors.

'Sure. He's a Scotsman I think. Doesn't say much but he is good.'

I was happy to hear that he didn't say much. It is a

supremely desirable quality in a dentist. When I finally returned home in 1962, the dentist who examined my wisdom teeth before extracting them, fixed my mouth in a wide open yawn and asked me probing questions about the Profumo-Christine Keeler affair. Since I was not in a physical state to say anything that made sense, I confined myself to dentist's chair sounds. But in my mind I was saying, 'Dirty old bugger. You think I was in their bedroom?'

I realize I am moving too rapidly towards Bristol and Teeth. They will come in due course. But before I go there, I must briefly backtrack to London and to my nose which, besides being a cannon for early morning explosions, also became a problem in a strictly aesthetic sense on one occasion.

11. The Nose

In giving this chapter the title of Gogol's famous story, I am not for a moment suggesting that my nose ever created a problem on quite the surreal scale that Major Kovalyov's did. It did not leave my face to get into a barber's breakfast nor did it presume to run about the city as an independent citizen of more worth than me before returning to its proper place on my face. My nose was leagues less dramatic; but it was dramatic nevertheless, both for its sound effects and the temporary contretemps it created in the make-up department of a Marathi amateur stage production in London.

First the nose as a cannon. The tragedy of the perpetual sneezer has been magnificently described by Chekhov in 'The Death of a Government Clerk'. I can do no better than steal its first inimitable paragraph to lift my own sad tale to the ranks of a classic:

> One fine evening, a no less fine government clerk called Ivan Dmitritch Tchervyakov was sitting in the second row of the stalls, gazing through an opera glass at the Cloches de Corneville. He gazed and felt at the acme of bliss. But suddenly... In stories one so often meets with this 'But suddenly'. The authors are right: life is so full of surprises! But suddenly his face puckered up, his eyes disappeared, his breathing was arrested... he took the opera glass from his

> eyes, bent over and…'Aptchee!!' he sneezed as you perceive. It is not reprehensible for anyone to sneeze anywhere. Peasants sneeze and so do police superintendents, and sometimes even privy councillors. All men sneeze.

And young women too. Except that I would sneeze as soon as my eyes opened to a new day. And I would not go 'Aptchee' which sounds inhibited. I would go 'Hashooo', like a clap of thunder. And, besides the puckered face, the arrested breathing, disappearing eyes and bent back, I would also raise my left knee to aid the firing of the shot. And I would not stop at one sneeze. I would do half a dozen or more in quick succession, all as hearty as the first.

I once took Usha and Rohini to Dahanu to my uncle Anna Mama's place for a brief holiday. This was the same Ghanashyam Narayan Behere of Behere's Industrial Works who had refused to have anything to do with Sindhu Maushi after she quarrelled with him and came away to Bombay. During the day we had enjoyed the bucolic pleasures of a small town that had still retained some of its erstwhile villageness. The evening meal had stunned both girls, particularly Rohini who even now remembers a fridge stuffed with five kinds of sweets led by shrikhand in a silver pot. We had chatted late into the night and fallen into a peaceful slumber. Usha and I were early risers. Rohini was not. The next morning, just as I had finished brushing my teeth I felt the familiar tickle in my nose. I took care to run to the extreme corner of the verandah farthest away from the bedroom where Rohini was sleeping. With my mouth already helplessly open, I was doing my best to protect her from the seismic shocks and after-shocks that were on their way; but three sneezes down the line, she came stumbling out on to the verandah all the same, looked at me bleary-eyed and mumbled, 'Do you have to?' Between sneezes I assured her I wouldn't if I didn't have to. 'It's like sleeping next-door to a cannon,' she grumbled and tottered back to bed. 'It's not over yet,' I warned, and delivered the next round of explosions. At which point she got up and brushed her teeth. I tried to tell her later that the thing I suffered from was photic sneeze reflex, otherwise known as Autosomal Dominant Compelling Helio-Ophthalmic Outburst Syndrome (ACHOO). I was expecting sympathy. But her early morning sleep, the sweetest as we all know, had been ruined and her mood was not kind.

My allergy to the first rays of the sun disappeared in London probably because the trigger rarely made its appearance in the city's skies. But in spring the pollen blew about and I became a natural victim to its collateral effects. Half the city's population suffered from hay fever in spring in any case; so my watering eyes and red nose simply became part of the general scenery. Not so the robust sound of my sneezing which, to my great embarrassment, rang out above the polite sounds Londoners made in their handkerchiefs. Comically, even after the pollen had settled, I still went around with an imaginary tickle in the nose, waiting for it to turn into a sneeze. It didn't. In the summer the sound effects department temporarily wound up. But the nuisance value of my nose continued in another department.

In order for the reader to understand the context of the event I am about to describe, some plain-speaking needs to be done. The shape of my nose is described by the unkind amongst my Marathi-speaking brethren as a bhaja (fritter). A bhaja-like nose is large where it should be small, and flat where it should be high. This is quite the opposite of the ideal nose that my Marathi brethren refer to as chafekali—champak bud. This nose is straight, narrow and refined. Having a fritter in the middle of my face had never bothered me; but it seriously bothered the director of the first Maharashtra Mandal play I acted in in London—P.K. Atre's comedy, *Sashtang Namaskar* (Prostration). The director Chandrahas Paigankar, whose own nose was as close to a champak bud as a man's nose could or should be, ordered the amateur make-up man (we were all amateurs so no offence meant) to build on what Nature had given me and create a thing of beauty. The make-up man did what he could. He spent two hours moulding and sculpting putty onto my nose to raise its flat bridge. The moulding was then covered with pancake and powder, with a darker shade of the pancake running down the sides of the nose to create an illusion of narrowness. Watching myself in the green room mirror, I wondered why a simple fact that had struck me when proceedings began didn't strike the make-up man—that plastering an object with putty would add to rather than reduce its dimensions. Finally, the make-up man set down his tools and bleated, 'Come and see.' Chandrahas Paigankar came, and what he saw was a large lump that could not, by any stretch of imagination, be called a chafekali, or even a nose for that matter. 'Take it off,' he said in despair. So off came the putty, leaving behind my natural organ, somewhat bruised by the mouldings and scrapings it had suffered, but in working order. Despite my nervous trembling in the wings before my entry, I had the pleasure of delivering a performance in which my unencumbered nose must have played a convincing part, for both of us got cast together twice more in subsequent Maharashtra Mandal plays before I went to Bristol. The first of these was M.G. Rangnekar's *Majhe Ghar* (My Home).

Humourist P.L. Deshpande, who was in London at the time, saw the play and wrote to Father to say his daughter had been the only open window in that home. The second was P.L. Deshpande's *Tujhe Aahe Tujapashi*, which, in the context of my nose, most appositely meant you have what is yours.

In the audience that saw *Majhe Ghar*, was a British film-maker who was planning to make a film on Gandhi. He had been told by my stage mother-in-law Mrs Kusum Pandit—aunt to Dilip Adarkar who had fed me mousse to check out his theory about allergies—that I might be just the young Kasturba he was looking for. The day after the play, Kusumtai called to say the film-maker would like to audition me for the role. I told her politely that I was not looking to change tracks from Eng Lit to films. She said she fully understood. And so ended my chance of beating Rohini Hattangadi to it. The film, as far as I know, never got made.

My stage fright on stage was nothing compared to my stage fright off it. Speaking a playwright's lines was a cakewalk compared to giving tongue to my own thoughts. Put me before ten unknown heads even now and my stomach feels like a playground for mice. I have looked for and felt vastly reassured by worthier women who have confessed to similar feelings of intimidation. J.K. Rowling began her speech at Harvard Commencement in 2008 with words that I make myself recall every unavoidable time that I have to speak publicly. (Avoidable times are strictly and happily avoided.) 'The first thing I would like to say is thank you,' Rowling begins. In the video on YouTube, you can see her swallowing nervously as she pronounces these words. But she presses on. 'Not only has Harvard given me an extraordinary honour, but the weeks of fear and nausea I have endured at the thought of giving this commencement address have made me lose weight. A win-win situation! Now all I have to do is take deep breaths, squint at the red banners and convince myself that I am at the world's largest Gryffindor reunion.'

I have found that it does help to pretend. You may not have created Hogwarts, but it is always within your capacity to tell yourself you're in a play by Wesker or Synge; and if you don't recognize your voice as yours, it only means you are playing your part extraordinarily well. Somehow, this strategy failed when I faced an audience of merely three during my first tutorial at Bristol. Lectures were where you listened. Tutorials were where you spoke. I was sitting across from my tutor with two fellow-students all waiting to hear my analysis of 'The elasticity of time in Conrad's *Nostromo*'. Young Mr Preston, dark, handsome, soft-spoken, a 20th-century Percy Bysshe Shelley no less, waited for me to begin. Gerry Seager and Peter Chapman waited for me to begin. I waited for myself to begin. I shuffled the pages in my hand to give myself time to pretend I was playing G.B. Shaw's Jack Tanner, who was 'prodigiously fluent of speech'. But Shaw turned his back on me. Finally, a sound issued from my mouth. It was not a word, only an attempt to shape a word. Mr Preston looked concerned. Messrs Seager and Chapman looked confused. When I made two more similar sounds, Mr Preston said, 'Are you having trouble with your voice, Miss Gokhaalay?' Hallelujah. Saved. I nodded vigorously, put my hand to my throat and signalled what I hoped would suggest a severely sore throat. Almost diphtheria. Much collective sympathetic tut-tutting followed and the baton was passed on. Messrs Seager and Chapman read out their well-argued essays. Although I hate speaking, I love arguing. And there was much in those essays to argue about. I was itching to challenge some of their statements. But a woman who cannot read her essay because she is stricken with diphtheria, cannot argue either.

Tutors are not ogres I told myself all the way back to Goldney House where I occupied a special single room during my first two years before moving to the palladian style Clifton Hill House in the third. After that attack of vocal tremens, I behaved better. I faced all future tutors, Charles Tomlinson, Susie Tucker, Henry Littlewood, with outward composure although an inner gale continued to toss my intestines about. Back in Bombay three years later, I walked into a class of hundred young females and males at Elphinstone College to teach them 'Compulsory English'. Miraculously there was no churning of intestines. No trembling of limbs. No clammy palms. I realized then that the me in a classroom was a different creature from the me on any other platform before any other audience. In that realization lay my first sighting of my vocation.

Although the tongue was reluctant to say what the mind thought during the first term of my fresher year at Bristol, the rest of my body was doing marvellously well. The University had a badminton club. That is right. A proper badminton club with a proper indoor badminton court. Rusty after three years of an enforced layoff in London, I turned up for membership and team trials with some trepidation. But muscle memory combined with the euphoria of a homecoming of sorts, was enough to bring the game back. The women's captain Pam Lewis, a student of medicine, and the men's captain Les Rigby, an engineering student, watched, confabulated and offered me a place on the university team. My body was alive once again. It stretched, bent, leapt and won full colours for two years running. This honour for sporting excellence, the redbrick university equivalent of the Oxford and Cambridge 'Blues', was meant to be displayed on ties and badges. I have no recall of how I displayed mine if I did so at all. In my final year, when I could spare little time for matches, I had to be content with half-colours, a lesser honour.

In England, badminton is a winter game. In Bath where we played often, the badminton court was laid over a swimming pool. Every time we arrived at a tournament venue with me generally riding on the back of Les's bike, I had to be dumped before the fire to thaw out before I could be allowed on the court. Winters in England were my worst ordeals, when my fingertips, toes and the end of my nose went into a permanent deep freeze. Once, returning from a victory at Exeter University, the cold did more than numb my extremities. It attacked my kidneys. I confided my symptoms to Pam. She looked concerned and directed the coach driver to stop whenever I asked him to. I asked every fifteen or twenty minutes, to get off in deep embarrassment and deliver to the local toilet the few drops that I could painfully squeeze out of my bladder. Back in the Hall, I was packed off to bed to await the coming of the large, gruff and grey-haired Dr Victoria. Mild kidney infection she announced brusquely and equally brusquely prescribed a week's bed-rest on a diet of liquids, fruit and pills. It was a week of much attention from friends, including a basket bursting with seasonal fruit delivered to my bedside on Otto's behalf, he not being allowed into the sick bay. The fruit basket was topped off by a coconut. I never did figure out whether that touch was aimed at an aesthetic effect or was there to make me feel at home. For a long time afterwards, the coconut stood on my mantelpiece. There was no coconut grater in the Hall kitchen, so it could not go into my curries. Sitting on my mantelpiece it looked forlorn and out of place. Finally it went into my trunk in the storeroom and was apologetically offloaded when I packed up to move out of the Hall in the next vacation. Meanwhile, at the end of one week in bed, I was back on the badminton court. Kidneys? Never heard of them!

12. Teeth

Mr Nicol turned out to be just as taciturn as Otto had led me to believe. When he spoke it was with a barely distinguishable burr that pointed north to his place of origin. He did a long and leisurely inspection of my teeth. Then he straightened up from the back-destroying dentist's stoop and pronounced in throwaway fashion, 'Orthodontically speaking, you are an ancient ruin. But let us see what we can do for you.'

What he could do for me began with a plaster cast of my entire set of twenty-eight (the remaining four, the wisdoms, emerged and were knocked off much later). In my next sitting, the cast was demonstrated to me. For the first time, I saw my dental malocclusion grinning at me. It had made me such a slow eater at school that Usha and Rohini would go home, have a full lunch and return, and I, much to their disgust, would still be chewing through my two chapati-ghee-and-sugar rolls. Mr Nicol was now explaining his modus operandi. 'The bottom set is fine. Nothing to be done there. The upper needs rearranging. For that we will have to knock out this molar and this molar. That will allow us to push back these canines and incisors and make place for these molars to gradually shift into position so as to connect with their counterparts down here and make you a more efficient eater.'

A diagram of the cast went home in my weekly letter with

arrows pointing to the problem areas. Mother was a little upset that all the care she had taken of our teeth had somehow not prevented malocclusion in mine. Father said, 'Go ahead. Get it done.' For once I felt no guilt in following his orders. The treatment, bless the National Health Service, was free. So out came the problematic molars in two sittings. Meanwhile a plate was being constructed to push the incisors in. Mercifully, my worst fears turned out be unfounded. I was not going to be fitted with a permanent plate, the kind that every other child in a British school wore. My plate would be inserted only at night, doing its good work while I slept.

The plate I received consisted of a pink palate piece with wires attached, the whole slipping into my mouth as smooth as butter. For the next two years this ritual added a few more seconds to my bedtime routine. At the end of post-dinner coffees in my room, friends would get up, stretch and say, 'Locking up time for Shanta, girls.' Once the plate was in, I couldn't talk except in a lisp that reminded me of the time I was five. Had I tried, I would have been back to 'Lokabhilamam lanalanga dheelam lajeevanetlam laghuvanshanatham'.

Mr Nicol readjusted the wires of the plate at every sitting in accordance with the current position of my teeth. His fiddling had a perceptible effect on the speed at which I ate lunch in the Refectory. Lunch was with Lee Prandle who did Philosophy with me; or Margaret Hall and Mary Hooper who were in the English Honours class with me; or Poppy Aiyer who was doing research for a PhD; or Chandrakant Patel, who was also doing English but was a year ahead of me.

Lee was an Anglican and asked me with great concern what it was like being a non-believer. One had to believe in god, didn't one? Not this one, I would reply gently. But, in order not to upset her further, I would desist from telling her that non-belief, aka atheism, was just as strong a belief as Belief. In Philosophy class, Mr Kirkham, who lectured on Plato, threw questions about Truth and Justice at the high window across the room, not once meeting our eyes. I argued with Lee that if god was a given, why did philosophers bother to delve into the nature of truth and justice? Surely in god's world, what was, was and no questions asked. After this she would walk into the whole tangle of free will and lose her way. That was good for me, because my arguments at that stage were also tentative and could not have been pushed further.

With Margaret and Mary, lunch was accompanied by heated debates about the morning's lectures interspersed, once in a while, with caustic analyses of what we were eating in the name of food. 'How could Leavis so arrogantly start his book with the sweeping statement, "The great English novelists are Jane Austen, George Eliot, Henry James and Joseph Conrad"?' Margaret fumed one day. I was in total agreement with Leavis and had chosen precisely those authors as my essay subjects for tutorials. F.R. Leavis was the reigning god of Eng Lit in those days. 'Where's James Joyce then?' Margaret demanded. She was a diehard Joycean. Not so Mary who said, 'Nothing wrong with the statement. They are great novelists, aren't they?'

'But Mary, not the only ones.'

'So who else is there? You say Joyce. I say Hardy.'

'Laying down a canon is only meant to open up the field for discussion,' I argued. 'That's how we ask ourselves the question Leavis must have asked himself, "Who are our great novelists?" Our answer will inevitably lead us to question our criteria for saying so. Leavis makes his criteria quite clear. Let us decide what ours are. *The Great Tradition* gives us a chance to find out.' Passionate lovers hate balance. Margaret and Mary, for once in agreement, rolled their eyes at me.

With my third set of lunchtime companions, we rode our separate waves of nostalgia. Poppy was from Calcutta and although not a Bengali, something that Bristol's Bengalis never failed to underline in conversations with her, was deeply attached to the city. Chandu's heart was in Sri Aurobindo's ashram at Pondicherry and the ashram school in which he had studied. Mine was in Bombay, its music, theatre and dance, its beaches, bhelpuri and badminton, its local trains and BEST buses, its textile mills and cinema houses where men came round in the intermission with trays full of potato wafers and fizzy drink bottles.

The Refectory was also where Osmond Ward of the engineering school collared me in December 1961 demanding to know how I was going to explain Nehru's annexation of Goa. 'And don't call it liberation. It was aggression.' At that point in my political consciousness, I was unable to produce a convincing argument against his charge. He beamed.

So did I, generally speaking. For by then my incisors, canines and molars had found their new places and Mr Nicol was planning my final sitting. Also, I was barely six months away from my final homecoming.

13. Dance Again

It was in the Refectory too that I was discovered to be a 'dancer' by Dr Charles McIness, a friend of India. Bristol had an Indian Association which celebrated Diwali and other such occasions every year with 'variety entertainment' programmes for which a variety of entertainers was required. While there were, during the years I was there, several singers, there were no dancers. When I was told confidently by the Secretary, Mr Dey, that as a middle-class Maharashtrian I was bound to know how to dance, I rashly admitted I had a smattering of the art. A smattering would do for Bristol, he said. I panicked. I pointed out that I could not dance without music, hoping desperately that music could not be provided in Bristol. But where there are Indians, there is music. Hope turned to horror when Brij Sharma of the square face, curly hair and soulful expression was produced as the resident harmonium player, and the elderly Mr Govindasundaram as the tabla player. The Indian Association even owned the required instruments. Mr Dey did not look obviously triumphant. Mr Dey who was on study leave from IIT-Kharagpur, did not easily display emotion. What he displayed was the origin of all emotions, the sthayi bhava of the rasa theory, an inscrutable arrangement of facial muscles that distantly suggested the presence of all the nine rasas but never allowed them to show themselves.

The evil day inevitably arrived. I togged myself out in a red Mysore georgette sari loaned to me by a non-university member of the Association and performed Bhairav Prasad's todas and Keshav Sahasrabuddhe's 'Debdasi go ami pujarini'. Mercifully alaripu and thillana were out of the question because that music required players and singers with years of training, which neither the UPite Sharma nor Govindasundaram, despite being a true-blue Tamilian, had. The only song Govindasundaram sang at all Indian Association get-togethers was the Carnatic krithi 'Himagiri thanaye hemalathe'.

That evening, all the furniture in the Refectory was pushed back to clear an arena for my performance, with the exception of two tables on which Mr Brij Sharma and Mr Govindasundaram perched lugubriously with their respective instruments and their joyous Diwali expressions. At the end of the evening, a woman in a sensible beige skirt and a twin-set in a lighter shade hurried across to say Dr McIness would like to meet me. I had not the vaguest notion who Dr McIness was or what he did. The woman in beige led me to a blind gentleman who said he had enjoyed my dance very much. How? But I thanked him profusely and he invited me to 'his rooms' for Tea the following day. The lady in beige, who turned out to be his secretary, nodded happily and I accepted.

Dr McIness was a rotund, rubicund man with a ready smile which caused his sightless eyes to recede far into the folds of his chubby cheeks. His shirt was generally spotted with drips of gravy caused by glitches between fork and mouth. Tea at his rooms was standard British, comforting in its constancy. Cucumber sandwiches, tea-cakes and tea. I hated tea so I loved what the British served as tea. It was tea-flavoured hot water in a pretty cup. Why did I not have coffee then? An academic question, since Tea always meant tea in England. No coffee was offered. Anyway I disliked coffee more than I disliked tea.

On one occasion my Hall mate Pam Williams, taking me for a cool babe, served me Turkish coffee. She had just returned from a summer holiday in Turkey with a cezwe and finacans and the rest of the Turkish coffee hardware plus the knowhow for making the stuff. I asked her how one was supposed to drink the thick residue left at the bottom of the tiny cup after the top was drunk. If that wasn't a cool question to ask, I rubbed my uncoolness in further by confiding in her that the only coffee I liked was the one served at Satyanarayan pujas in Maharashtra, made with full-cream milk and lots of sugar, flavoured with cardamom and nutmeg. I liked it precisely because it was not what anybody would call coffee. Utterly disgusted, Pam upturned my fincan over the saucer, lifted it off, studied the dregs and pronounced my future: 'You will forever remain a barbarian, and not find a single civilized man to marry you.'

The tea at Dr McInness's rooms held no such dire predictions. Rather, it heralded the beginning of an unexpected life outside the university which was to add much to my cultural knowledge and joy. Dr McInness was a close friend of Arnold Haskell and a regular visitor to his second home in Bath, his first being in London. To my huge embarrassment, Dr McInness called me soon after the Tea to say he had talked of me glowingly to Mr Haskell who had promptly invited me to lunch along with him and his secretary the following Sunday. I was awed. Mr Haskell was a distinguished ballet critic who counted Alicia Markova among his friends. Through her he had become a friend of Ram Gopal's with whom she had recently collaborated to create the duet 'Radha-Krishna'. And I was to eat at this man's table on the strength of the few todas and gats old Bhariav Prasad had taught me!

It was my first introduction to a home where the table was laid just so, knives and forks in their proper places with an unseen presence in attendance to serve us delicately flavoured French onion soup, thinly slivered lamb with mint sauce, potatoes and carrots, followed by rhubarb tart for dessert. Nothing that Nancy Mitford would have categorized as non-U happened at that table. You never put a serviette on your lap, always a table napkin. You never referred to the vegetables as greens, nor did you say, 'Pass me the cruet.' Indeed it was non-U to possess a cruet at all. You had salt-cellars, pepper-mills and mustard pots which you asked for independently by those names. How you held and drank your wine was also governed by the strictest rules of what was U and non-U. Whether it was in Mr Haskell's house in Bath or in London where I spent a Christmas with his large Russian wife Vera and sons Francis and Stephen, Mr Haskell kept a well-stocked cellar, full of vintage wines and whiskies. He took it upon himself to educate me in wines, the temperatures to serve them at, the glasses to serve them in. I was taught the importance of swirling the pale gold liquid around in its goblet, sniffing delicately at it to savour its subtle bouquet and rolling the first sip on the tongue to enjoy again the sensuous experience of its aroma. I absorbed all this knowledge assiduously, strictly as knowledge, with the relieved thought that it was not going to be part of my life back home. But I appreciated Mr Haskell's generosity in opening the door of an aesthete's life to me, with its exquisitely understated culture.

One of the cultural treats Mr Haskell invited me to was Dame Alicia Markova dancing *Giselle* at the Bristol Old Vic.

My winter coat was a camel-coloured rough wool thing with a large collar and no buttons which I had bought in a sale. It had to be held together when you walked to stop it from flapping open in the wind and letting the freezing air in. The most attractive thing about it had been its price. Four guineas. While it was warm and good enough for university, it was hardly fit company for the furs and lambswools that floated into the Old Vic that evening. Acutely aware of its inappropriateness to the occasion, I marched into the theatre with extra swagger, telling myself that clothes did not make man. Or woman. At the coat check in the foyer, the attendant helping people off with their coats and hanging them up behind the counter, was discretion itself. Not a line moved on his face as he received my coat after an expensive black lambswool. British politeness never failed.

The ballet was magnificent and Mr Haskell full of good spirits and information. At the end I was taken backstage to meet the great dancer herself. She was fifty, thin and gaunt. The *Giselle* we had seen was perhaps one of her last performances before she retired two years later. I didn't deserve any of these rich encounters on merit. Some people are just damned lucky Joan Pick said good-naturedly when I returned to Hall with the story. That is what I was. Lucky.

14. Rag Day Shivers

Although I sneezed through the whole of the British spring, I didn't mind the season as much as I did the winter. In London I had saved every shilling to put into the ever-empty maw of the tiny heater in my digs and gloomily counted the winter months I would have to spend on this chilly isle getting myself an education. Out in the open, the wind would slap my face right and left while the icy air screwed straight into my bones. My nose dripped, my eyes smarted and my toes turned into senseless protuberances that made me stumble. I was always at risk of skidding on the frosted roads and falling flat on my face. There were ways and ways of falling flat on your face, some more humiliating than others. Once, wearing a brand new white silk sari, faux fur-lined winter boots and a defiant look, I was walking down Picadilly Circus with my date, when my frozen toes stepped on the hem of the sari causing a flood of billowing white to drop onto the frosty footpath around my feet. My date caught my horrified glance and murmured, 'Is this a disaster?'

'You could call it that.'

'So what do we do?' He was probably wondering what the modern follow-on to the Walter Raleigh act could be.

'We do nothing. I alone do. You stand by and pretend you have nothing to do with me.'

I turned to face the grey wall we were passing. With the natural protection of my flappy coat to hide my manoeuvrings and assured that people passing by and looking my way (though the English never did that) would assume I was engaged in some mysterious Eastern ritual, I managed to gather up and tuck back the fallen pleats where they belonged. That evening led to a resolve. In winter, I would wear my saris ankle length and to hell with elegance. I had looked comical before in this country when I went camping in Cornwall where the weather changed every few minutes. Rosemary Devin had taken a picture of a thoroughly confused me in a raincoat topped by a summer straw hat, wondering which to keep on and which to take off.

In Bristol, Otto found my winter depression amusing. He got his sister Lillemor, who lived and worked in Oslo, to make a little red ski-cap for my nose. He proposed I should wear it when I stepped out. Norwegians speak fondly of koselig, or 'coziness' in winter, which comes from lighting candles and fires, drinking warm beverages and snuggling under blankets. They find great joy also in bundling up and sallying forth into the great outdoors where dire winds are blowing and snow piling. They have a saying: 'There's no such thing as bad weather, only bad clothing'. I wore the nose cap Otto got me in my room and laughed at myself in the mirror. How I wished I had the nerve to wear it outdoors and allow the world to laugh at me while I enjoyed my koselig.

Spring was something else. To see the first snowdrop poke its head above the earth was nothing short of understanding the miracle of life. In Bombay, the koel's call heralded spring and musicians broke into raag Basant. A few peepul trees put out delicate, fluttering shell-pink leaves which turned the sunlight filtering through them into a rosy blush. There was also the appearance of raw mangoes in the market which meant pickling. But there was nothing like a shoot breaking the earth and emerging into a brave new world.

After winters spent sitting on radiators or turning my room into an oven that made my hardy English friends throw open the windows and let the freezing air in, I went a little crazy each spring. Laughed for no reason, sang for no reason and began planning for the summer vacation. Once, sitting out on the downs during lunch, I put a daisy behind Otto's ear. He forgot it was there and walked back into the dental hospital like a male version of France Nuyen in *South Pacific.* He came to himself only when he saw the half-amused, half-horrified expressions on his batchmates' faces and heard the professor roar, 'Thank you, Mr Tokvam, for bringing the spring in.'

But spring wasn't really the beginning of warm weather. At least not warm as I defined the word. March, supposedly the beginning of the season, was also the month in which Bristol University and the city came together for Rag Day dedicated to the charity selected for the year. On that day students, representing Halls of Residence and University departments, went around the city in specially designed floats, and the citizens dropped coins for the charity into their rattling tins. I'm not certain whether I was on our Hall float or the English department float on my first Rag Day. But I do know that, had I had the choice, I would have been on any other float but that one. The theme of the float was 'The Haunted Castle' and we were the haunting spirits. Our costumes were what all self-respecting ghosts wore, whatever the season—loose white sheets with holes for eyes and nose. Although I had worn three layers of woollies underneath my sheet, the wind merely laughed at them and brazenly climbed up my legs and into the interiors of my body. The floats were open and the ride through the city long. The only compensation for being a ghost on a float in March was the eerie sounds we got to make. As a frozen ghost with chattering teeth, my blood-curdling sounds were made less to arouse dread than to express sheer misery. By the end of the ride, we had managed to collect a tidy sum for the charity. But before I could join in the celebrations, I had to thaw out and return from my stalactite state to something approaching humanhood.

Summers, except when it rained which it did all the time, were my great guarantees that all was still well with the world. Summers were the time for strawberries and for the wisteria vine on the back wall of the Hall dining-room to burst into light purple, headily fragrant blossom. Summers were for croquet on the lawns of Goldney House. Summers were for travel. Travel meant money which no student could eke out of her stringent budget. My middle-class parents, who were so generously (for me) and problematically (for themselves and Nirmal) funding my education in the UK, could hardly be expected to cover my holiday travel. I needed a summer job to finance it. With Otto's contacts in a travel agency in Oslo with whom he had worked one summer, my destination had to be Scandinavia. Father was thrilled. Scandinavia was where the institution of the parliamentary ombudsman had been first developed. I found myself a job at Will's cigarette factory in Southville, on the south bank of the River Avon. It entailed taking an early morning ferry across the river and another back in the evening.

The six weeks I worked in the factory, deftly taking cigarettes with faulty filters off the conveyor belt, sharpened my eyes and quickened my fingers. I thought of my childhood years when I was the family's butter fingers. If something needed dropping or breaking, my hands were the chosen instruments for the operation. Father's occasional endearment for me was 'vendhalabai', which, bluntly put, meant Miss Scatter Brain. This basic meaning was extended in my case to cover other gaucheries, like my habit of twisting myself in the living-room curtain when a visitor asked me which school I went to. Once in a while this caused the curtain to slip off its rod and expose me to my interrogators. But most times it stood solidly by me.

My chirpy conveyor-belt-mates at Wills, Linda and Tony, and my supervisor Fay with her curly mop of salt-and-pepper hair and grey eyes that twinkled when she grinned, encouraged me along as they would a promising race horse. And I was soon working as fast as any veteran. Come Friday Linda would say, 'So what are you doing over the weekend? Will you come dancing with us?'

And I'd say, 'Afraid not.'

'So what'll you do?'

With the greatest difficulty I'd bring out the word, 'Read.'

'You mean mags and things. How long does that take?'

I'd drop my voice further and say, 'No. Books.'

It took Linda a while to understand that I'd rather spend time with books than go dancing with her and her gang dressed in a white mini, gold belt and stilettos which, she said, would look just fab on me.

The brothers W.D. and H.O. Wills, who did lungs much harm, were good to me. They financed my trip to Scandinavia—

two days in Bergen, ten in Flam on Sogn Fjord with Otto and his old parents, three in Oslo, three in Copenhagen and two in Gothenburg. At the beginning of my second year I was writing about the trip for the *Times of India*. Paula Kahn, sitting across the library table from me, grumbled, 'How can you get into a national paper with stories about catching trout in Flam and getting sick with boiled prawns on Oslo Quay? And get paid on top!'

It astonished me too. I was just being a normal student doing normal student things. But in those days the Sunday edition of *The Times of India* did publish stories of this kind. Why, even the daily Times published funnies called Middles in which people wrote about their spouses and pets and strange neighbours and stranger aunts. I was to contribute to this feature for nearly a year after my return from Bristol until Vatsal, who later married Tulsi Mehta, a student at Elphinstone College when I was doing my stint there, asked in his gentle fashion, 'Do you intend to die writing middles?' I saw his point and stopped.

But I will say in my defence that I wrote the article on Scandinavia on request. This is how it happened. During my six years in England, I wrote long letters home every week and got long letters back at the same frequency. After my traumatic experience on Rag Day, I wrote a longer than normal letter describing the entire thing. Father's colleague in the Times, M.V. Mathew who, besides doing his editorial duties also wrote theatre reviews out of personal interest, read the letter as he had read many others, and said to Father, 'This I will publish.' After that, he asked me to write about my Scandinavian trip, then my fortnight in Italy the following year and then the Edinburgh Festival in my final year. But Paula was right when she said, 'Some people have all the luck.' How many young women had fathers who were assistant editors in a national newspaper with colleagues like Mr Mathew?

15. Dark-skinned in Gothenburg

Nirmal and I were born dark-skinned. In Maharashtra you were either fair or dark or wheat-coloured. Fair was best, wheat was acceptable, dark was sad. Arvind Terdalkar, my badminton mate from the Municipal Club, had once asked me to choose a sari for his sister. It was going to be his Bhau Beej gift to her. Not having met his sister, and men not being observant of their women relatives' tastes in dress, I had no clue what to look for. I fingered the pile of saris that the shop assistant of my favourite sari shop had thrown on the counter with, what I hoped, looked like an expert touch. The shop was owned by a Gujarati but the counter assistants were all Marathi. Marathis are clerks and poets, playwrights and actors, singers and sermonizers and, in their very heart of hearts, warriors, descendants of the great Shivaji, ready to pull out imaginary swords to lay low anybody who dared breathe a word that suggested the warrior-king was after all a human being, not a god. What they were not, if they could help it, were persuasive sellers of goods. Novelist-playwright Shyam Manohar, who lives in Pune, told me in the course of an interview for my book on Marathi drama, that he once went to a shop in Pune to get a refill for his ball-point pen. The shopkeeper offered him one which didn't work. When he asked for another, the shopkeeper said, 'You just have to hold this one against a flame for a moment. That'll make it flow.' In short, if you were paying for goods, it was your responsibility to make them work.

The shop assistant showing us saris in my favourite sari shop belonged to this tribe. At one point he began sweeping all the saris off the counter and suggested we try the next-door shop. Then, in the brusque way that comes naturally to Marathis, he relented and said, 'What is her skin colour?' With the greatest delicacy Aru said, 'She's wheat-coloured.' The man looked suspiciously at him and said, pointing to me, 'You mean like that?' Aru nodded uncertainly. 'Then that's called dark.' The shopkeeper then proceeded to fold up all the bright-coloured saris, leaving behind the dull, pastel shades. 'Anyone of these will suit her,' he said, his nose very much in the air.

Mother had grown up in a joint family full of fair to wheatish women who shared the shop assistant's sense of colour coding. My grandfather, as dark-skinned as they come, would bring back from his business trips vari-coloured saris and sometimes khanns—those jewel-coloured woven blouse pieces with broad borders in contrasting colours that came from Dharwad and Hubli. The seniormost aunt had the right to open the bundle and distribute the contents according to age and skin colour. The brightest and best went to Mother's aunts and cousins. Mother got self-effacing shades that, she was told, would bring a glow to her skin. When Nirmal and I came along, she took revenge on her aunts, many long since dead and gone. She dressed us in vibrant shades of red, yellow, blue and green, and parkar-polkas (traditional long skirts and blouses) made from Dharwad khanns, against the aesthetic judgement of the solidly middle-class Shivaji Park neighbourhood. Across the road from our house, dark-skinned women from Andhra worked on construction sites wearing shocking pink and flaming orange saris with beaded blouses in contrasting colours. Look at them Mother said. How beautiful they look.

Shivaji Park was not convinced. But we were awarded Maharashtra's favourite consolation prize for being the wrong colour: we were 'dark but smart'. That phrase has been one of the two most frequently used currencies in the Marathi marriage market, the other being, 'dark but sharp-featured'. In the old days, the Indian Railways used to have four classes of carriage: first, second, intermediate and third. If one were to classify women according to those categories, the 'dark but smart' would be the intermediate class; the fair would be the unquestioned first; and the wheat-coloured the second. Wheat-coloured was never further analyzed according to species of wheat between which, if observed closely, Khandwa was a shade lighter than Punjab Pisi.

On the Municipal Employees' Club badminton court, Vijay Joshi, who had preceded me to the UK, was always told with some envy and a lot of admiration that he looked like an Englishman. He didn't ask which kind: pasty, lobster or cream. All set to be part of the general English colour scene, Vijay was shocked when he was asked there if he came from southern Italy. In Italy, where I went on my second summer holiday, I was asked repeatedly if the Indian sun had made me brown. 'Molto sole,' they said, nodding wisely. At Bristol, Mary Barwell once asked me if I was pink inside. 'Inside?' I asked, wondering if she meant all the way in, like my stomach and intestines and all of that. If so I would not know because I'd never seen myself inside out. 'No no,' she said answering the question in my eyes. 'I mean where your clothes cover you. Where the sun doesn't get to you.' Mary was pure Anglo-Saxon, pink inside and out. To her mind, I had to be at least a caramelized Anglo-Saxon. 'No,' I answered kindly. 'I'm evenly dark, inside and out. I can live in the Arctic all my life and still be this colour.'

At New Year in Edinburgh, where we were staying with Otto's friends the Dobys, my skin colour made me a very special person. Mrs Doby looked at me on New Year's Eve and said to her husband, 'We've got our first-footer for Bertie and Carol right here, love.' Bertie was the Dobys' only son; Carol his wife; and first-footing an old custom in which, if the right person was the first to set foot in your house on New Year's Day, you were going to be blessed with good fortune for the rest of the year. Traditionally, the most desirable first-footer was a tall, dark-haired male. Allow a woman or a fair-haired male in and you were inviting a year of bad fortune. I was not only dark-haired but dark-skinned as well, compensation enough for not being male. So I was like a bonanza. That year I brought luck to Bertie and Carol, and to several other good friends of the Dobys' to whose homes we went first-footing.

In Gothenburg, at the end of my Scandinavian holiday, I met a Bengali student who said, 'Let me show you a sight that will make your eyes pop.' He took me to the University common room where a man with skin the colour of black coffee, hippie hair and a wide grin was lolling on a settee with three blonde women draped around him. 'He's from Ceylon,' said my escort, 'and women find his vacker hud sexy.'

'What hud?'

'Vacker hud. Beautiful skin.'

'You sound bitter.'

'With reason. Back home I'm dark. Here I'm not dark enough.'

In India, even gods have to live with the knowledge that their colour is wrong. Chapter 48 of the Book of Ayodhya in Valmiki's *Ramayana*, says Rama, 'whose face is like the full moon, of dark brown complexion, whose collar-bone is invisible, a conqueror of foes, whose arms descend to his knees, whose eyes resemble lotuses, the elder brother of Lakshmana, who takes initiative in speaking and expresses with sweetness, truthful of speech and possessed of extraordinary strength, is benevolent to all, delightfully charming as the moon. That tiger among men, as mighty as an elephant in rut, that great warrior, will surely adorn the woods, while roaming through them.' Rama was 'of dark brown complexion' and all the other virtues were additional to the colour not compensations for it. What happened then between Valmiki's description and the image of Lord Rama as it has come down to us? Why has he been painted blue? Why has Krishna, also called Shyam, both names meaning dark, been painted blue? One of the dozens of answers offered by scholars for this betrayal of truth is that blue rather than brown or black is more likely to arouse devotion in people's hearts. After all, the malevolent planets in our horoscopes—Shani, Rahu, Ketu—are painted black while the other planets are painted white, yellow or red.

We have it from the Kannada scholar, novelist and playwright Adya Rangacharya that the 16th-century saint-poet Kanaka Dasa once wrote a play called *Rama-dhanya-nataka* (Play of Rama and the cereals), in which a bunch of light-coloured cereals argued with ragi, the dark-skinned finger millet, over who was superior. The argument went back and forth till Lord Rama was asked to settle the dispute. He told the cereals to bury themselves in the ground for two years. At the end of that period all the light-coloured cereals had rotted. Ragi came out shining.

I like to think this was Lord Rama's revenge against artists who have turned his glorious dark skin blue.

16. Adipose Tissue and the Mating Game

In 1959 March, I had flown back home in a Super Constellation for a five-month break. Three years later I returned in a Boeing, with a not particularly brilliant 2B degree in English Language and Literature in my pocket. My second-year dissertation for Susie Tucker had been on the New English Bible. Published in 1961, this translation had filled reams of columns in the Press. It was seen by most scholars and lay correspondents as necessary but a comedown from the Authorised Version which had contributed so richly to the English language. I questioned the necessity of the modern translation. The Authorised Version translated from Hebrew had been necessary because Hebrew was an alien tongue. Not so Elizabethan English. Further, religion was not merely a matter of comprehension. Biblical stories were not just factual events, if they were that. More often they were metaphors which deepened the believer's understanding of religion in a subliminal way. I believed a sacred text needed to keep its distance from the everyday. Brought down to the level of the everyday, the multiple meanings created by its metaphors were destroyed without being replaced by anything of equal value. My dissertation, a linguistic comparison between the Authorised Version and the New English Bible, could no more than hint at this argument which verged on the theological where I had little knowledge. So I confined myself to looking at the two texts only as forms of the English language to see what was gained in the contemporary and what was lost. The dissertation had pleased Ms Tucker who gave me a good grade, putting a silver lining around my 2B cloud.

Before returning home, I had to get rid of all the acquisitions made during my three years at University that could not be accommodated within the stipulated 20 kg of baggage I was allowed. Although most of my books came back with me, I was forced to junk, in a final wrench, six years of weekly letters from home. I possessed a pair of expandable suitcases made of light fibreglass that did not add weight to the contents. Everything that I simply had to take home was packed and I was still weighing the large bundle of letters on my trusted spring scales, standing by the window, switching on all the lights in the room to see better, postponing the final decision to the following day when the sky might not be so cloudy (fat chance), hoping to discover that the bundle did not weigh 3 kg as the arrow had persistently shown but… Actually, I was avoiding admitting that the arrow had to stand still at zero to let me include the letters in my baggage. I wept when I put them out with other accumulations, including the lovely Modigliani print that had hung in my room for three years. The letters were the only written record of life in Shivaji Park during the six years that I was away. I know my parents had scrimped and saved to keep me at Bristol, although their letters had said not a word about it. I was determined to make sure I earned enough when I returned to keep myself and contribute a little something to the household.

Teaching. That was where my first bit of money came from. Father's friend Professor Mahishi, who taught English at Sydenham College, asked me practically the day after I returned, whether I would take classes in remedial English at the college. Sydenham had many students from schools where the medium of instruction had been an Indian language whereas the medium at college was English. The remedial English classes were meant to close the gap. The classes brought me enough for myself, but left nothing for the home. Fortunately there was something else at Sydenham. It was full of Dawoodi Bohra boys from wealthy business families. One day Professor Mahishi called to ask if I would teach conversational English to one of the daughters of the Syedna (or was it the wife of one of his sons?). The Syedna is the Dā'ī al-Mutlaq, or absolute missionary of the Dawoodi Bohras.

'With pleasure.'

'One hour twice a week, two hundred rupees a month.'

'Gulp.'

'Are you there?'

'Just about. Two hundred? So much?'

I need to put two hundred rupees in perspective to explain my amazement. The year was 1962. The month July. When I joined Elphinstone College in September to fill a maternity vacancy, I was paid Rs 288.30 per month for a six-days-a-week, five-hours-a-day slog.

'So much? You'll go to Saifee Mahal to teach. When you see the place you'll know what so much means. Just take the money, okay?'

Saifee Mahal was a sprawling three-storeyed palace painted cream, up a steep incline off Nepean Sea Road. It had an imposing porch with pilasters, doric columns, mouldings and balustrades leading up to the entrance. The rest of the edifice stretched as far as the eye could see, punctuated by rows of shallow-arched windows on the first and second floors. Lots of little boys in crocheted Bohra caps were on their way to school on the morning I arrived for the first lesson. Predictably I lost my way. Someone directed me to a room at the far end of the edifice. By the time I found it, I was a quarter of an hour late. A woman of about thirty-five, dressed in a plain ghagra-choli and an odhni with an embroidered border covering her head, was waiting for me. This was Zehra. She was a good soul, diligent and full of good intentions; but, as I was soon to discover, unteachable. Conversational English is a slippery thing. You don't do grammar except incidentally. You don't have a textbook for support. Nobody has taught you to teach it. You're on your own with a student whose expectant gaze is fixed on you, waiting for you to do your magic. Every tuition day, as I climbed up the incline to Saifee Mahal, I would ponder over a subject we could converse about. The idea was that Zehra would talk and I would gently point out mistakes, explain why they were mistakes and get her to construct similar sentences minus those mistakes. With this method, I expected her to be in full flow soon with me sitting back admiring my skill. Unfortunately, by and large, Zehra had nothing to say about any of the subjects I suggested. I ended up doing most of the talking which of course was not the point. So then I thought I would bring along simple plays for us to read aloud. Plays are conversation. In reading her lines Zehra would learn English as she was spoke. But Zehra read so haltingly, with so many pauses in the wrong places that English as she is spoke flew out the window.

At the end of the month Zehra led me downstairs to an enormous hall lined with steel cupboards. She plucked the huge bunch of keys dangling from a silver ring hooked into her ghagra, and opened one of them. Inside were wads and wads and wads of notes from the bottom of the cupboard to the top. My jaw got unhinged and hung flaccidly while my eyes flew out of their sockets. Zehra pulled out one wad and nonchalantly peeled off two hundred-rupee notes. They looked totally ridiculous before that obscenely stuffed cupboard. Professor Mahishi had only hinted about how my ideas of money would change when I saw Saifee Mahal. He knew nothing of the cupboards inside. From next month on, I carefully averted my eyes when Zehra's hand reached for the keys.

That tuition lasted four months at the end of which Zehra knew and I knew that, much as we liked each other, conversation in English was not happening. So we called an end to the farce. The next tuition I did was with a Japanese woman—unforgivably, her name slips me entirely—who had no English at all. It may have been Adrian Stevens the photographer who recommended me to her. We struggled together to find something that would take us beyond sweet noises and sweeter smiles. Once, in desperation, I told her of a wonderful Kobe steak restaurant that had just come up in town. My friend Mahrukh Irani's people had started it. Eureka. I had hit the right spot. From angry signs we went slowly to words and then sentences, all about Kobe steak. The Bombay restaurant was rubbish. No place could possibly serve the real Kobe steak. Do you know how those cows are looked after? Since she spoke very haltingly, it took her many lessons to give me the whole lowdown on the lineage of the cows and steers that yielded this highly prized beef; about where they had to be born and raised and what grasses and grains they had to be fed before we could enjoy real, meaning REAL Kobe steak. It was clear then that no restaurant anywhere in the world other than in Japan could ever serve the REAL Kobe steak, whatever its pretensions. With Kobe steak as the centre of our lessons and assiduous mutual application to our task, we had gotten to a point where she could put together an English sentence—with only a prod or two from me, on other subjects too—when the time came for her to return to Japan, and I to a strictly vegetarian conversation with my next student, Kalpana Mody. Kalpana knew English but her pronunciations were atrocious. I spent many lessons trying to get her to pronounce her mother's name Susheela right. She got what I was trying to say but the name always came out as Shuseela.

Meanwhile, I was putting on weight. The euphoria of being home had made me reckless. I ate here, I ate there, I ate everything I was offered everywhere. Nirmal had meanwhile got engaged to Balu (Mukund) Limaye. She had returned home after her 'O' levels, suffocated by the formalities of British life. She was a kho-kho player, an athlete, a national-level basketball and table tennis champ, someone who belonged to the open cheering fields, not to the mincing prunes and prisms of England. She was not equipped with a filter between thought and word. In England it was all filters. Nirmal's two years in England would make a very different story from mine. Always on the lookout for odd jobs which would bring her pocket money that Mother could not carve out of the allowance Father sent us, she did newspaper rounds and waited tables in a Siamese restaurant. While she excelled at her school work, she was never perfectly happy under London's grey skies. At last, it was decided she would return to Bombay after her 'O' levels and return to England for a postgrad degree if she so wished. She was keen to do medicine and would have done so too had she not fallen in love with the dashing Balu, a past student of her college and a fine cricketer. The medical college plan was ditched. She graduated in Science, doing superbly well as always, winning scholarships and awards. And then she married.

Nirmal and Balu were married in Lalit Estate according to Vedic rites in keeping with the wishes of Balu's family who were orthodox. Only close friends and relatives were invited. Babu took pictures. Babu was Queen G's find, a good-looking, soft-spoken man with a passion for photography. Amongst the prints he delivered a week later was one which featured a fat arm in the foreground with Father's friends in the background. That arm, I realized in horror, was mine. During my six years in England my weight had fluctuated between normal (112 lbs) and low (96 lbs). I had never touched the heights I had unwittingly reached now. Mother's friends said I was at last looking healthy, the Indian matron's term of ultimate approval. Slim young women were encouragingly assured they would fill out and become healthy after marriage. Usha and Rohini were both healthy. But they carried their health well. I was not made to carry so much good health. The moment I added a couple of pounds I felt I was not walking but waddling. I had already started feeling that by the time Babu's pictures arrived. When I saw my arm filling the picture frame, I knew drastic action was called for. Once a week badminton, which is all I had time for just then, was not enough. I added early morning bending, stretching, jumping, skipping, sarvangasana, dhanurasana and tadasana. With firm though regretful self-denial of ghee and sweets, I was down to 112 pounds within a month.

In the three years that followed, life was all mind and little matter. Father's friend Professor Mangesh Vitthal Rajadhyaksha called to say there was a vacancy in Elphinstone College and would I like to fill it? I jumped at the chance of earning something more regular than the flood-and-drought pattern of English conversation tuitions. Elphinstone provided security of sorts and more. It revealed my vocation to me. I was, I told myself rather sententiously, 'born to be a teacher'. The final break-up with Otto happened during those years. I admitted to myself that I didn't have the makings of a world citizen. Otto's plan of six months in India and six months in Norway did not fit with my desire to be rooted. So, what had been a beautiful relationship of mutual love and respect, came to a deeply regretted end.

Father said why do you want to marry at all. Come live with us in our retirement home in Talegaon, teach at Pune University, read, write, forget marriage and babies. The prospect seemed attractive; but I was being wooed. A table tennis friend took me out to a seaside cafe where he played 'Yeh mera prem patra padhkar' on the juke box. As the song bounced along, he looked at me significantly. I thought it rather odd that, having so much to catch up on after my years away in England, he was totally tongue-tied when we met. The song ended. He said, 'So?'

'Nice song.'

'Yes. The words are so beautiful.'

'Words?'

'Yes. Ke tum meri zindagi ho, ke tum meri bandagi ho.'

Dummkopf I told myself. He's proposing to you for God's sake. Can't you see?

But he was an old pal whom I had slapped on the back and laughed with; whose home I had visited dozens of times. He would be one of the first friends I would invite to my wedding if ever I got married. But did I see him standing beside me in a silk kurta, wearing the garland I had put around his neck? I shook my head. 'Sorry yaar. Really sorry.'

'It's okay,' he sighed. Two months later he came over to invite me to his wedding. He was marrying his medical school classmate.

A badminton player, mixed-doubles partner to the great Nandu Natekar, asked Queen G if she thought I would be interested in marrying her brother, also a badminton player. Excited by the prospect of being a matchmaker, Queen G invited me and the sister (not the man himself) to tea. I had seen the man play. He was in the habit of looking at the tramlines or net or shuttle or racquet reproachfully every time he lost a point. When his sister gently probed me about the possibility of meeting him 'with a view to marriage', I said, 'Sorry. Really sorry. He's a wonderful player and I'm sure a lovely person. But I'm not planning on marrying just yet.'

Another old friend, mine at first but of the whole family later, wrote to me with a formal proposal. He was small and tense and rarely laughed. He was also a brahmin who was proud of his caste, while to me being brahmin was an accident of birth. So again I wrote back saying, 'Sorry. Very sorry,' adding a few elaborations on the theme. He wrote a brief nine-word note back: 'Mea culpa. Peccavi. But I hope we'll remain friends.' He was otherwise a lovely man and we did remain friends, and soon enough he married his cousin and the three of us became friends together.

I was turning down proposals, but I guess I was also looking for a mate. It was not a powerful, insuperable urge; but I would not look away if a suitable man swam into my ken. My old friend A.V. Bharath, whose acquaintance we had made on a summer holiday in Kodaikanal, the same holiday during which I had written verses about poor solitary girls drowning in the deep, and whose friend Madhav Vaidya had left Paula Kahn heartbroken, was now posted to INS *Hamla*, the Navy's logistics and training establishment located in Malad, a western suburb of the city. It is a beautiful, peaceful base with its own beach of silver sand. Bharath invited Nirmal and me to Sunday lunch. It was the day I had my first Indian Navy trifle pudding which I will not presume to describe. I did not know then that trifle pudding was to become the central motif of my lunches and dinners for many years to come. Along with trifle pudding in *Hamla* came an introduction to Lieutenant-Commander Vijay Kumar Mohan Shahane, Viju to friends, a pleasantly 'healthy' man who spoke of books and little else. Later there were evening parties where dance bands played. At the first one I was invited to, Viju stamped all over my toes doing what he thought was a fox-trot. He also told me, not the least apologetically, that he did not speak Marathi. For me, brought up to be bilingual, this sounded like an affectation, an unforgiveable one considering his maternal uncle was poet Madhav Julian (born Madhav Patwardhan), member of the Ravikiran Mandal and initiator of the sonnet in Marathi poetry. But I let it pass and we sat out the remaining dances, talking books. In the course of several more lunches and dance parties in *Hamla*-by-the-sea highlighted by trifle puddings, I must have come to the conclusion that Viju was the mate I was looking for, notwithstanding that, on his first personal invitation to me that did not involve Bharath, he had kept me waiting at Malad station for forty minutes, before he turned up on his Vespa to ferry me to the base, a half-hour bumpy ride away. Did I think there was something wrong here? No. I waited cheerfully, transferring my weight from one foot to the other, thinking generous thoughts about how his scooter had probably broken down, poor fellow, or how something urgent must have come up, poor fellow. Hope he's not unwell poor fellow was the worry that occupied the last ten minutes of waiting. Not for a moment did it strike me that he had been sleeping off a hangover. When he did turn up, he was cheerful as he said sorry yaar and I totally forgiving.

One evening we were at a terrace party in the middle of Bombay, I with my fruit juice and he with his favourite Old Monk, which was then, in 1965, celebrating its eleventh anniversary as India's only dark rum. He sauntered up to me where I was leaning against the parapet watching the crowd from a writerly distance. I could tell by his uncustomary shuffling and silence that he was priming himself to do something he had either never done before or done badly and earned a rebuff for. Wanting to ease things for him, I said, 'Why don't we get married, Viju?' Nearly dropping his glass, his light skin reddening, his green eyes popping, he made a brave attempt at nonchalance. 'Yes, why not?'

In Pune, where his much-travelled parents had built themselves a dark little retirement bungalow called Mamita, there was much relief at the news of his decision to 'settle'. At age thirty-five, he was well into the no-man's land that precedes confirmed bachelorhood. There was even greater relief that he was not, as his father put it quaintly in his congratulatory letter, marrying 'a decorative doll'. Presumably Dada, as he was called, had imagined his son cavorting with many such in wicked Bombay, any one of whom he could have sprung on Mamita as the second Shahane daughter-in-law, the first being Lilu, married to his older brother Squadron-Leader Ajit of the Indian Air Force.

Despite the fact that a war with Pakistan was looming on the horizon and we were soon to cover our windows with black paper and knit sweaters for our jawans, the date set for the wedding was 15 August 1965. This allowed Viju's friends to joke, each as though he was the first to think of the witticism, 'So you're losing your independence on Independence Day!' I was financing the wedding. It didn't strike me as odd that Viju wasn't offering to share the costs. Nor did it strike me as odd that, despite belonging to the armed forces, he was persuading me not to follow the government order, part of the austerity measures then in force, that put a cap of hundred on wedding guests. He had hordes of close friends, so did his family, my family and I. But we were building the nation and what was good for the nation had to be good for us. If I had any doubts about my decision to marry at all (women with too many principles make bad marriage partners), or to marry Viju, they were swept away under the naive assumption that love would conquer all. Viju's bachelor quirks like drinking himself silly and being financially irresponsible would vanish in the warmth of family life, which his mother Mai regretted he had been deprived of for too long. A well-run home with babies scampering around would usher into his solitary life a sea-change that he didn't at present seem to realize he was yearning for. Little did I know that his grip on the bottle would grow stronger in self-preservation (being married to someone as prickly with principles as me was so much more complicated than being single); his grip over finances would remain slack, and that nothing was more likely to make him run a mile than babies scampering around. He told me good-naturedly that he did not want them. I told him lovingly that I did. So the babies came, first Renuka, then Girish. The body was back in play.

17. The Babies Are Born and How!

I was in my eighth month and so big that I couldn't see my toes when standing, and I was still riding pillion on Viju's Vespa. We had been invited to Suresh and Sulu Samant's place for dinner. They were old friends of Viju's and now mine. When I had married Viju, Suresh had taken upon himself the responsibility of getting him to the wedding venue on time and had kept his promise. It had been part of Viju's life as a bachelor to be generously fed and equally generously scolded by friends' wives. Sulu was a member of that system. She was horrified to hear that we had made the journey from the Naval Flats in Colaba to the Samant home in Mahalakshmi on Viju's Vespa. Dressed elegantly as always and looking ethereal, she proceeded to scold Viju now. 'How could you let Shanta ride pillion in this condition?'

'What condition?' inquired Viju innocently.

'Perhaps you've noticed she's in her eighth month. Perhaps you've noticed our roads are festooned with potholes.'

'No yaar.'

'What are you saying "no yaar" to Viju? To her being pregnant or to the potholes?'

Viju was caught. So he simply laughed, hoping the question would go away. But Sulu wasn't letting go so easily. She made a stern face, wagged her forefinger and said, 'This is the last time you're taking her on your chariot. We don't want her delivering in a pothole.'

I'm not sure if anything Sulu said penetrated Viju's good humour. But I was cautioned. After that, I only did short runs on the Vespa.

On the afternoon of 6 October 1966, the pains began. I called Viju at his office—he was posted then at INS *Angre*, Shahid Bhagatsingh Marg—to inform him, as father of the child, that the child was coming. He was very gracious. He said, 'Carry on. Take a cab. I'll see you later.' Mother was at Nirmal's place helping her with her second born, Vikram, who had arrived a fortnight before. I did as I was encouraged to do. I carried on to the sprawling INS *Ashwini*, the hospital 'ship', arrived at the maternity ward which was at one end of the campus and registered my presence. As W/O (wife of) a naval officer, a certain amount of toughness was automatically expected of me. 'Wives of' didn't fight at sea, but they fought to stay afloat in life, moving from one borrowed flat to another, living out of boxes while they waited wistfully for their rightful accommodation to be allotted to them. I had never figured out why the Navy recruited more men than it could accommodate. But that was how it was. You were compensated for the inconvenience by the lifelong bonds you forged with friends who offered to share their homes with you.

It was evening. I had Muriel Spark's *The Prime of Miss Jean Brodie* to keep me company. As an aside I have a suspicion that part of Miss Brodie, the non-fascist part, leaked into a character I created for my second novel *Tya Varshi*. The pains were still few and far between. Viju came with a gang of friends later to wave me on in my birth-giving endeavour and departed. He had already made his contribution to the raising of the child that was coming. If it was a girl she was to be called Roza after Comrade Dange's daughter or Renuka after Renuka Ray Chakravarty or Kamala after Kamaladevi Chattopadhyay. But unlike these women of substance, she was to elope at sixteen and not bother us with marriage expenses. If the baby was a boy, the choice of name was to be mine.

At some point in what Indian journalists love to call the 'wee hours' of the morning, I was woken up from sleep with a wave of pain that was clearly a signal of things warming up. I lay patiently waiting for the next wave. Having read up abundantly on labour and delivery, I was on top of things, recording mentally the intervals at which the pains were coming. Around five o'clock, they began to come at five-minute intervals. I trotted over to the nurse on duty and said, 'Excuse me but I think it's coming.' Without even looking up from her work she said, 'Walk.' I started pacing the floor. In fifteen minutes I was back. I said, 'I'm sure it's coming.' She clicked her tongue impatiently and ordered a ward boy to see me to the labour room. His manner of doing that was to walk me out and hoist me onto the back of a three-tonner, instructing the driver of the hulk to drop me off outside the labour ward. I held on to the strap of the truck with one hand while supporting my stomach over the bumps with the other. I had seen troops travelling that way in films, not holding their stomachs of course. So I knew how to do it.

Outside the labour ward, I was waved into the ante-chamber of the labour room, told to lie down and wait. I waited. The pains grew more urgent. When the gynaecologist Dr Ghosh walked in on his morning rounds, he said, 'What are you doing here?'

'Having my baby.'

Shaking his head, he examined me briskly and said, 'Why aren't you in the labour room?'

'Because I was told to wait here.'

'Why?' he asked furiously, as though I was head of the labour ward in INS *Ashwini*. Then he hollered for the nurse and ordered her to take me in. As I climbed onto the delivery table, things began to move fast. It was six o'clock and Renuka (I'd decided Roza was too alien and Kamala too characterless for my child) popped out within the hour, all six pounds of her, bawling so lustily that you couldn't see her face for her mouth. Meanwhile, Mother had arrived and was waiting outside to receive the bundle. My friend Mona Shahane, from the other clan of Nagpur Shahanes, visited in the evening and said, 'This is the mouse you dug out of your mountain?' Mai, Viju's mother, came from Pune the following day. She was disappointed that I had not produced a boy. Ajit and Lilu had already given her two lovely granddaughters, Neelima and Charu. She peered at Renuka and said, 'She's dark.' Really? The Shahanes had a thing about skin colour. When we visited Viju's hometown Nagpur after our wedding, one of his aunts, the same shade of skin as me, gleefully said, 'Good you've broken the Shahane obsession with white.' Later, however, Mai made much of Renuka whom she called Sanuli.

As soon as I was discharged from hospital, Nirmal, I, Bharat her firstborn and the two newborns left for Talegaon with Mother to be pampered and indulged. Talegaon was where she and Father had built their retirement home and where Father was devoting his life to his poultry. Mother had decided that Renuka was too harsh-sounding a name for someone so small and delicate. So she named her Uma.Vikram and Renuka-Uma were as different from each other as night and day. Vikram was born eight pounds, a happy, contented baby who nursed like the next feed wasn't coming. Renuka was tiny, colicky and nursed like an ascetic, a bit here, a bit there and done.

Raising Renuka was a breeze with Mother beside me and Dr Benjamin Spock's *Baby and Child Care* to guide me. I liked the respect Dr Spock gave me as a parent. The opening line of his book was: 'Trust yourself. You know more than you think you do.' I liked his view that each child was an individual; so, while you gently coaxed it into a routine, you didn't force a one-size-fits-all regimen on it. I liked the fact that he believed babies should be hugged and kissed, not treated like soldiers who needed toughening. Add to this the fact that he was a peacenik and stood firmly against the Vietnam war, and I knew here was a friend, guide and counsellor after my heart.

If raising Renuka was as natural as growing up myself, dealing with the physical effects of having her was more difficult. My digestive system, touchy since that fateful fig-orchard trip, went for a toss and my hair fell like rain in July. This was an acceleration of a process that had begun the moment I stepped on British soil, despite washing my hair with Tomco which Mother believed in so fervently that two large bottles of it had travelled with us on the *Arcadia*. There was little choice in shampoos back then. Who knew that three decades on, young models would be swinging sleek, waxy, washed-in-X-Y-Z-shampoo hair at us from every television screen in the country. Tomco was like the Ambassador car: solid and dependable. It came in a large, functional plain-Jane bottle and had little noticeable fragrance. The story goes that Jawaharlal Nehru, feeling concerned about Indian women spending too much foreign exchange on beauty products, had asked J.R.D. Tata to start manufacturing them in India. Tomco hair oil and shampoo were two of the outcomes.

When my hair had started falling in England, Mother said it was because I had stopped using Tomco coconut hair oil which also she had carried. I told her coconut oil froze in my hair. So she said there you are. Why won't your hair fall then? Having a baby had only accelerated this process. One day, disgusted with the limp strings that hung around my face and went by the name of hair, I hacked them off. It didn't matter to the people of Talegaon, nor to my parents, nor to me what my hair looked like. The cynosure of all our eyes were Vikram and Renuka. Three months later when I returned to Bombay to our very own flat in Kaka Court on Dinsha Vaccha Road, I took myself off to Dolfre's near Regal Circle. There Peewee, the man with the magical scissors, shaped my hacked hair into an elegant bob. A pre-hacking photograph taken with Father near his Alsatian Khandu's kennel in Talegaon, told me of another action I needed to take tout-de-suite. Once again I needed to shed weight. So back I went to my daily morning regimen of bending, stretching, skipping and the three asanas ending with tadasana which made me feel as slender as the tree that had given the asana its name.

In Bombay, Renuka settled into a non-troubled life. She was small and sprightly, happy to sit in her spacious playpen, custom-made by a naval carpenter, tearing sheets of paper into shreds. Apart from newspapers, a piece of silk sari which she called mau-mau had to be left in the playpen. When she was sleepy, she hugged it to herself and slept. When my niece Vasanti, Baban Bhau's daughter, came on a visit, she said, 'The child should be walking now. She's just being lazy.' Vasanti picked up a pair of shiny scissors—she had noticed Renuka's great interest in them as she watched me cutting fabric for our clothes—and held them before her as an incentive to motion. It worked. As Vasanti moved the scissors backwards, Renuka moved forward in high excitement, unmindful of the tumbles along the way. Somewhere in her little brain she must have decided that if she could grab the scissors it would make tearing paper easier. Years later, when Viju was posted to Visakhapatnam, she spotted the same pair of scissors lying near a piece of cloth that I had just cut into a front for her dress. Interrupted by a call I had rushed away, forgetting to move the scissors to a safer place. Renuka had swooped on them and run them neatly through her dress front. When I returned from the call, I found her looking approvingly at her handiwork, scissors in hand. I asked Dr Spock telepathically what I should do about this. Was this a sign of a congenitally destructive bent of mind? Dr Spock said soothingly, follow your instincts. So I laughed, picked her up, gave her a light tap on the hand and said, 'See? Now Aai can't make you a pretty dress.' But of course I did make the dress. All I needed to do was turn it into a front-buttoning one. Inventive tailoring came to Nirmal and me easily because of Mother. The same went for cooking. We had never been told to cook when we were studying. But when the time came for us to do it, we did it. Chapatis, which were many women's nightmare, were a dream for us. The rolling and the roasting had its own hypnotic rhythm. It was a fertile time for creative thinking. Many of my ideas for stories were conceived over the chapati rolling-board.

When I was in my third month with Renuka, I had sat for my Masters degree from Bombay University. A 2B BA degree from Bristol was not qualification enough to teach at college. Now that Renuka was walking and talking and generally enjoying life, and I had found Savitri and Ramchandra to join us as her minders and general factotums, because the Kaka Court flat had a servants' quarter, I put word out that I was interested in returning to the teaching force. My two years at Elphinstone College had convinced me that this was my vocation. Nissim Ezekiel had lectured to us in MA Part 2. He had invited me to join Jhunjhunwala College where he was head of the English department. Even as I was planning to meet him to find out if the post was still vacant, Viju's transfer orders came. We were off to Delhi.

Viju's favourite posture when not in uniform was horizontal with a book. On the rare occasion that he found himself without a book, he had been caught reading newspaper wrappings off parcels. Naturally, packing for the shift to Delhi became my job. Living with Viju had taught me one thing. You didn't request him to do this or that. Being full of goodwill and desperate to get you off his back, he would promptly agree and return to his book. You could not fight with him. His unfailing good humour was like a shield against all attacks. If he found you were determined to make him move, he would heave himself up with mock weariness, throw a pair of shoes into a box and return to position. If you were wise, you saved your breath and got on with the job yourself.

I asked a friend of Viju's to get a dockyard carpenter to make me wooden boxes. All naval families possessed them. Having your own set of six was like a rite of passage. When you were allotted your accommodation, you unpacked your goods and arranged the empty boxes in threes, draped them with colourful coverings and you had settees to augment the standard issue furniture which came with your flat. When the next transfer order came, you whipped off the coverings, filled the boxes with your worldly goods and off you went to the next borrowed or shared home.

In Delhi, we shifted accommodation three times. Borrowed homes were organized on a personal level. You sent word to friends posted where you were going. They nosed around to find out who was going to be away on annual leave and booked you in. Annual leave was sixty days which gave you time to settle down and feel at home. Settling in a borrowed home meant unpacking only the box that held your basics for survival. The remaining five boxes were unpacked only when you had your own home. Our first home was in Pandara Road in the heart of the city. The second was in Moti Bagh and the third in R.K. Puram. In R.K. Puram, the owners of the flat had left us their pet dog Peeko, short for Peekaboo, to look after. Peeko was a mixture of the worst features of several breeds and ugly as hell. But he was sweet natured and came in handy as an ally during Renuka's lunch and dinner times. She had continued to be a reluctant eater; so I would mould the rice or rotis into bite-sized pellets. Renuka would then intone, 'Peeko one ball, Nenuka one ball.' And that is how dog and daughter got fed.

My second baby was now on the way. Viju had found two bachelor friends to drink with. My next-door neighbour, a senior naval officer's wife, told me I should not put up with such nonsense. Wednesdays and Saturdays were half days for the Navy when officers trooped down to the bar and stayed put. It was assumed they discussed the state of the Navy and/or the country. My neighbour would call the bar on the dot of two-fifteen on both days. Everybody knew who the call was from and whom for. Commander X of the Indian Navy dutifully took it. The voice at this end said, 'Bolu, I'm waiting.'

The voice at the other end said, 'Yes dear.' The Commander walked back to the bar, downed what was left in his glass and headed straight home. In Bombay another wife had told me, 'I hide my husband's bottles. When he gets home, I pour him just two drinks and that's it.' Did she not know or knew but turned a blind eye to the fact that her husband stowed bottles under his car seat from which he helped himself on the way back from work with the result that he was already merry when he came home and most grateful for the two extras he got from his loving wife? I nodded my appreciation of her methods but I was not made for nagging or for wifely wiles. I was not, as it was turning out, a professional wife.

In December 1968, just before we were due to be allotted a house in Delhi, Viju was sent to Odessa as a member of the commissioning crew for INS *Amba*. She was to be the only submarine tender ship in service with the Indian Navy, thc mother ship that was to provide operational and administrative support to the Russian submarines which had been simultaneously commissioned. Every time Viju was transferred, I would return to my own mother ship to wait for accommodation. For a couple of years it had been Talegaon. But before the shift to Delhi, Father had suddenly died and Mother had had to sell their lovingly built retirement home Abhang, and return to Bombay. Nirmal had shifted to Lalit Estate, away from her in-laws' house, after our parents had left for Talegaon; but she had offered to shift back, insisting that Mother should return to where she belonged. And so it was that I, well into my ninth month of pregnancy, was back in Lalit Estate. I was to have the second baby in the private hospital next door, where Nirmal had had both hers. When the pains started, I walked across to the hospital, an experienced second timer. I was put on the brown rexine-covered delivery table while Mother waited outside. The baby was taking its normal time emerging. But the doctor had an operation lined up and could not wait. She decided to accelerate labour with a shot. In the natural course of labour, the gaps between pains decrease gradually, allowing you to build up resistance against each successive wave. If you're going to be injected with something to accelerate the process, you need to be warned. I wasn't. So in went the needle and out came Girish. The scream I emitted then sounded like a jungle animal caught in a trap. I did not know I had it in me to produce such a scream. Mother shot up from her seat in panic. When the nurse went out with the baby, her face wreathed in the special grin reserved in India for announcing male births, and said, 'Boy!' Mother said, 'Why did she scream?'

'Not she. It's a he.'

'I'm asking about my daughter. Why did she scream?'

'Women do that. Boy,' said the nurse again, thrusting the baby at Mother. Mother was supposed to fall in line with the country's cultural norms and gush. But she took the baby absently and said, 'Why did she scream?' The nurse gave up. 'No problem. Just like that. You can go in after she's stitched up.'

The induced birth had produced a jagged tear in my vagina that still hurts.

Mai would have fulfilled the nurse's highest expectations in the gushing department had she been present. But she was in hospital, only a few days away as it turned out, from her last. I was discharged from hospital when the baby—I was going to name him Girish—was nine days old. I asked Viju's friend Bandu Karve to drive me down to Pune so Mai could see her much longed-for grandson. Bandu Karve was famous for two things. He did not sit down when he was drinking at a party. Alcohol travelled faster to the feet when you drank standing up, making room for more at the top he said. He was also famous for seeing *Sound of Music* twenty-two times. Bandu was not much of a conversationalist but he was obliging to a fault. He drove me down to Pune and back in one day. Mai gazed upon Girish with profound contentment and passed away in peace two days later. Within a month Mother and I were in Mamita, to be with Dada who was now all alone.

The hospital where Girish was born was known for passing on assorted infections to its patients, including newborns. What fell to Girish's lot was a runny stomach and a predilection for throwing up dribbles of feed. Every time Dada wanted to pick him up for a cuddle, he would ask, 'Is he dry at both ends?'

We had a small but celebratory naming ceremony for Girish. Poor colicky Renuka had howled through the larger part of hers. When it was time to put her in her cot and have her name whispered in her ear, Naloo Maushi had said, 'Wait a minute. We can't have her howling like that. I'll quieten her with a song.' Naloo Maushi had trained under Pandit Sharadchandra Arolkar, doyen of the Gwalior gharana, and had a lovely, ringing voice. As soon as she began to sing a soothing cradle song, Renuka stopped crying as though a switch had been flicked. It was no surprise that she grew up to have an instinct for pitch, melody and rhythm, and a grasp so quick that our guru, Pandit Jal Balaporia, regretted forever that she had not devoted herself to music, but chosen to become an actor instead.

Girish, on the other hand, was calm and smiling in his decorated crib. The tension was elsewhere, between his mother and grandfather. My understanding with Viju was that I would choose the baby's name if it was a boy. But a boy was a family's kuldeepak, expected to bring it glory. It was paramount that he should be appropriately named. I had decided to name him after Girish Karnad who had won a Rhodes scholarship to Oxford, and had written *Yayati* and the magnificent *Tughlaq*. He was one of the group of brilliant playwrights whose plays my friend Satyadev Dubey had directed and made memorable. However, Dada had other ideas. He was keen to name him Dnyanesh, a shortened form of Dnyaneshwar, his father's name. With much heartache, I submitted to the elder's wishes; but Dnyanesh remained Girish's cradle name. Nobody ever called him that, not even Dada; nor did it appear on a single official document. Years later, by one of those incredible coincidences that makes even a rationalist like me wonder if there is indeed some design at work in this chaotic world, Girish Karnad was on the interviewing panel that selected Girish for a Rhodes scholarship.

It was 1970 and Mother and I were still in Pune. That was the year *The Female Eunuch* was published. I had grabbed a copy as soon as it was out and was reading it every spare moment I got. When Dada read the title, his eyes widened in horror. 'Why are you reading this vulgar book?' He looked disgustedly at the cover image of a naked female torso hung up on a clothesline with handles on the sides. I said, not at all confrontationally, 'It's an important book about feminism.' To him the word feminism was like an ugly toad that had hopped into the pretty garden people had spent centuries creating. If he had been younger I would have needled him with Greer's thesis that women were castrating themselves in the service of their femininity. But he was not young. So I covered the book in a newspaper jacket and didn't tell him that the line I had just finished reading was, 'Women must humanise the penis, take the steel out of it and make it flesh again.' I was becoming a feminist, in theory at least if not always in practice.

Viju had returned from Odessa in June 1969 and was posted to Visakhapatnam. Mother accompanied me there when he had found accommodation, and stayed for a couple of months before returning to Bombay and her old home. Renuka and Girish, bright and lively, full of questions, became the lights of my life, lifting the shadow that was lengthening over my marriage. Before I joined Viju in Visakhapatnam, he had discovered rummy. Rum and rummy were his companions at the club. The wife and children had full freedom to do what they liked with their lives. The children were well-behaved and agreed to let me write when I wanted to. Our understanding was that when I said I was not Aai but Shanta Gokhale, they were to entertain themselves and not bother me.

I discovered translation as a serious and deeply satisfying occupation in Vizag. Satyadev Dubey first pushed me into it. We were staying in a place called New Entry Camp, a kind of halfway house to a proper accommodation. The house was built like a train with four sequential compartments, a breezy corridor running their full length facing a large garden, and a kitchen attached at right angles to the fourth compartment, by a covered passage. I wasn't doing much with myself except writing fiction in Marathi, directing plays for the local Maharashtra Mandal and playing badminton. In the midst of this leisurely life came Dubey's letter. Polite as always, he wrote, 'You are vegetating there. You've become a cow. Do some work. Translate the play that's coming to you by separate post.' The play was poet-playwright C.T. Khanolkar's *Avadhya,* hailed by Marathi theatre's reigning drama critic Madhav Manohar as 'the first adult play' in Marathi and condemned by the cultural orthodoxy as obscene. The play exposed the hypocrisies of middle-class morality with brutal insight. Three men in a lodge are informed by the room boy that a peephole has been obligingly made behind the calendar on the wall through which they may, if they so wish, watch the young couple next door make love. The men were utterly revolting; but converting Khanolkar's sharp dialogue into something equally punchy in English gave me a high such as I had not experienced before. Dubey liked the translation and sent it to his friend Rajinder Paul in Delhi, editor of the theatre magazine *Enact*. *Avadhya*, The Invincible, was the first of many of my translations that *Enact* was to publish.

Comrade Godavari Parulekar, a friend of the family, had written a book about the Warlis of Dahanu and the surrounding areas amongst whom she had worked and for whose rights she had fought for many years. The book was called *Jenwha Manus Jaagaa Hoto*—When Man Awakens. A fellow comrade had translated it into English, but Godutai was not happy with the translation. She sent me the manuscript to correct. The translation was so bad, I did a fresh translation instead. My version got published, but it did not carry my name. It carried the original translator's name. It would have been awkward for Godutai to explain to her colleague what had transpired with his draft. A reward more precious than having my name on the book lay in having had the chance to translate it in the first place. Translation forces you to engage intimately with a work; and this was a book about people whom I had known from childhood. Dahanu was my mother's home. That is where I was born. That was where I had spent many summer holidays, surrounded by Warlis who worked in my grandfather's home and factory. To know the oppression and exploitation that they had endured was to know the other, darker side of the lives of these people whom I adored.

When I chose to do English Literature in England, Mother had asked me how I intended putting my knowledge to use back home. I had said I would teach. 'That is one way,' she had said. 'But there's another which you must consider. Translate the best Marathi literature into English.' With *Avadhya* and *Jenwha Manus Jaagaa Hoto*, I had set off on that path.

18. Back to Bombay

When Mother visited us at Visakhapatnam, we were living in a small flat in town. She saw how distant Viju and I had grown from each other and how much time I was spending doing nothing but housework and minding babies. There was no help to be had in this provisional accommodation. I must admit I was also being bloody-minded. I remember an occasion when Viju needed something vital to be picked up, and would not go himself, wasn't really asking me to go either, but I went, not by a rickshaw which, with some patience I would have found, but trudging there and back on foot in the heat of the summer sun, forcing my body to submit to my angry mind. Mother went away anxious and depressed. 'This is not the life for which your father and I struggled to put you through the best education we could give,' she wrote when she returned to Bombay.

In a couple of months, we were shunted to our next provisional accommodation in New Entry Camp before being allotted our rightful house in the Naval Base. At last I could unpack all our boxes and settle down. I found a delightful pair of sisters, the ever-smiling Rajamma and little Parvati, to look after the children in the evenings and a dour but hard-working Rangamma, whose only Hindi was 'parva nahi', to wash and clean. With only cooking to do, I began looking around for a college lecturership. I was interviewed twice. I was told I had the required qualifications. But a friendly interviewer told me the university had an unwritten policy to hire only Andhras.

Suddenly we were in the midst of a prolonged agitation. Two movements had torn united Andhra Pradesh apart—the Jai Telangana movement of 1969 and the Jai Andhra movement of 1972. It was going to take another forty-two years for the state to be officially split into Andhra and Telangana. Meanwhile, one of the focal points of the ongoing agitation, the one that had generated the greatest bitterness, the most number of strikes, brutal police action and student revolts, were the mulki rules. The seed of the rules which mandated jobs for sons of the soil, had been sown by the Nizam in 1919 to appease disgruntled Telugus who were seeing their jobs being taken by Muslim and Hindu elites from outside Hyderabad. After the states were reorganized in 1956, the Telugus realized that the mulki rules had stopped being applied. That was the starting point of the Jai Telangana agitation. In 1972, the Supreme Court ruled that it was obligatory for the state to enforce the mulki rules. This judgement launched the Jai Andhra agitation, the one in which we were unhappily caught. The slogan that tore through the streets of Visakhapatnam was 'Mulki rules down down'. Schools and colleges shut shop. My itch for teaching was unexpectedly fulfilled at home. The neighbourhood children gathered in our living room for lessons and fun activities. They played spelling bee, wrote descriptions of each other, drew, painted, sang, danced and acted out the little skits I wrote for them. It was joyous to have them around me. But the Jai Andhra agitation put paid to any ideas I might have had of working out my marital problems through professional fulfilment.

I kept myself busy with other things though. I played badminton every evening and edited the *Eastern Naval News*. As its editor I was introduced to the then president V.V. Giri who had come on a visit to the Eastern Naval Command. I have a picture of me greeting him, while, as newspaper captions like to say, the then Chief Minister of Andhra Pradesh, Shri Narsimha Rao, 'looks on'. The *Eastern Naval News* was a four-pager for which most of the material came to me from the Admiral's office. I was responsible for filling the space that remained. This meant getting after talented but lazy pens to contribute. On the rare occasions that my tenacity failed, I would produce the space-filler myself. One of these was a supposedly funny thing called 'The Spouse That Snored'. Viju, good-humoured as always, found it amusing. Dada did not. He wrote to me telling me off for making public fun of my husband. What I would have loved to make fun of in fact, which would not have amused even Viju, was the way menus were decided for the get-togethers that the Naval Officers' Wives Association (NOWA) regularly had. As editor of ENN, I was invited to meetings of the organizing committee chaired by the First Lady of the base. Discussions about the menu went like this:

'Let's have sandwiches and cake. I can make the cake.'

'Or chaat.'

'Yes yes, chaat.'

'Bhajias. Onion bhajias and halwa. Lovely gajars in the market.'

The First Lady would listen patiently, nodding impartially at all suggestions with as much enthusiasm as a First Lady was allowed to show without losing rank. Then she would announce with mild surprise at her own imagination, 'Why not idli-chutney? Best.'

Everybody would then nod till their heads fell off. And idlis it would be. Or vadai-sambar or upma. The First Lady always won. Democracy never.

There were other activities to preoccupy naval wives while their husbands conducted the serious business of protecting the nation's coast from the enemy. (They did a marvellous job of it during the Bangladesh war which was fought while we were in Vizag.) Some wives met to play mahjong. Some to play cards. Some taught at schools which had reopened. Some threw dinner parties, making khao swè, baked cauliflower or bharwan bhindi, paneer and pulao. Rama Sinha fed us crisp masala dosas on Sunday mornings. Lata Lohana served delicious Gujarati snacks. She also tried to teach me to drive—there's nothing to it, she said—and failed. I bathed her surprise third bundle of joy, Jyotsna, because my experience of bathing babies was more recent than hers. Occasionally, charity sales were organized. I made girls' dresses in all sizes and had the pleasure of seeing little naval girls running around in them. I also made part of Damini Ahluwalia's trousseau because there was no decent tailor to be had in Vizag. In season, tomatoes sold at Poorna Market at two rupees a kilo. Wives went into a red tizzy making and bottling ketchup. My family did not care for ketchup. So I sat out the frenzy. All in all, it was a warm community life. I grew fond of Viju's friends and their wives. The affection that was born then, has lasted till today. But beneath it all I was restless.

Around this time a bachelor friend of Viju's was transferred to Vizag. I shall call him VF for convenience. If Viju's preferred position was horizontal and inert, his was vertical and active. He chivvied Viju into getting up on weekends and going with us on long drives to the beautiful places surrounding Vizag.

Viju's Air Force brother Ajit once told me a story. When he was posted to Agra, he invited Viju for a holiday. Viju went and spent nine days in bed with books. On the tenth day, his last, Ajit felt obliged to show him the Taj. Viju stood before the great monument and said, 'Ah!' Then they came home, Viju with relief that he could return to his book and Ajit with a sense of duty done. In Vizag, Viju came more or less happily on the long drives VF planned, once to the splendidly verdant Araku Valley and often to Bheemli beach with its lighthouse dating back to 1830, overlooking the confluence of the Gosthani river with the Bay of Bengal. He also agreed to cross the Andhra border into Orissa for a few days to visit the magnificent sun temple at Konark, the Jagannath temple at Puri, Chilika Lake with its migratory birds of myriad hues, shapes and calls, and the beautifully carved temples of Bhubaneshwar whose sculptures had provided the great pioneers of Odissi three-dimensional references to the history of their sensuous dance. These were days of pleasure mixed with pain. We were in the constant company of VF, Viju's exact opposite in every respect—a responsible, unaddicted family man. And the inevitable was inevitably happening. A feeling was growing between us that could neither be denied nor accepted. I was confused and upset with myself. I knew VF was in love with the wife of another friend of his in Chennai. (Was he a wife-snatcher then?) I had met her in Bombay and knew of their relationship. He was only waiting for her to divorce her husband before they married. Then what were these signals he was sending out to me? I wanted none of it. I wanted out. Life was complicated enough without an extra-marital relationship thrown in. So I would deliberately ask him about the woman in Chennai. He would say she was fine. Met her last month.

So is the divorce coming through, I would ask. Soon, soon, he would say and reach out for my hand. And I would give it to him! My feminist self looked on aghast. But the other self seemed not to care. Viju was oblivious to what was happening. Or pretending to be. He didn't want to challenge either VF or me. Emotional complications were not his cup of tea. Years later I would look back and feel deep compassion for him in a situation he had never bargained for when marrying me. All he had ever wanted in life was to be allowed to do his job, which he did exceptionally well, drink, play cards and read. That was not asking for much. But it was if you were married. Or married to me.

Two years later, in Bombay, I saw VF in perspective. He had wanted to marry, whether it was the woman from Chennai or me, whichever was free to do so first. But I had no intention of divorcing Viju. Even if I did, had I not had enough of marriage already? Did I not want only to work and look after my children now? And see theatre and dance, hear music and watch films—the Indian New Wave cinema was burgeoning then—translate and write? Did I also not know that if I ever did divorce Viju and marry again (perish the thought) VF would not be the man for me? With all his virtues, there was one he lacked, which overrode many for me. A sense of humour. I could live a Spartan life with two meals a day and four saris to wear, but I could not live without laughter. After a few months of not wanting to hurt him, I made it clear to him that I wasn't going to divorce Viju. He then married his first love and they are still together.

Viju was transferred to Hyderabad in early 1973. We joined him in May. Renuka was six and Girish four. Viju had not found them places in a decent school. So they went to one nearby which could just about be described as a school. In April 1974, Mother wrote to me enclosing an advertisement for a junior lecturer's post in the English department at H.R. College of Commerce, Bombay. Her covering note was cryptic. 'I suggest you come here and apply for this.' It was not a call to walk out on Viju, but one to give myself a chance at a more fulfilling life in the profession I had come to love. Viju would continue being transferred all over the country. If I could come to Bombay like a homing pigeon each time he was transferred and not allotted family accommodation, why could I not make Bombay my permanent home where he visited us whenever possible?

I arrived in Bombay with the children on 7 May 1974, one day before the great railway strike called by George Fernandes began. I carried with me a single trunk that contained our clothes and little else. If the children were not able to settle down in Lalit Estate, missed Viju and wanted to return, I would pick up the trunk and leave. Or Viju could try for a Bombay posting so we could be together again. But he had decided that my coming away was a permanent break. With that, he absolved himself of all responsibility towards the children. Not in so many words. That was not his style. But in effect. He did not ask how much money I would need each month for the children's expenses nor did he offer any that he thought reasonable. On my part, I did not insist that he should. My logic was simple. He had not wanted children. I had. He had not asked me to come away. I had come against his wishes. Ergo, I must live with the consequences of my actions.

I sent in my application to H.R. College as soon as I arrived in Bombay. An interview followed and the post was mine. I grabbed it with both hands. The joy of having a job was indescribable. Finally, I was going to teach, albeit at a commerce college where English was as low as you could fall in the academic hierarchy. Accounts mattered. Statistics mattered. Economics mattered. English was the class to bunk. A senior lecturer in the department would hold her book up before her eyes to shut out the students' bored faces. Another would enter the class by one lift, take attendance—the thing for which the students were there in the first place—and escape home by the service lift. For early morning English lectures students would rush to catch the seats by the walls so they could lean their heads against them and snooze.

My challenge was the Intermediate year, to which I had to teach a novel that should have topped the list of worst choices for future bankers, chartered accountants and businessmen. E.M. Forster's *A Passage to India*. 'What actually happened in the Marabar caves, Miss?' was a natural question for students dealing with quantifiables to ask. 'I believe Forster wanted that to remain a mystery. Perhaps it was a mystery to him too,' was not an answer to satisfy them. Like the rest of the world, they too believed that a writer's job was to tell convincing tales, not pitch riddles at readers.

In my first *Passage to India* lecture to a class of hundred and fifty in which some boys were 6 feet tall with sizeable paunches, I heard a loud mooing from the back of the room accompanied by suppressed laughter. I had learnt to handle student tricks at Elphinstone. Kumar Shahani, the film-maker, told me of one that I had not had to face. He and a group of his classmates were once heading for my class where they had no business to be. They intended sitting in the front row and freaking me out by rubbing their eyes through their spectacle frames which I wouldn't know were empty. The plan was foiled by the formidable Miss Homai Shroff who intercepted them and sent them packing to the class where they belonged. The mooing from the back of the class in H.R. was a far less clever prank. I closed E.M. Forster and waited till there was silence. I told the class I had been hired to teach, not to police them. I was not going to waste my time finding out which buffalo had mooed. What I wanted was for the entire herd at the back of the class to file out quietly after I took attendance. I informed them to their incredible delight that henceforth I would mark attendance at the beginning of the class, not the end, so that those who were not interested in Mr Forster could leave. The students who left told everybody up and down the college corridors that I was a fantastic teacher. The class was now reduced to a group of fifteen bright sparks whom it was a pleasure to teach.

It was also a pleasure to be made responsible for organizing the cultural events for the college's annual days. An item into which I threw myself body and soul for the first annual day was a ballet I choreographed for Kathak and contemporary dance, using passages excerpted from Andre Previn and Ravi Shankar's concerto for sitar and orchestra. I was also happy to edit the college magazine, until 25 June 1975, when Indira Gandhi declared the Emergency. Then I had to make tedious monthly trips with the students' outpourings to the office of the Director of Information and Publicity of the Maharashtra government where Binod Rau, former resident editor of the *Indian Express*, held fort as the censor. He was a pleasant man doing an unpleasant job which he had not had the courage to turn down. He smiled in embarrassment each time I stepped into his office with my file of student poems about first love and sunrises, anecdotes about pet cats and fervent articles about the generation gap. We went through the farce till 21 March 1977 when the Emergency was lifted.

But did I have time to celebrate? Not for a moment. On the heels of our regained freedom of expression came a bolt from the blue. Or perhaps not from the blue at all. A change in the system of higher education had been mooted for many years, and now it was upon us. The magical new formula was 10+2+3, the 2 representing the buffer years to be spent at school before students could be considered mature enough to handle the dangerous freedoms that college offered. Typically, despite all the discussions that had preceded the implementation of the scheme, no study had been made of the capacity of schools to extend their space and facilities to accommodate the two extra years. No teaching staff had been trained and no funding for advanced laboratories in schools organized. As a result, only a few well-endowed schools were able to create the new eleventh and twelfth classes. Students from other schools went to Junior Colleges, sharing the campuses and facilities of senior colleges. And who would teach there? At H.R. and probably everywhere else, the junior-most lecturers from the senior college were subpoenaed for the job. As the junior-most recruit in H.R., I was informed of my altered status. I was also given to understand that, till the salary structure for junior colleges was fixed, I would be paid by the clock hour. In short, I was to be a daily wage earner. This meant not only a cut in my monthly income but no salary during vacations. Help! How was I going to look after two children and myself on what those clock hours would bring me? The answer was: by being optimistic. When there was so much reason to worry, there was no point worrying. A corollary to not worrying was believing that something promising would soon turn up.

Something did. As once before, my deus ex machina was Nissim Ezekiel. I ran into him one day after the bolt had struck, and he said, 'You don't really want to teach at a commerce college all your life, do you? Why don't you trot over to *Femina*? They're looking for a sub-editor.' I trotted over and got the job after writing a piece, I forget about what, as a formality. I resigned from H.R. (sadly, I must say) and joined *Femina* in June 1977. The first Status of Women report, *Towards Equality*, had been released in 1974, and had become a turning point in the women's movement. Dina Vakil, the assistant editor at *Femina*, had brought to the magazine a political consciousness it had lacked before. Vimla Patil, the editor, was open to change. It was a very good time to be at *Femina*. Those were years of awakening for urban women all over India. The women's movement was gaining strength. In my limbo state of being married and yet not married, I found a title to replace Mrs. I became Ms. Earlier, while I was still in Vizag, it was *Femina* that had informed me women were allowed legally to retain their maiden names. I had made a dash for the court on one of my visits to Bombay, with an affidavit which said I wanted to return to being Gokhale. The men in the office were deeply doubtful. It would mean losing out on my husband's property they warned. What property, I thought. No problem, I said. My name, my name, a kingdom for my name. I still have a copy of the Gazette in which I was declared to have changed my name from Shahane to Gokhale. So when I returned to Bombay it was with my maiden name.

In the late seventies and early eighties, women's groups were blooming everywhere in Bombay. I was a member of some. The Forum Against Rape was formed in 1980 to protest against the judgement in the Mathura rape case. This organization later widened its scope and became Forum Against Oppression of Women. Another group to which I belonged did women's plays—I wrote them—sang women's songs, danced women's dances and spoke and wrote about women. Suddenly we were talking about ourselves, our lives, our experiences and discovering that a common thread ran through them all, originating in patriarchy. What had begun for me with Simone de Beauvoir's *Second Sex* and Germaine Greer's *The Female Eunuch* grew into a personal ideology in the company of women like Sandhya Gokhale, Lalitha Dhara, Chhaya Datar, Jyoti Mhapsekar, Sonal Shukla, Vidya Bal and many others.

In *Femina*, I had taken Olga Valladares' place. She had moved to *The Evening News* where she was looking after, among other things, a weekly column for women called…er…well… 'Milady's Boudoir'. The person who had been writing the column had quit and Olga wanted me to take over. *Femina* was going to pay me marginally more than H.R.; but during those hard-up, hand-to-mouth times, more money was more money. Even then I could not see myself writing a column under the slug 'Milady's Boudoir'. Suggest something else Olga said, but remember it is a lighthearted column for women. I suggested 'Woman to Woman'. The name was approved and I was on—450 words every Tuesday on any subject of my choice. I decided my women readers would be amused by anything I found amusing. So I wrote about things beyond cooking, sewing and parenting while keeping the tone light. There was not much feedback; but I do remember a male reader writing in to say, 'Why call the column "Woman to Woman"? Even I read it regularly.'

With Olga's move to the *Evening News* I had taken over her portfolio in *Femina*—fiction and cookery. Both were up my street. I love cooking; and reading fiction by women from all over the country was going to be a pleasure. But I had to wait for that pleasure. At the time I joined, the fiction file I had inherited bulged with some fifty accepted stories. For the next six months I returned, unread, every new story that came, with a polite note to say this was not a rejection. Please resend next year. By the beginning of 1978, the fiction file was down to ten pending stories. Time to begin reading new ones, making sure they did not exceed ten at any given time. This gave writers the chance to see their stories published within six months of their being accepted.

The cookery page was mostly fun. We shot Thangam Philip's food at the college of catering and ate it afterwards. But there were a couple of goof-ups I will never forget. Once an agitated woman called up. 'I'm making Sylla Bhaisa's recipe for kheema,' she said. 'There's kheema in the ingredients, but not in the instructions. I've fried the onions, garlic-ginger and spices. I've added the tomatoes. But when do I put in the kheema?' Leaving the woman on the line (was her masala burning?) I quickly called up Sylla Bhaisa. She was one of our most meticulous contributors which must have made me careless in my editing. I was told Sylla was abroad. I returned to the kheema woman and said, 'Dump in the kheema now.' I mean come on. If the masala is fried that is when the kheema goes in. But thereafter, I went through every recipe we published three times before sending it in for setting.

Those were stimulating years on the fourth floor of the Times. There was Bachi Karkaria down the corridor at the *Illustrated Weekly*. Khushwant Singh, the editor, dropped in regularly to see Vimla Patil. Dr Dharamvir Bharati, editor of *Dharmayug*, occupied the centre of the hall. Across the passage from us was Surendra Jha, editor of *Science Today*. Next to me in *Femina* was Padma Prakash who moved later to *Economic and Political Weekly* and now edits eSocialSciences. Then came Shailaja Ganguly who did more things than I can remember after she quit *Femina*. But meanwhile, after I left, she conceived a two-page section called Literatti. Its focus was fiction written in English or in other Indian languages and translated. She asked me to guest-edit it. Literatti lasted for two years during which I made the acquaintance of interesting writers like Mridula Garg, Subhadra Sen Gupta, Lakshmi Kannan and Dalip Kaur Tiwana.

My time at *Femina* ended in the summer of 1979 when a bolt, similar to the 10+2+3 one at H.R., struck. There was a lockout at the Times. Old hands told me cheerfully that that could mean anything from half a month to six months of sitting at home. Help! How was I going to look after two children and myself etc., etc. The answer was by being optimistic. When there was so much reason to worry, etc. A corollary to not worrying, etc. Something would turn up. And it did. This time my deus ex machina was Shanti Aaron from the art department. She had been part of my second memorable disaster at *Femina*, also to do with the cookery page. The issue that was scheduled when I joined was a cookery special. I had dealt with all the concerned pages and gone home. I got a call from Vimla Patil later in the evening to say two of the pages were missing. There was panic all round. The missing pages were found in Shanti's drawer the following day. That is how we became friends. She now brought me a newspaper ad that said Glaxo Laboratories was looking for a public relations executive. The ad also said the applicant had to be under thirty-five. I was forty. And the application had to reach Glaxo by 20 May. We had just sailed past that date. Shanti said don't waste time over numbers and dates. Type out your application and send it in. I was seeing Arun Khopkar then and he offered to hand deliver my application to save time. It had taken H.R. College a single brief interview to hire me. It had taken *Femina* a token written test to hire me. Glaxo started with a written test, supervised by a tall, elegant woman, Jyotsna Parulekar, who was to become a dear friend later. Then came a group discussion and finally a one-on-one interview with Mr Jehangir Khambata, Glaxo's first Indian managing director.

Glaxo's PR department had been seven women strong. One flew away and then there were six. The company was keen to hire a man in her place. So one man from amongst my co-applicants was kept in the running till the group discussion stage. Not only was he a man, he was also the right age and had sent his application in before the last date. But the group discussion exposed his limited understanding of public affairs and his underwhelming communication skills. So he was let go of. The interview with the MD was a mere formality I was told; but in the brief exchange I had with him, I had the opportunity to display my singular ignorance of corporate affairs. One of the questions Mr Khambata asked me was, 'What do you think of the working environment in the company as you have seen it?'

'It's pretty informal,' I beamed.

'Why do you say that?'

'The men are sitting at their desks with their shirts off.'

Mr Khambata nodded non-commitally. The interview ended. I was offered the job. After I joined I was told that the men were shirtless because they were protesting against the management for not granting the union's demands made during the annual agreement negotiations.

My leftist friends at the Times were disgusted with me for joining Glaxo. How could I think of joining a multinational corporation, the biggest bad boys in business? It had been only two years since the Minister for Industries in the Janata government, George Fernandes, had thrown Coke and IBM out of the country. The company I was joining not only had a forked tale like those two, but, as the biggest producer of infant formula which was killing Third World babies, it had three horns in place of two. I stared down my friends. 'Excuse me,' I said. 'I have two children to support and can't afford to be picky.'

I gave *Femina* a month's notice. I was locked out so I wasn't going to work. The children were on summer vacation. I had to do something to fill up the time. The body chose this opportune moment to remind me of its existence. I had chicken pox and passed it on to the children. My attack was mild and so was theirs. But people kept asking me how I had managed to contract chicken pox at my age. 'I had to work very hard for it,' I said, leaving them feeling vaguely confused.

Twenty years later I was to discover that once the chicken-pox virus has entered your body, it takes up permanent residence there. Some day in the future, it might emerge as herpes. Herpes happened to me when I was in my late sixties. Three little blisters under the right arm. I rushed to the doctor and within a week they had disappeared. But the virus is still there, lying dormant, waiting to strike. I heard a story from Sharayu Vahini about how it can strike. One day, a niece of hers found that she could not remember a thing about her immediate past. It was a blank slate. Wiped clean. The family took her to half-a-dozen doctors all of who shook their heads, mystified. The eleventh asked if she had ever had chicken pox or herpes? The husband said yes. The doctor said the virus is continuing to do its work. I can treat the patient against future strikes; but what is lost will remain lost.

19. Divorce and Marriage No. 2

Once bitten twice shy? Never. Or, as far as I was concerned, not shy enough. Here's a rapid read account of how I fell once more for an unsuitable man. I met Arun Khopkar on 4 February 1978. It was the day he and his wife, Gwalior gharana singer Neela, were celebrating the birth of their son Tapan, with a concert by Neela's guru, Pandit Sharadchandra Arolkar. Tapan was six months old that day. Pandit Arolkar was known to his disciples (Naloo Maushi was one of them) and his close circle of admirers as Buwa. I had met Neela at a terrace dinner given by Buwa's landlords, the Pusalkars, who were family friends of ours. She and I had had a long, warm chat about men, marriage and music. That could have been the reason why I was invited because I had neither met nor seen Arun. The concert was my first cultural evening out after I had returned to Bombay in 1974. Renuka was now eleven and Girish nine. I didn't have to be home for them every evening. I could begin to have a life of my own.

There was a slim man with abundant hair and whiskers at the concert who came up to me in the interval and told me a joke about a Marwari woman and an umbrella. Although I promptly forgot the joke, it was amusing enough at the time and I laughed. After the interval, the man came and sat beside me. He was still in the mood to be funny but now I was not amused. The only voice I wanted to hear was Buwa's. I asked Naloo Maushi between items who the man was. She whispered back, 'Neela's husband.' This was Arun Khopkar who had once been pointed out to me in Samovar as Kalidas from Mani Kaul's film *Ashadh Ka Ek Din*. But I hadn't turned round to look.

The concert was brilliant. The outcome wasn't. Arun started calling me, which bugged me. Why should Neela's husband call me so persistently? I told our maid I was out any time a man named Arun Khopkar called. One day he didn't call but dropped in and found me at home. He had been to a party in town and thought he would look me up. I sat in an armchair with my arms folded. He said I looked like a stern teacher. He was right. I was feeling stern. That didn't stop him from telling me about the book he was reading and funny tales about sundry friends. He continued to call. Once it was in the middle of a party I had invited my old Elphinstone College friends to. He must have been drunk because he did not stop at one call. That really bugged me. When he next dropped by, he hinted that he and Neela were parting company. A woman who came to Mother's sewing class told her he had been thrown out of Neela's house, a story that she believed and I didn't not believe. Arun was now back in his parents' home and continued to call and come over. He had read much, seen much and thought much. His conversation began to excite me. Soon we were going out together. I remember a particularly scintillating concert by Amjad Ali Khan that we attended at Tejpal Auditorium. Arun had bummed around a lot. He had a large circle of interesting friends—painters, poets, musicians, film-makers. He was a film-maker himself. But he was also a womanizer, a fact known to many in the city. So when he proposed to me in a bohemian kind of way, I responded in a middle-class kind of way. I told him I did not think he was the right man for me to marry. To begin with he was six years younger. And more importantly, he was a womanizer. He believed in marriage as an open relationship. I did not. Extra-marital flings were not something I was prepared to put up with.

Arun took two days to think over my response. On the third day we went for a walk on the beach. He said, with the setting sun as witness (I can't resist using that trope from sentimental Marathi fiction), that he had had enough of open relationships and was ready to commit himself to me; and the difference in age did not matter to him. I thought I was being very careful and sensible when I said, 'But old habits die hard. If at any point you feel you are slipping back, tell me and we will part as friends.' Today, I can't believe I said that and meant it. Did I really think a man who was having flings was going to say to me I'm having flings so let us part? I thought I had safeguarded my interests when he agreed to my transparency clause. I trusted him. There was no point marrying someone I was not going to trust. I had not policed my students at college. I had not policed Viju. I was not going to police Arun.

Divorcing Viju was painful. I was very fond of him. We agreed to part by mutual consent. Mother distrusted and disliked Arun. She had heard stories about him that made her intensely afraid for my future. She said, 'Not in my house' to my decision to marry him. But when I said I'd take a loan from Glaxo for a flat I could afford, she said angrily, 'You can go where you like. I won't let the children go with you.' It was not really a threat. If it had been I would have backed down. I would not have allowed anything to part me from the children.

But saying she would keep the children was only her way of saying she hated what I was doing but for the children's sake she would put up with our living together.

The children had not expected their mother to marry the man they had been calling Arun Kaka. I asked them if they would be alright with it. Girish who was ten, thought about it carefully and said, 'I don't want him to be my Baba.' I assured him he would not be. 'Will Baba still come to see us?' Of course he will. That was enough for him. Renuka took much longer to come around. I did not pressure her but she must have felt the pressure. In the end she consented. My heart went out to both my children. Was I doing the right thing by inviting into theirs and Mother's peaceful lives this wild, erratic element? Living in middle-class Shivaji Park which had seen Arun and me together for several months, it was too late to ask myself that question. I had to take forward what I had started.

We married in December 1979. Then the inevitable happened. Arun continued his flings. If I got to hear of one, I faced him with it. He laughed it off. I told myself I had to trust him. That made him complacent. In June 1992, I stumbled upon concrete proof of a relationship he had been in that he could not deny. This was no mere fling. He had been talking of renting a room in Delhi to be close to the Ministry of External Affairs which had been funding his films on artists. The woman in question lived in Delhi. I called her up in his presence to ask if Arun had told her he was married. She said he had but had given her to understand that we were splitting. I told her we hadn't been, but would now. She was shocked and full of regret. She was a fine, intelligent woman. It seemed to me then that many fine, intelligent women were also prize idiots. I certainly was.

That was the end of our marriage. But Arun had nowhere to go. He had never earned enough to buy a place of his own. Nor for that matter had I. It was lucky Mother had the rented flat in Lalit Estate in which we lived. We had spent twelve years together. Along with Arun's flings there had also been enrichment with the music, books, films, ideas and laughter we had shared. He had opened up cinema for Renuka, Girish and me. I had loved sitting in on his edits with that patient magician Rajesh Parmar cutting and splicing negatives at old, unwieldy Steenbecks. *Lessons with Eisenstein* was the most perfect introduction to everything that was important in film-making, including that very slippery concept, mise en scène, which Eisenstein analyzed with astonishing lucidity. With all this behind us, I could not throw Arun out.

I sat down and thought realistically about my situation. I had never been able to live in muddied water. It had to be clear. Although I had howled before Mother's framed photograph (she had passed away in 1986) in remorse for having foisted Arun on her despite her dislike of him, I was now quite unemotional. First, I was going to quit my job. After her Masters, Renuka had made herself a good career in television. Girish was away in Oxford on a Rhodes scholarship. Both children had been persuading me to quit my six-days-a-week grind at the Times and give myself time to read and write. I resigned. I told Arun that his continuing to live in Lalit Estate was only a temporary arrangement. He would have to move out as soon as he found a place. Meanwhile, we were not, by any definition, husband and wife. It was important for me not to live with negative feelings about someone who was going to share my room and table. The only way I could overcome the anger and the pain that was in me was by keeping our creative relationship going. I had written most of Arun's documentary-film scripts. Now that I had given up my job and had more free time, I wanted to write a feature-film script. He had often said he would like to take the plunge into a feature film one day. Well, this had to be the day. He could choose the story and I would write the script.

While we would work together amicably, he was to treat me as a professional colleague and forget his habit of making unreasonable demands on my time and energy. When I attended his shoots, it would be as his writer. I would expect to be accommodated in a separate room. While I had loved, I had loved single-mindedly. Now that I was breaking off, I was breaking off single-mindedly, putting into practice Mother's favourite phrase, 'Ek ghav doan tukde'. One stroke, two clean pieces. No messy edges. Sounds brutal. Not easy to do. But it works if you can do it. Frees you totally.

Arun said he would like to make a feature film based on Gogol's short story, 'The Tale of How Ivan Ivanovich Quarrelled with Ivan Nikiforovich'. I got down to work. It was a heady feeling relocating a hilarious and ultimately tragic Russian story to a place and time in Maharashtra. I was very pleased with what I had done. Arun too was pleased. He paid me my professional fees (he had always been punctilious about that) and the script passed into his hands. Dilip Prabhavalkar played the thin Ivan (Ganpatrao Turay-Patil) and Mohan Agashe, much padded, played his fat friend Ganpatrao Moray-Patil. If I felt disappointed with some of the directorial decisions Arun took, I wasn't the first or last script-writer in the world to feel that way. Kumar Shahani liked my script and that was reward enough.

A couple of documentary scripts later, I was hankering

again after a feature film. This time I kept suggesting stories and Arun kept knocking them down. Knowing there's nothing people love more than themselves, I suggested we make a children's film about his boyhood friendship with the raddiwala downstairs who loaned him second-hand books to quench his hunger for reading. The Children's Film Society accepted the script and it was made with Parzan Dastoor as the boy, Renuka Shahane and Tushar Dalvi as the parents, Heeba Shah as the mausi, Shrivallabh Vyas as the raddiwala and Ir(r)fan Khan as the raddiwala's not-quite-so-straight brother-in-law. The film wasn't a roaring success but it was fun.

My next project with Arun was what I consider to be my piece de resistance—a one-hour long documentary film on the Kabir Sanman winning Dalit poet, Narayan Gangaram Surve. From the day the poet and I had walked down Madame Cama Road after attending a seminar at the Yeshwantrao Chavan Centre, and a group of mill-workers had saluted him and stopped to chat, I knew I had to write a film on him. It wasn't the number of awards he had won—and the number was large—nor that I loved his poetry—and I had done so for years—but the fact that he was read and admired by people like those mill-workers. He was, in every sense of the phrase, a people's poet. His poetry came directly from the streets of Bombay's mill district where he had been abandoned as a baby to be brought up by a mill-worker couple as theirs. Having no biological family, and no ancestry in the upper caste middle-class that dominated the literary world, he converted his hard life itself into robust, well-crafted poetry.

Narayanrao was seventy-five when we proposed the film to the funders. He was not in the best of health either. Shooting for the film would have been stressful. So I wrote a script in which I had him appear only in a few crucial scenes while the versatile actor Kishor Kadam, also a poet, played him in the rest of the film.

During the eight years following that terrible day in June 1992 when the huge Delhi skeleton had tumbled out of Arun's cupboard, Arun had been denied a housing loan. Neither his bank nor housing-loan organizations had felt convinced that one film every two years was enough guarantee for them to offer him a loan. Then suddenly he had three documentary film contracts in hand and the loan situation changed. He found himself a lovely, airy flat on the twelfth floor of a new building in Goregaon and moved. The Narayan Surve script was still underway. I was keen on following this up with a script on Charles Correa in whose work I had become interested after I wrote about his British Council building in Delhi. I had already collected a large amount of background material on him and his architectural ideas and practice, and had talked to a couple of young architects to try and understand what his work meant to them. But I did not get around to writing that script. Arun was in a new relationship. It was time to snap even our professional ties. He went on to make a film on Correa without a script. It was the last film he made. He is now married and has become a writer of high repute in the Marathi literary world. His marriage has enabled him to have all the things he had always craved: a large luxurious home, world travel, plenty of time to read, see films and learn more languages. He had learnt French, German and Russian when we were together. He has now learnt Spanish and is inching his way towards Persian.

Just as Viju and I had remained friends until his death in February 2004, Arun and I have remained friends over the past sixteen years. I presume he is happy in his new life. I am certainly happy in mine. I needed a room of my own to be the person I was. I had managed to write my first novel *Rita Welinkar* during the dribbles of time and slices of space available to me while I was married and working full time. I would let chapters write themselves in my head as I travelled to work by bus; then sit under a tree on the lawn at Glaxo during lunchtime, my back to the main gate to dissuade friends from saying hello and rapidly scribble down what I had thought of on the bus.

I wrote *Tya Varshi* seventeen years later, sitting in my own room unoccupied by any other body but mine. Rarely are women blessed with such blissful singlehood. The pleasure is not confined only to having my own space, my own work table and my own bookshelves. It extends to having my own cool bed. I consider a cool bed a vital part of my singlehood. A cool bed in which I can stretch my body any which way I like, throw my arms about, sleep leg on leg or legs wide apart. A body by itself, no move it makes arousing thoughts of possession in another. The independence to be yourself, complete in yourself, is very heaven.

20. Hair and Heart

Almost as soon as I joined Glaxo, I was sent to meet Praful Bidwai who was writing against pharmaceutical MNCs. I was supposed to sell him the manufacturers' story against the government's Drug Price Control Order. Sitting in Samovar, I repeated the story that had been fed to me, neither with nor without conviction. Praful peered at me through his glasses and took an hour-long class with me, knocking down every argument in the story. Having come into public relations from journalism, my natural inclination was to disbelieve big business. I found Praful's argument totally convincing. I decided I was not going to allow Glaxo to use me for my contacts in the Press and destroy the credibility I had won there. I told my boss Mrs Jane Swamy that I wanted press relations to be taken out of my portfolio and returned to my colleague Ruby Dharamsey who had been doing such an excellent job of it. I would work on the company's communication programme with its employees along with the quietly efficient Jyotsna Parulekar and our bouncy colleague with a big smile and a big heart, Hilla Sethna.

In the next nine years I was to gain much knowledge of the affairs of men who went about corporate corridors with flapping ties and bulging files, looking as though the profit motive which drove them was the most sublime force that anybody could desire to be driven by. However, our department was so placed that we were witness to how even the most high-flying managers of the company were brought down to earth by the call of nature. The men's washroom was next to our department. The body has its own compulsions unconnected with human dreams and delusions; and piss is a great leveller. We saw daily evidence of how vulnerable powerful managers looked when they came out of the washroom under the gaze of fourteen female eyes. Had they remembered to zip up?

Meanwhile my hair was greying. A well-meaning supervisor from the factory floor drew me aside to the back of a filing cabinet one day, and said confidentially, 'I have a stone that does the trick.'

'The trick?'

'Hair.'

'Hair what?'

'You're going grey.'

'I know.'

'But you're young.'

'Really?'

'You shouldn't go grey so early. I have a stone. I use it myself. Simple to use. Just rub it in after washing hair. Colour doesn't come off on pillows.'

'That's really kind of you. But I have made a promise to our family goddess that I will never dye my hair.'

The man looked immediately respectful. I had used this trick on a couple of occasions before to avoid arguments and it never failed. Once when the commander-in-chief of the Eastern Naval Command got friendlier than necessary on the dance floor, I did a scared intake of breath and said, 'Oh my god. Our lunar fortnight for not singing and dancing began this morning. Please excuse me. I can't go on.' He held on to my hand. 'It's a vrat we keep for our family goddess,' I explained. He let go of my hand immediately, respectfully bowing me off the floor. That's the advantage of living in a 'spiritual' nation which believes in thirty-three crore deities; each to be worshipped with her or his own esoteric rituals.

It was not the greying but something else about my hair that was worrying me. Having grown too lazy to go regularly to the hairdresser, I had allowed it to grow and was now afflicted with the dropping bun syndrome. The dropping bun is not a bakery product. It is a condition in which, however many pins and clips you use—ironmongery as one of my friends in Bristol used to call it—your bun refuses to hold. Renuka said, 'Chop it off.' One lunchtime I sped over to Century Bazaar. A Chinese hairdresser used to run a salon in its basement till it got flooded one monsoon and all the establishments had to close down. Renuka came up from Shivaji Park to give me moral support. Standing behind my chair she chanted, 'Shorter, shorter,' which pleased the hairdresser mightily. Twenty minutes later, I emerged from the basement bunless, feeling wonderfully light-headed and free.

Greying hair wasn't the most important bodily change that was happening to me during my nine years at Glaxo. That honour must go to 'ischaemia' and menopause. I put the first condition in single quotes because I had suffered no symptoms till the time Dr Lech, who was given to making you undress down to your shoes if he wanted to inspect the stye in your eye, looked at my annual medical check-up reports and said, 'Ischaemia. Please have a stress test done.' Really? I mean did I need more stress in my life than I already had with Arun? We were living in Mother's house but Arun tended to look through her, occasionally even flaring his nostrils at her. She disliked him intensely because he seemed to have more female friends than male and did not appear to do much 'real' work. Making a film once every two years was hardly work. She had tried hard to stop me from marrying him and failed. When I sorted out her things after she died, I found a song in her diary that she had adapted from an old Marathi bhavgeet. The original song went, 'Shant sagari kashas uthavilis vadale' (Why have you set up this storm in a quiet sea?) She had retained that line and added her own stanzas of personal anxiety to it. One of the bitterest regrets of my life is to have caused her so much pain with my second marriage.

Inquiries revealed that the best man I could consult for my ischaemia was Dr Tushar Medhekar whose clinic was in Mahim, a fifteen-minute walk away from my home. A soft-spoken man, who was just friendly enough not to seem unconcerned and professional enough to give you instant confidence, he said, 'You don't need a stress test,' and put me on Inderal. Dr Lech was offended. Who was this physician who had contradicted his advice? 'I will have to put this in my report about you Ms Gokhale,' he said, with an expression that said, 'Just you wait, Henry Higgins.'

'Will they throw me out because of that?' I asked, all pretended innocence.

'They might. They might,' he said in a playful sing-song. I smiled and left. It was an ego thing I decided. Doctors who had their offices in the basement of large industrial buildings might easily delude themselves that it was they who drove the tablet-making and financial wizardry that went on upstairs. Dr Lech's general swagger reminded me of Francis Bacon's fly which 'sat upon the axle-tree of the chariot wheel, and said, what a dust do I raise!' The man was not to be taken seriously.

Glaxo's organizational planning system, MBO (Management By Objectives), did not include plus or minus marks for ignoring doctor's reports. It was for the employees to set their annual goals in consultation with their bosses, and it was for the bosses to appraise them against those goals at the end of the year. My great triumph was managing to persuade my boss Mrs Jane Swamy to include the plays I was doing with the workers as one of my objectives for improving the company's relations with its internal publics. She allowed herself to be persuaded on condition that I did not ask for a budget for the activity (theatre is used to not having budgets!) or for time off from work for the actors. This was going to challenge my management skills and that excited me.

The dramatic activity came about as a result of my disappointment at the dreary lack of culture in Glaxo. I had once suggested to a union leader that they ought to fight for participation in inter-company music and drama competitions instead of always going on about more money. The union leader had laughed. There was no point responding to a suggestion that was so palpably naïve. But the personnel manager had deigned to do so. 'Ms Gokhale, our employees have no talent and no interest in culture.' Aha I thought. He's putting me in my place for the conversation we had had over EST. EST had come on the heels of Transcendental Meditation and before Landmark Forum as a way to self-fulfilment and eternal happiness. The personnel manager was sold on it.

'Where's the time Mr X?' I had said when he had tried to persuade me to do the course.

'We'll let the company worry about that.'

'But what's it for?'

'To fulfil yourself and be happy.'

'But I'm already fulfilled and profoundly happy.'

'So you think. But you'll discover when you do EST that you aren't.'

'You mean EST will first make me feel unhappy and then happy?'

I thought I was joking. He had not laughed.

It got my goat that this gentleman, who was sending managers off by the bucketloads to fulfil themselves at the company's expense, was summarily squashing an idea that would guarantee some self-fulfilment and happiness for the workers. Whatever else the Marathi manus cannot do, s/he can sing and act. Girish Karnad says he envies Maharashtra its acting talent. It is said that if you put two Marathis together on a desert island, they'll do a two-hander play.

Ignoring Mr X's dismissal of the histrionic abilities of Glaxo's workforce, I had sent word around the following morning to say I was starting a drama group. Ten men and women from the factory floor and offices had registered during tea and lunch break that day and more were on their way. I worked out a plan for lunchtime plays which ensured that neither actors nor audience went without lunch or entertainment and were still back at their desks or conveyor belts on the dot. We couldn't afford to have managers and supervisors complain.

Glaxo had three staggered lunch breaks of forty-five minutes each. I chose playscripts that could be pared down to thirty minutes. Employees would eat their lunch in ten minutes, rush to the auditorium, see our play and still have five minutes to return to their workplaces. We would stage five shows over two days to cover all lunch breaks. The employees came in droves and went away asking for more. I cannot claim they worked better for having seen a play in their lunch break; but seeing a play altered their view of the company. They had regarded Glaxo as a stodgy, po-faced employer. Now they conceded it had some human features.

Even before we put up our first play, casteism showed its dark, dank, narrow mind. A true-blue Maratha who had been one of the first I had cast for the play said to me, 'Why have you cast Sanjay?'

'Because he's a very good actor.'

'But you know what he is?'

'What?'

'Not one of us.'

'I don't know what that's supposed to mean. But he is in the play.'

'You might find others withdrawing.'

'Just too bad if they do.'

Nobody withdrew. Not even the true-blue Maratha.

News got around about our conversation. A clerk stopped by my desk casually and said, 'These Marathas think no end of themselves. And here's we, brahmins, who don't dare say a word.'

Two Dutch journalists had come to interview me about caste. Their assumption was that it was a thing of the past in cities. I told them my Glaxo story. They made me repeat it twice before they were willing to believe it. When they sent me a translation of their story, I found I was the only one who had said caste was alive and kicking in Bombay. Everybody else had said it was dead.

One of the highlights of my Glaxo years was escorting

Ian Jack to the company's plant in Ankleshwar. Ian was then a feature writer for the *Sunday Times*, London, with a special interest in South Asia, particularly India. He had been asked by the parent company in the UK to write about the Indian company's expansion covering the new plants it had set up at Nashik, Thane and Ankleshwar. These establishments were aimed at boosting the company's image as a producer of basic drugs as against formulations and infant formula, both of which had become increasingly suspect in the eyes of the pharmaceutical-industry watchdogs. The precisely observed piece Ian wrote on his return did not please the Indian company overmuch. Ian had not bought everything he had been told and he had made what was seen as an unwarranted comment on the blue- pink- and yellow-coloured dogs of Ankleshwar, evidence of the dips they had taken in local water bodies polluted by factory effluents. Although he was not pointing a finger at Glaxo, he was implying criticism of the laxity of rules governing industry in India.

Ian and I kept in touch for several years after his visit. He even sent me a copy of his first book *Before the Oil Ran Out: Britain 1977-86*. Then I lost touch with him and also lost the copy of the book.

Glaxo's proximity to the Bombay Doordarshan Kendra allowed me to do a number of interesting television programmes, particularly book programmes and interviews, for producer Kunwar Sinha. I met Gieve Patel on one of these programmes, leading to a lifelong friendship. Two interviews I most enjoyed doing for Kunwar were with journalist, cartoonist and environmentalist Abid Surti, and with the grand old man of Indo-Anglian literature, Mulk Raj Anand.

It was during my Glaxo years too that Govind Nihalani

asked me to do a two-minute scene in his hit film *Ardh Satya*. It took half a day to shoot because I kept tripping over one word in the speech about police atrocities that I had to make as an activist at a public meeting. I do not remember the treacherous word itself. But I do remember the words that preceded it, 'dil dahalta hai', because I had halted at them in confusion so often through that long and trying afternoon.

21. Mother

1986 was a year of great distress. Mother had been diagnosed that February with cancer of the colon that had metastasized to the liver. She was seventy-three. Dr Arun Samsi, Balu's friend, operated on her in March at K.E.M. The mass in the colon was removed but nothing could be done about the liver. She was in hospital for ten days. I had taken leave to watch over her during the day. She was under sedation and would doze most of the time. Nirmal would come in the evening to take over the night watch. During those ten days I sat beside Mother and wrote the last chapters of *Rita Welinkar*. Back home, Mother tried to go about her work. But the cancer grew. She, who had been such an exceptionally strong woman in body and will, grew subdued. A point came in June when her legs would not hold her up. She took to her bed. During those last two months, when she saw no hope for herself, she would turn to Father's framed photograph on the wall and say softly, 'Gopalrao, please take me away.'

Touch remains the last vital connection between bodies. When Mother became physically dependent on me, she said, 'Now you are the mother and I am the child.' We had never been a touching, kissing family. The overwhelming love we had for each other was expressed through action alone. For the first time during that illness, before her voice became too weak to be audible and her mind began to wander, Mother said, 'Come here Taiday.' I was Tai, elder sister. Taiday was Mother's transformation of the word into an endearment. I bent towards her. She lifted her skin-and-bone hands to stroke my face and kissed me on the cheek. She had never kissed me before. Then she turned to Nirmal who was sitting on the other side and kissed her too. In the last week of life, just before she began to hallucinate, she said, 'Hug me.' She was so fragile, I was afraid to lift her up for a hug. But her fading eyes appealed to me and I held her lightly in my arms where she lay, and put my cheek against hers.

Mother had faced many crises in her life without flinching, but she did not once ask what she was suffering from. Sensing that she suspected what it was but did not want it to be spoken about, we said nothing. She had gone through surgery without questions hoping this was the end of the disease. Two months later, she started getting temperature every day. We dosed her on paracetamol. That would bring the fever down; but soon it would rise again.

'What kind of doctors are these,' she would say angrily, 'who can't cure an ordinary fever?'

She had had great faith in homeopathy. It had been her practice to make a monthly visit to see the taciturn Dr Habbu at Sion. He was treating her for rheumatism. With her went Mr Dattaram Palekar and his wife Leela for their respective health problems. Palekar Kaka was Father's school friend from Belgaum and the eldest brother of Dr Vitthal Palekar who had pulled out my recalcitrant molar. After the three had seen Dr Habbu, they would amble down to Hanuman Cafe on the corner of Sion junction for a leisurely breakfast of idli-sambar.

'You are right about doctors,' I agreed. 'Let me consult

Dr Ganesh Rao.' Dr Rao was her homeopath of choice after Dr Habbu's passing. He prescribed a mother tincture to be administered to her at regular intervals through the day. Within a day her temperature came down and stayed down. Dr Rao suggested something else. A Parsi homeopath named Dr Kasad, whose clinic was located opposite the Khada Parsi statue in Byculla, had been doing research on cancer for a long time. Dr Rao said since allopaths had nothing more to offer Mother, it would do no harm to try Dr Kasad's therapy. The doctor came home and spent an hour with Mother taking down her medical history. That in itself was a comforting change from allopaths who came, examined her cursorily and prescribed paracetamol. This doctor prescribed injections which contained metals. They had to be imported from Switzerland and given subcutaneously every day. Dr Rao had agreed to administer them. The routine had continued for just about a fortnight when, on 21 August, just as the doctor had turned away to fill his syringe, Kamal Mami, Mother's favourite brother Ananta's wife who was with Mother said, 'Doctor, I don't think she needs that.'

In the split second between the doctor's preparing Mother's upper stomach for the injection and turning away to prepare it, she had passed from being into nothingness. Renuka called me at the office. She was sobbing so hard that 'come home' was all she could say. I rushed home expecting to see Mother in the last throes of life. What I saw was a body at rest. The lines of pain had dissolved from her face and she looked as calm and dignified as she had been in life. I looked at her and thought, peace at last.

22. Menopause, Eyes, Fibroids and the Arts

My menopause started in the year of Mother's passing. I waited for the hot and cold flushes to begin. They had been a dramatic feature of all menopausal tales I had heard. None visited me. I had also heard of excessive bleeding, a last hurrah of sorts before the end. It did not happen. Instead, the monthly leak turned into infrequent spotting that turned into nothing. And then I was free. It was like the last-day-of-school rhyme 'No more Latin no more French no more sitting on the rut-put bench.' The original, and much less evocative version, 'hard school bench' had been replaced by some Indian poetic genius of yore with the onomatopoeic 'rut-put bench' which suggested not only the age but the incurable rot of school benches. I hadn't minded periods—one learned to live with them—but I was happy to see the last of them.

I made much of the few menopausal symptoms I did develop. After all, it was a major life-changing event and could not pass without manifesting some signs. 'Occasional palpitations and dizzy spells,' I told Dr Medhekar who had been monitoring my health since the ischaemic scare. 'Pins and needles in my palms,' I said, half-wondering if I should mention them at all. They reminded me of Dr Oliver Sacks' patient whose complaint about someone stabbing the soles of her feet with pins turned out to be a hallucination. Was I making up pins and needles to give my condition the drama that it lacked? This is a major problem with the body. You never know for sure whether it is controlling the mind or the mind is controlling it. Dr Medhekar received all my complaints with a sage nod, duly recording them in my file in his small, neat handwriting. A sage nod is reassuring. It tells you the nodder knows what is what and you can relax.

Meanwhile, the heart was ticking away merrily. Dr Lech's veiled threat that his report to Glaxo's personnel department might get me dismissed was never heard of again. What was giving way though were my eyes. Glasses came to me at the textbook age of forty-five. In Marathi, the age and the accompanying spectacles are denoted by the same word, 'chalishi', the forties. But chalishis are for reading. I could read even a 6-point type with my naked eyes. Strictly speaking then, my glasses could not be called chalishis. They were for seeing distant things which had begun to acquire double edges of late.

One day I discovered a lump in my left breast. I rushed to my gynaec with it. I shall not reveal her name because of what transpired later. She assured me there was nothing, nothing at all to worry about. It was just a fibroid. Biopsy? No need. Prognosis? Nil. Much relieved, I proceeded to live.

It was the summer of 1988. I had been with Glaxo for nine years. One morning Darryl D'Monte saw me waiting for a bus. He gave me a lift. In the course of catching up, I disabused him of the generally held notion that Glaxo was a generous paymaster and that nobody who joined the company left before retirement. I told him while the latter was generally true, I was ready to up and leave anytime. Perhaps he knew even then that he was rejoining the Times as resident editor.

Dileep Padgaonkar had already been appointed editor. They were now looking for an editor for the Arts Page that the Times was planning to start. Dileep asked Arun, a film-maker, to edit it. Arun and he were old pals. Arun laughed off the idea. When he told me about it I asked if he had thought of mentioning to Dileep that he was married to a dyed-in-the-wool journalist-editor who would love to run an arts page? It had not struck Arun to do so; but now he did and Dileep seemed interested. I began to behave as though I already had the job in my pocket. My Glaxo colleagues told me not to be silly. One more year in the company and I would be eligible for gratuity and other benefits. But in my scale of values, when challenging work was weighed against money, the former won hands down. Dileep suggested my name to Mr Sameer Jain. Mr Sameer Jain called me for an interview. He said, 'Why don't you do Public Relations for us instead? You'd be more useful there.' The devaluation of editorial work had already begun. Knowing what public relations meant in the world outside Glaxo where Mrs Swamy had introduced professional PR which did not involve fetching VIPs from the airport or wining and dining the Press but building relationships with communities most affected by the company's products, I suggested someone younger would be more useful to him than me. He said forty-nine wasn't old; and anyway I didn't look forty-nine. But I was forty-nine I said, and eager to get back to journalism.

When I re-entered the portals of the Old Lady of Boribunder, this time as Arts Editor of the *Times of India*, it was with a body that was in pretty good shape. Everything was present in its appointed place and functioning. Hair was cut and out of the way, distance lenses in cheap plastic frames (salmon pink I think) sat on my nose, the heart bounced, menstruation was over and done with and the lump in the breast was nothing more worrisome than a fibroid. All set to make the Arts Page an informative, invigorating, provocative read, I began to look for young contributors. The old guard who had been reviewing music, dance and art for the Times for decades, sounded like Victorians. Their style of reviewing had long since passed. I needed contributors with new ideas, a fresh perspective and critical language that did not smell of mould. There was change all down the third floor of the Times. My friends Bachi Karkaria and Kalpana Sharma had joined as senior editors and Rajdeep Sardesai as assistant editor. At the end of the corridor were Darryl, Dina Vakil and R.K. Laxman the evergreen elder. The floor was fairly buzzing with new energy.

That year the old lady was gearing up to celebrate her sesquicentennial year, but she hadn't yet tricked herself out to look like a Rajasthani dowager. That would come later. I began my work at a table and chair in the open hall where the reporters and subs sat. I did not have a telephone. My calls were routed by the board to the news editor's desk. When my first call came, I pushed my chair back to receive it, causing it to do a backward flip and go down noisily with parts of me attached. Righting myself and the chair I noticed a ragged-edged pothole behind me, measuring roughly 20 cm in diameter. I worked out the critical distance to which I could push my chair when I leapt to receive a call without it toppling over. Aided by the nimbleness I had developed on the badminton court, I was able to negotiate this distance every time someone called till the day I was allotted a cabin and a telephone line of my own.

Since I've mentioned badminton, I would like to put on record that the last time I played the game was in my farewell week at H.R. College. My routine at *Femina* had left little time for it; and marriage to Arun, none. With a heavy heart I had had to put away the stringed companion of my merry youth and mature adulthood, never to pick it up again. I was once tempted to give the game a try at Veenapani Chawla's theatre centre Adishakti in Pondicherry. It had left me with a stiff right shoulder that had taken months to mend.

The Arts Page was exciting to conceive, design and bring out, not least because no template for such a page existed in the Times. Reviews used to be strewn around the paper wherever and whenever and plonked in as they were because nobody except the critics themselves knew what they were about. So I was free to imagine and execute the Arts Page according to my ideas. Happy to be back with dance, music, theatre, art and architecture, my eyes were skinned, my ears pricked for new writers. While I was still in the newsroom with the tricky pothole behind me, a student from the J.J. School of Architecture came to discuss his final year submission, 'Theatre and Space', with me. I am not sure what he got from the discussion, but what I got was my contributor on architecture. Himanshu Burte's interest in spaces for theatre and art continued beyond architecture school. He later wrote *Space for Engagement*, an absorbing study on the theme. He brought to his articles for the Arts Page a lively analytical style that instantly engaged the reader. A woman I met in Dadar's vegetable market told me how much she was learning about architecture from his writings. 'We live in houses that we don't know how to look at or experience,' she said.

Ranjit Hoskote, who was then at Elphinstone College with Girish, brought me a remarkably well-articulated response to Vivan Sundaram's show that had opened at Chemould Art

Gallery across the road from the college. I read it and knew instantly that I had found my art critic. The reigning art critic of the Times, Dnyaneshwar Nadkarni, a friend of my father's and someone I had admired, was miffed at this addition to the table and soon withdrew from the feast. Darryl once said to me, 'People say they have to sit with a dictionary to understand Ranjit's reviews. Can't you ask him to make his language less difficult?'

I said that would be interfering with the writer's individual expression. But I would pass on the feedback to him. Ranjit's love for words did not produce fluff. He wrote with great precision. And if readers needed to consult dictionaries to understand him, that was good news. Dictionaries had never done anybody any harm.

The much-acclaimed poet Arundhathi Subramaniam, who had been a student of Bharatanatyam, interviewed dancers for the page. The Chhau dancer and alumna of Kanak Rele's Nalanda Dance School in Juhu, Prakriti Kashyap, reviewed dance. A young man named Rajan Varadarajan wrote to me about a Carnatic music concert he had heard in Ghatkopar which he said we should have reviewed. His response to the concert was so knowledgeable and sensitive, that I instantly grabbed him to review concerts in the northern and eastern suburbs where Mr Hariharan, the old TOI music reviewer, never went. Naresh Fernandes who was on the staff of the Times wrote on jazz for the page. *Taj Mahal Foxtrot*, which he went on to write years later, has become the definitive book on the Mumbai jazz scene in the forties and fifties. Jerry Pinto, author of the multi-award-winning novel *Em and the Big Hoom,* wrote only a couple of pieces on literature for the TOI arts page, but contributed more regularly to the arts page of *The Independent* which I went on to edit later. I found other writers like Sharmila Joshi, Parag Trivedi, Jiten Merchant, Roshan Shahani and Mukta Rajadhyaksha to write on theatre, music and art. Mukta was the eldest daughter of Professor M.V. Rajadhyaksha who had told me of the Elphinstone College vacancy thirty-seven years ago. My discussions with these young writers and the writing they produced for me were enriching enough to compensate for the meagre salary of five thousand rupees a month that I was drawing.

I too contributed to my page occasionally. Translation, one of the missions of my life, was part of my concept for it. I translated a passage from Durga Khote's autobiography when it was released. Her elder son Bakul persuaded me later to translate the whole book. It has become one of my most read translations. I also translated the first essay from artist Prabhakar Barwe's collection on his creative process, *Kora Canvas*. His artist friends persuaded me to translate the whole book which I did, again years later. Another small translation that led to my doing the whole book was Lakshmibai Tilak's description of how she lost her way in Byculla, excerpted from her voluminous four-part autobiography *Smritichitre.* I did this translation for TOI's special sesquicentennial issue devoted to Bombay city. It took me sixteen years after that to find time to translate the whole book.

The Arts Page was doing swimmingly well and garnering a loyal readership when it was suddenly scrapped. The year-long sesquicentennial celebrations, during which TOI had become a supporter of the arts, were long since over. There was no need now to cover the arts. The ostensible reason for the scrapping was the imminence of the First Gulf War that was darkening the horizon. Reams of newsprint would be required to cover it. How could any be spared for the arts? Darryl said to me one Saturday morning, don't bring out the Arts Page from tomorrow. Orders from above. And that was that.

Then another story began doing the rounds, according to which Alyque Padamsee was behind the closure. There was a background to the story. Our critic for English theatre, Jiten Merchant, had informed us that Padamsee was about to open his new production *Othello* at the National Centre for the Performing Arts and had instructed the institution not to send free passes to the Press. We wondered why. Was it because he was not open to criticism? An investigation was called for. None of my regular contributors could have done it. So I requested Manjula Sen, one of TOI's sharpest reporters, to put her nose to it. She came up with a brilliant piece aptly titled with Desdemona's query, 'Come, how woulds't thou praise me?' Manjula had talked to other critics besides Jiten about the ban and also tried to get Alyque's comments. The article ended as follows:

> 'After he learned the purpose of the article, he interrogated, "You are doing a story on *Othello*?"
>
> "Yes."
>
> "When are you writing it?"
>
> "As soon as I finish speaking with you."
>
> "What are your credentials?"
>
> "I am a staff reporter with the *Times of India*."
>
> "Tell Darryl D'Monte to ring me up."
>
> Slam went the phone.'

It was generally assumed that Alyque, the big boss at Lintas, known as God for the power he wielded, was upset by Manjula's article and had turned the screws on TOI. I found that an unlikely story. However big Alyque was, the Times was surely bigger. Had they wanted to keep the page going, they would merely have warned me not to mess with him and continued the page. But it had clearly been TOI's intention all along to start the page for the sesquicentennial year and stop it once it was over. The Arts Page of the *Economic Times*, edited by Sadanand Menon, was also scrapped soon after and there was no Alyque Padamsee involved there. If Padamsee was upset by Manjula's article, he was even more upset by the story linking him with the demise of the Arts Page. He wrote to me:

> Dear Shanta,
> Enclosed is a xerox of the letter I have sent to the Editor of the *Times of India*. I believe there is a rumour running around the TOI office that I spoke to the top brass to get the Arts Page stopped. This is a complete fabrication. (I believe there is a mischief monger in the TOI who has been gunning for me through a series of nasty articles in various publications under different Pseudonyms). I would be grateful if you could share the enclosed letter with your colleagues (in case the TOI does not print it...Press censorship?).
> Many thanks and regards.
> Alyque Padamsee

Alyque's letter to the Editor read:

> Dear Sir,
> I read recently that you are thinking of dropping your Arts Page. This will be a great disservice to the cultural community in Bombay. We all look forward to this page with excitement, and sometimes with trepidation, but always with expectation. It serves as a forum for vigorous discussion on the arts. Long may this continue.

In spite of what some uncharitable people may have written recently, I am and always will be a supporter of free speech springing from intelligence and experience.

Alyque Padamsee

My response to his letters was:

Dear Alyque,

Thank you for your letter of January 11th. The rumour you refer to was rife in the tight little media world outside the TOI. In here we were quite certain that you couldn't have asked for the Arts Page to be dropped. Managements can be callous without outside help. What we are sure of though is that you 'expressed your displeasure' to the management. This was quite unnecessary because (a) you could have answered all the uncharitable accusations people were making about your manipulation of the Press directly to our reporter when she called you or (b) you could have written as long a rejoinder as you pleased for the Arts Page and we'd have happily published it. The outcome either way would have been happier for all of us.

One thing that struck me during the post-Manjula Sen and Arts Page scrapping episodes was how many of the people who called to congratulate us on the article and sympathise with us over the scrapping, insisted the latter was your doing. It reminded me of a lovely story Vijay Tendulkar tells. There's this chap he met in some prison who'd been sentenced to death. He wore a beatific smile although he insisted he'd been framed. "Aren't you angry with this miscarriage of justice?" Tendulkar asked. "No," he grinned. "I didn't murder anyone this time. But I did a few years ago and got off scot-free. So I'm being punished now."

With Kind Regards

Shanta Gokhale

For the longest time I had wanted to write a book on the history of Marathi drama. With Renuka and Girish encouraging me to quit the Times, I began reading up for it. I was making plans for my research, when an unasked-for opportunity came my way. Girish Karnad, who was then chairman of the Sangeet Natak Akademi, invited me to present a paper at the Festival of India in Berlin which was to open with a German production of his play, *Nagamandala*, directed by Vijaya Mehta. Would it not be wonderful to tag on a visit to London, to see what was happening in British theatre? After all, modern Marathi theatre had been seminally influenced by Shakespearean tragedy and Shavian realism. Was Marathi theatre still running in tandem with them or had the colonial influence worn off? Rupa Patel, head of the culture department at the British Council, offered me a small grant to cover my fare from Berlin to London and my theatre tickets. Accommodation was not a problem. The Bank of India had posted Usha's husband Shantaram Jategaonkar to London. By the most fortuitous of circumstances, their next move, which was supposed to have happened before I arrived in London, had been postponed. So I had a warm and welcoming home in St John's Wood for the entire length of my stay. This was March 1992, thirty years after I had said goodbye to England. During my fortnight in London, Girish, who came up from Oxford, and I saw a play practically every day. We would queue up in Leicester Square for half-price and discounted tickets that were made available on the day of the show and up to a week in advance. There were a couple of shows we saw at half-price from the very best seats. Ariel Dorfman's *Death and the Maiden* was one of them. During that fortnight we even managed to wedge in a day trip to Bristol where I drowned myself in nostalgia.

Ajit and Lilu's daughter, Charu Shahane, was with the BBC in Birmingham. She heard that her friend, storyteller Vayu Naidu's husband Chris Banfield, was directing my translation of Mahesh Elkunchwar's *Pratibimb* (Reflection) for the Birmingham University Drama Department. When Chris heard I was in London, he urged Charu to persuade me to go up to Birmingham to see the production. The show was scheduled for the day after I was to fly back to Bombay. But I had an open ticket and Girish saw no reason why I should not stay on an extra day to take in the play. The ultimate pleasure for a translator is to see her work on stage. The University Drama Department's production was sensitive, imaginative and thoroughly professional. What most chuffed me was Chris telling me afterwards that neither he nor his actors had felt the need to change a single word in my translation. I returned to Bombay on an extra pair of wings.

I quit the Times in July 1993, a year and a month after Arun's Delhi bomb had exploded, to continue research on my book. The management said why quit? You can write your book sitting here as others do. Suddenly I was not dispensable as I had been when the TOI arts page was scrapped. I was now editing the arts page of the new TOI baby *The Independent.* I said I'd rather sit at my own desk to write my book, and quit. It was sweet revenge for what the TOI had done to my baby.

I started writing my book in 1995 on a small grant from the National School of Drama, facilitated by Kirti Jain who was then director of the school. I was working simultaneously on the script for *Katha Doan Ganpatraonchi*, Arun's film based on the Gogol story. The film was released in 1995. I completed writing the book in 1998. It was published in 2000 by Calcutta's Seagull Books under the title *Playwright at the*

Centre: Marathi Drama from 1843 to the Present. Arun moved out of Lalit Estate the same year into a beautiful, spanking new flat in Goregaon. Finally, we were mistress and master of our own independent spaces and looking forward to our new lives.

23. The Body Politic Fractured

On 6 December 1992, an old mosque in Ayodhya, popularly known as Babri Masjid, was demolished by right-wing forces. It was a watershed moment in India's history. It drove a wedge through the country, separating Hindus from Muslims almost as traumatically as Partition had done. A new and terrifying face of my city was revealed during the months that followed. Madhusree Dutta caught it painfully in her first film *I Live in Behrampada*. Underneath the warm and welcoming surface of the country, politically incited rage had been gathering strength since L.K. Advani's rath yatra in 1990 which had left behind a trail of blood. The demolition was a correction of an unproven 500-year-old wrong. Babur, the first Mughal invader and emperor of India, was popularly believed to have razed a Rama temple that had stood on the very spot where Lord Rama was believed to have been born, and built a masjid in its place. The spot was called Ramjanmabhoomi. The right-wing political party, the Bharatiya Janata Party, made the building of a grand Rama temple on the exact spot where the mosque stood, its election plank.

The demolition of the Babri Masjid was followed by riots of a ferocity that my city had never witnessed. Being neither a historian nor an archaeologist, I have no right to an opinion on the matter of whether the mosque had indeed been built over the ruins of a temple. However, a passage in Vishnubhat Godse's *Majha Pravas* (My Travels), considered a classic of chronicle writing in Marathi and arguably the only eye-witness account of what is now known as the first war of independence, throws light on Ramjanmabhoomi which needs to be taken into account. In Part Six of the book, the erudite priest Godse describes the rituals that attended worship at the Ramjanmabhoomi in Ayodhya as prescribed by the shastras.

He says: 'It is recorded in all the holy books that those who bathe in the Sharayu before two o'clock in the afternoon, and pay their obeisance at the Ramjanmabhoomi, are released from the perpetual cycle of birth. That is why the pilgrims bathe in the Sharayu at noon and hurry to the Ramjanmabhoomi with holy basil leaves, betel nuts and money. The place is an open park with many trees and very ancient walls standing at a great distance. The site of Kaushalya's room is about fifty arms length long and forty arms length wide. On it stands a solidly built waist-high platform surrounded by a parapet that is not more than two arms length high. Some seven or eight hundred thousand pilgrims gather there. Despite the vastness of the place and the horse-guards and elephants that the government deploys to control the crowds, four or five people die there every year. We had our darshan and on the following day we bathed at Swargadwar where Lord Lakshman abstained from food and meditated till he went to heaven.'

Nowhere in Godse's description of Ramjanmabhoomi does he mention a mosque.

Vishnubhat Godse was writing about the events of 1857. Babur had died in 1530. If Babur had indeed built a mosque on the ruins of a temple at Ramjanmabhoomi, then there had to be two Ramjanmabhoomis in existence—the one that Godse and thousands of pilgrims worshipped at in 1857, where no mosque existed, and the one where the Babri Masjid, built before 1530, stood.

The demolishing of the Babri Masjid was a body blow to the nation. We have continued to feel the aftershocks of that event till today.

24. Glaucoma and a Fracture

I finished writing *Playwright at the Centre* in 1998. With bibliography, notes and index, it had run to five hundred and eighty pages. Naveen Kishore of Seagull Books said it was like Hanuman's tail which would not stop growing.

Writing the book had taken a toll on my eyes. I had worked ten hours a day for months. But there was also something other than eye-strain wrong with them. I went with my complaint to my opthalmologist whom I will not name because of what followed. I told him I occasionally experienced a searing pain around twilight that felt like my eyeballs were being pulled into the back of my head. The doctor said, 'Nothing but eye-strain. You work too much at the computer.' He gave me soothing eye drops and sent me home.

A fortnight later, I was back in his clinic with the same complaint. The twilight pain had become more frequent. The doctor said, 'Don't worry. Don't work at the computer for a few days. And continue with the eye drops.' How could I, a writer, not work at the computer? I ignored the advice and decided to continue working while I watched and waited.

In October that year, I was in Pune staying with Baban Bhau. Sharayu Vahini was in her mid-eighties then and still interested in cricket, sewing, reading, thinking, arguing and joking. She would remain that way till the end of her ninety-four-year-old life. During that visit, I was to read my new play to the students of Pune University's department of music and drama, headed by playwright Satish Alekar. He was present for the reading and so, by chance, was the other eminent playwright of our times, Mahesh Elkunchwar. Halfway through the reading, shadows had begun to gather in the room. The twilight hour was at hand, coinciding with the entr'acte of the play. We took a break. Exactly on cue I felt the familiar stab of pain in the eyes, but that evening it was so acute it was almost unbearable. I shut my eyes tight. After a while the pain passed. But when I opened my eyes again and began to read, I noticed that the words were blurred. I pressed on nevertheless. The reading ended. The feedback was mixed. The students had nothing to say. Satish did not like the play. Mahesh did. But now it was my eyes, not the play, that occupied my mind. I was sure I couldn't see as well with my right eye as I had done before that stab of pain.

Back at Baban Bhau's, I described my ocular condition. Without a moment's pause he said it must be glaucoma. What's that, I said. Resourceful as ever, Sharayu Vahini hurried to her room and returned with one of her many files of newspaper cuttings. This one was on health. Running through it rapidly, she found what she was looking for—an article that contained all the information anybody could ever want on glaucoma. The least cheering bit of information in that article was that the condition was irreversible. The right medication could only maintain status quo. Baban Bhau said, 'Now just go back to that doctor of yours and tell him to give you a test for glaucoma.'

I went back. The doctor said, 'Glaucoma test? What for? Do you have a family history of glaucoma?'

'Not that I know of. But couldn't I be the pioneer?'

The test was simple. It lasted two minutes. But the findings were dire. The normal pressure of fluid in the eyes is 17 or under. Both my eyes had registered a pressure of 50. The doctor was stunned. He reproached me, 'You had no family history, no headache, no vomitting, no red eyes and yet you have glaucoma!' I turned on my heels and left his clinic for good. I found Dr Nisheeta Agarwala at Dr Natarajan's Aditya Jyot Hospital. She was to move later to Hinduja Hospital nearer to my home. She ordered a field of vision test that confirmed my worst fears. I had lost vision around the periphery of my right eye. Only tunnel vision remained. Fortunately, my left eye was fine. Under Dr Agarwala's care, I have managed to read, write and translate with one eye and a half for the last twenty-five years. All I have needed to do is put one drop of a rather expensive medication in each eye every night and live with the fact that no pair of spectacle lenses will ever balance the difference in the two eyes to give me a sharp, consolidated vision. Sometimes I close my left eye to see better and sometimes my right.

In 1999 I turned sixty. That year, at the end of a seminar at SNDT college, Churchgate, I stopped at the gate to talk to a group of fellow seminarists. Among them was the scholar and political activist Pushpa Bhave. She was roughly my age so I thought I would share my sixtieth birthday resolution with her. 'We shall not fall and break our bones.' Pushpa seconded my pledge. We laughed heartily and parted. A few days later, I fell.

When I took the oath not to fall, I had forgotten the role that the city's municipal corporation could play in these accidents. I had also forgotten my general predilection for falling. I've fallen down the steps in an Italian pensionne; I've fallen over a carpet at Cairo airport; I have fallen on the road outside Nirmal's house waving out to Vikram standing in the window above; I have fallen twice on my morning walk round Shivaji Park and once off a horse, about which later. In my post-oath fall, the culprit was a loose kerbstone. I was waiting to cross the road after my walk. As I stepped off the kerb, the loose stone got dislodged. My leg buckled and I went down. A neighbour of Nirmal's, Vijay Godbole, who was passing by, picked me off the road and led me home. Jabeen, who has not appeared in this story so far, but is Girish's wife, wrapped my destroyed right wrist in a tight bandage and said, 'Off we go to the hospital.'

'Why hospital?' I asked brightly. 'There's a twenty-four-hour clinic right here in Shivaji Park, and I know the orthopaedic surgeon who runs it. His parents used to play badminton.'

I was to discover later that sons of badminton players do not necessarily make the best go-to people when your bones are in trouble. Chubby-faced Dr Y chortled and rubbed his hands to see my forearm. 'Classic dinner-fork fracture,' he announced. He sat down at his table and drew me a diagram of the radius which had broken in such a way as to lift one half of it over the other. 'See?' he said, viewing his handiwork. 'Doesn't that look like a dinner fork?'

'Yes, it does. It does. But what do we do about it?'

'Fix it,' he said, promptly summoning his nurse. Attaboy I thought, throwing a triumphant look at Jabeen. Hospital indeed!

I lay down on the brown rexine table. The doctor stood before me, the nurse behind me. Jabeen hovered anxiously in the background. 'This will hurt a bit,' said Dr Y. I remembered Girish's entry into the world and said, 'I can take it.'

The doctor took a firm grip of my palm. The nurse took an equally firm grip of my elbow. He pulled my arm towards him, she towards her at a perfectly coordinated moment of time. I thought I heard a click. If there was pain, I did not notice it because a disconcerting thought had hit me hard just then. Belying the framed professional certificates that decorated his wall, Dr Y was not an orthopaedic surgeon at all. He was a bone-setter.

'There we are,' Dr Y said, rubbing his hands together again. 'All fixed. Now the cast. Then you can go home.'

I went home with grave doubts about what was happening inside the cast. What if my bones were quietly turning to dust? I had to get a second opinion. Dr Shreedhar Archik, recommended by Dr Medhekar, was not a bone-setter. He took an X-Ray of my arm and said grimly, 'Operation. New cast for six weeks. We'll remove the screws, nuts and bolts after that. But let me warn you. Because of the first ah…umm… operation, you'll probably have to live with a slight distortion in the wrist.'

For the next six weeks my arm, full of hardware, creaked like an old ship. But it was rather spectacular attending a film society discussion in Pune about *Katha Doan Ganpatraonchi* which had just been released, with my arm in a cast. Gradually the bone healed. Kneading dough, my daily practice, was more useful than squeezing a rubber ball as prescribed by the physiotherapist, to return my hand to its normal functions. The distortion in the wrist was hardly noticeable. And anyway, I was not in the race for Ms Ponds-Femina Pretty Hands. What mattered was that I could write my weekly bread-and-butter culture column for the Times. And I could eat.

25. Horse Fall

Although Dr Archik had urged me to have a bone density test done, putting down my wrist fracture not to the municipal corporation's irresponsibility but to the fragility of my bones, I decided to ignore the advice. I am not one of those people who believe they are smarter than their doctor. In fact, I admire doctors immensely. But sometimes you need to take responsibility for your body yourself. Savita, a school friend, began to stumble a little when she walked. The doctor diagnosed her with incipient Parkinsons. The medication did not stop her from stumbling. Instead, it added other impairments to her body's functioning. Her voice grew weak. Her speech slurred. She became more and more depressed. One day she emptied her bursting pill box into the wastepaper bin. When I spoke to her a few weeks later, I was astonished at how strong and clear her speech had become. 'Congratulations. The medicine is working.'

'No. My commonsense is working. I stumble because I'm old, not diseased. I've thrown away the pills.'

My uncle Ananta, Mother's favourite brother, was told by his doctor that he needed to undergo a bypass surgery. 'I am sixty-five,' he reasoned. 'I have lived a life. Why spend lakhs on a heart that is bound to stop ticking by itself one of these days?' He lived an active life for ten years after that and died of galloping cancer of the throat that took him away within two months of diagnosis.

All I'm saying is, you don't have to jump when the doctor says jump. I didn't. And soon enough there was evidence that my bones were not in the seriously fragile state that Dr Archik had suspected. The hospitable Francis Wacziarg, creator of boutique hotels, had invited us, his colleagues on the board of trustees of the India Foundation for the Arts, to hold our biannual meeting at his heritage hotel, The Verandah, in Matheran. There was a choice of transport at the foot of the hill station beyond which cars were not allowed. You could do horses, palanquins or your own legs. We had some tough trustees who chose legs. I fancied myself tough and did likewise. But it was dusk. The swaying trees flanking the path threw shifting shadows on it. My glaucoma eyes went blind in this play of light and dark. I was inspecting every shadow closely to make sure it overlay level ground and not a dip in the road. Glaucoma prevents you from seeing depth. Staircases are murderous unless you are very careful. Noting my slow progress, one of the toughies asked delicately so as not to hurt my ego, 'Would you like to take a horse?'

'Would I not just,' I said in high relief.

I'm not a horse person. The only horse I had ever loved was The Pie in *National Velvet*. But the distance between the screen, the horse and me had been vital for the love to flourish. I had also had a crush on Montgomery Clift; but I wouldn't have known what to do with him had he dropped in and asked for a cup of tea. Distance is important for some forms of love. There are people who know instinctively what to do with animals. I am not one of them. Barbara Williams at school used to feed her forearm to Fido the school dog as a form of play while I watched horrified. I have some knowledge of cats. I stroke them, tickle them, even allow them to curl up on my lap. But dogs? Lovely, trusting eyes, sure. But tongues hanging out and slobbery kisses? No. And horses? I wouldn't go nearer than 50 feet from them if I could help it. That distance is just right to appreciate the gloss of their coat, the taut elegance of their flanks, the toss of their heads and the magnificence of their manes. From that distance what you do not see is their long, strong teeth, their flaring nostrils and their impatiently quivering skins.

The horse in Matheran that was hired for me, held no risks. Only promise. He was transport. And he was going to be led by his owner at a safe trot. His great height did make me a little nervous, and so did his owner's age. The horse must have been 6 feet tall, and the boy fifteen years old. But my fellow trustees encouraged me to take the leap; to trust the horse and the man. I clambered gingerly on to the horse's back and made myself as comfortable as I could with the reins in my hands as a placebo support.

We had trotted along happily for most of the distance to The Verandah when another horse, much shorter than mine, came up beside us. The two owners knew each other and got into a jolly old chinwag accompanied by, if I may say so, much horseplay: pushing each other around, slapping each other on the backs, that sort of thing. My horse did not appreciate this. He snorted menacingly, swinging his head this way and that and lifting his legs a little too high. I suspected he did not care much for the other horse either. Since both owners were still busy having fun, he decided to protest. Before I knew what his plan was, he bucked. I found myself at an angle I had never been at before. About 45-degrees from the vertical and sliding towards the horse's tail. I held on to the reins for dear life. The horse owner stopped fooling around and started making soothing sounds. But it was too late. The horse was not to be pacified. He bucked again and this time I slid down to his rump. One more bout of bucking and I was over his tail and flat on the hard, stony earth. Those who had gone ahead rushed back. I was helped up and escorted to a nearby rock. Ice was fetched from somewhere and held to the back of my head where a largish lump was beginning to form. The horse owner blamed me entirely for the fall. He said I had kicked the horse. I told him I should have kicked him instead. He went away laughing, the money he had earned jingling in his pocket. I walked the rest of the distance to The Verandah. For the next two days I was like a piece of rusty machinery, creaking with every move. But bones? Intact, every one of them. Not even a hairline crack.

Francis's warm hospitality included Manjiri Asnare singing for us for three hours while the stars came up in the sky behind her. It also included a face-reader who had predicted that Francis's properties were going to multiply exponentially. This had touched Francis. Hoping the face-reader would bring equally happy tidings to the rest of us, Francis set him up in a kind of secret grove beside the hotel where he was free to hold individual sessions with us. My fellow trustees went to him one by one and returned laughing from the tryst.

I was one of the last to go. I sat myself down before the gentleman. He studied my face for a few moments and said what would have been obvious to anybody with half an eye and no brain. 'You don't believe in face-readers.'

'You're right. But I'm curious all the same.'

He smiled and told me about the wonderful qualities of

mind and heart I possessed. I guessed the idea was to massage the pig with fragrant spices before skewering it on a spit. The gentleman noticed that my expression had not changed. He said, 'But there's one thing I must tell you. Whether you believe it or not, there's somebody up there looking out for you. Your past shines, you're future shines. That's because somebody up there loves you. You don't believe that, do you?' Obviously I did not. Now his expression changed. 'But you should. You need love. Because your present is clouded by someone with a round face and a mole who wishes you ill. I'm sure you know who it is.'

'No, I don't.'

'Round face? Mole?'

'Depends on where the mole is,' I said. 'Some moles are not on public view. But even a round face sounds improbable.'

His eyes went dead. 'I don't think I can tell you much more then,' he said.

'Perhaps you can,' I countered. 'Maybe you didn't mean round face and mole. Maybe you meant long face, large teeth and a swishing tail. If you did, then this creature did wish me ill but has finished doing his worst. I'm safe now.'

The man was too obliged to Francis to say FO to one of his guests. But his face said it. Such are the minor victories that make a rationalist's day.

26. Full-blown Cancer

Around 1992, the year of my marital crisis, I noticed that the fibroids in my left breast were multiplying. But my gynaec's assurance that they were harmless, was like a line etched in stone in my mind. And anyway, I had no time to worry about them while I was living under strange and stressful conditions with Arun. Arun moved out in 2000; and one day in October 2004, the fibroids oozed blood. Renuka was with me. She noticed the spots on my kameez. White-faced, she ordered me to the doctor immediately. I got an appointment for the following week with Dr Medhekar. He took one look at my pebbly breast and said, 'Cancer. You will see Dr Jagannath at Lilavati Hospital immediately. Here's a note for him.' This was Dr P. Jagannath about whom we had heard good things from Shilpa Tulaskar, a close actor friend of Renuka's whose mother he had treated.

The cancer was at Stage 3, but there were no secondaries. Dr Jagannath said, 'How could a well-educated lady like you not know what this was?' Thoroughly ashamed, I promised to tell him my idiotic story another day. Meanwhile, he discovered that the lump was so large it was practically sticking to the chest wall. Unless it came loose and decreased in size, surgery was impossible. So I was sent off to Dr B.K. Smruti, the medical oncologist, for pre-surgery chemotherapy. She offered alternative bouquets of drugs. Without second thoughts, Girish chose the imported ones which she said might cause fewer side effects although the Indian were equally effective. After the first round, I emailed the following to my friends.

Breast Bulletin: 1

27th November, 2004. After a day's reprieve—the chemo was supposed to have started the previous day, when I saw *Singin' in the Rain* instead—I woke up to the haunting melody of its theme song along with the early morning calls of sparrows, crows and pigeons. Good way to begin the first day of chemo.

Into Raheja Hospital at 10.30 on the dot to face nursing staff for whom the occasion doesn't demand any more attention than the normal—continue task in hand, in one case playing video games, throw half a glance at visitors, recount all the problems they have not been clever enough to anticipate on their own, finally relent and tell them what they are expected to do and where. Admission organised, height and weight taken, the latter on scales showing everyone 2 kg lighter, and finally in bed with an anti-emetic mixed with saline water going drip-drip-drip into chosen vein. I feel mighty pleased at the ward boy's sincere praise of my vein—it's been easy to find.

The doctor is told I'm on. She promises to be there in half an hour. The half hour turns to two, so the saline water drip has been turned down to practically nothing. The flow has to be kept up somehow till she comes.

I look at the drip and can't get Rajesh Khanna out of my mind, saying to Sharmila Tagore with his characteristic tilt of the head—Pushpa I hate tears. But what I want to get to is the bit about saline water and I can't for the life of me remember the exact words. Anyway Pushpa's quivering chin stops quivering and she wipes her kajalled eyes gently after allowing two last pearls to roll over her rouged cheeks.

The doctor arrives and a pink-coloured liquid is hung up on the hook chasing the last drops of saline water. Meanwhile I've tucked into cheese sandwiches and am all set to go. Girish has been sent off on one of the hospital's many get-this-get-that errands. Jabeen is with me smiling and running her hands through my hair. She has a lovely gentle touch.

The pink liquid begins to course through my vein. The nurses hover, the doctor hovers, each in turn asking me if there is any pain, any burning. There ain't none. How can there be when pink drug meets pink comrade. We just meet on our side of the boxing ring, shake hands and sock it to the unruly lumpen element trying to take over this true Marathi breast.

Off with the pink, on with the next drug—colourless, transparent, no ideological indications. 'I'm dreaming of being a boxing star in my new pink maidenform bra!' I hum to myself in unexpected recall of a half-century-old ad which I detested at the time but which has obviously made a permanent home in my memory. Dressed thus, I'm kind of leaning against the ropes, legs crossed casually, looking the transparent guy straight in the eye and saying come on buddy or whatever boxers say, I got no time to dilly-dally.

No spectators around now. Doctor's in OPD, Girish has been sent haring off on another errand, nurses back to video games and casual chatter in their room. Jabeen sits beside me gazing out of the window looking like Nefertitti (if that's the spelling). When suddenly, WHAM. I'm floored. My heart is trying to eject out of my mouth. My innards are slipping out of my feet. There's a ton of hot iron in my head and an elephant is standing on my empty chest. I tell Jabeen in a voice that comes out of some ancient cave that the countdown has begun and she'd better run for them before the bout is declared a knockout. She runs to the nurses, they run to me, the doctor runs to me, they unhook me from this dangerous, ideologically neutral drug and pump some efcorlin and avil into my vein. They wait ten minutes while the khatarnak's effects gradually wear off. Jabeen looks at me and says the redness has gone. What redness? I ask. Your face had gone red as a tomato she says in horror.

That's a real come down. Sixty-five years of attempting balancing acts in private and professional life so that I never have to go red in the face and suddenly this. The drip is now on again, reduced to a less dangerous pace, and all is well. The bottle drains away. Nausea? Ask the nurses at the end of it. No. No Nausea? Again and again, ad nauseum. No, no, no.

So the last saline drip is hooked up and goes in at a fast clip. Then I'm unhooked for the next three weeks. We're down in the canteen eating sandwiches and having hot masala tea. Back home, this woman with some wonder drugs in her and a hopefully quailing lumpen element in her left breast, sits back against the cushions, surrounded by loved ones, enjoying their pampering!

So far so good. I rise on the day after with this bulletin going round in my head. Under my window a cat caterwauls for her mate and in the corner of my verandah garden, two fledgling pigeons in an empty pot, chirp for their first feed. Life is good.

But the bad days, they are a-coming. Perfectly calculated to occur between the 8th and 10th day after chemo, they will fall on the 4th, 5th and 6th of December for me this time around. I shall counteract adverse effects with all the things I've not had time to do in the routines that have governed my life so far—listen to lots of music, read, see films. I've opted for all the funnies. Wodehouse stopped amusing me when

> I reached 14. But I've got a whole omnibus now, presented by Arun, riding on which I hope to return to my 14th year. He has also gifted me cheerers like *Pyar Kiye Jaa*, *Jaane Bhi Do Yaaron* and *Padosan* along with some old Prabhat films. It's going to be a rich life with enough pain injected into it to tell me what a complete life is all about.

On 10 December, four days after my infection-prone period between chemos was over, Renuka's second son Satyendra was born. I had been a hands-on granny when Shouryaman was born two years before on 23 October. With Satyendra, I could only look and hold, but not spend time. The best substitute for me was Nirmal. She was with Renuka in hospital and at home till she settled down with the new arrival. For the time being, I could not be with anybody but myself.

> **Breast Bulletin: 2 or the Case of the Dying WBCs**
>
> The thing to watch out for, the doctor had warned us over and over again, was fever. Or rather FEVER. That's how the upping of body temperature is regarded by chemotherapists. It was likely to strike between the eighth and tenth day after a chemo round, she said, when my WBC count would be at its lowest ebb, leaving me to the mercy of every malevolent germ that was passing by.
>
> How do you watch out for FEVER was the question I kept mulling over. I remembered the time of the Chinese aggression when Indian leaders, it appears, kept appealing to people to be vigilant. How do I do that, my father had demanded testily in his weekly letter to me in Bristol. Do I look under the bed every night for a lurking Chinaman? That about sums up how I felt about watching out for FEVER.
>
> Meanwhile, on the dot of the eighth day, as predicted,

my white blood cells began to give up the good fight. I remembered our physiology teacher calling them the body's police force. It gave me a picture of what was happening inside of me. I saw hordes of men in white behaving exactly like the Mumbai police on riot day. Erasing themselves out of existence.

While on the subject of policemen, I also recalled the sprightly traffic cop in Imphal who, on a balmy day, waved the traffic in from all four directions. Just for the heck of it I guess. Once he had got us into a satisfactory snarl, he quit his post, sauntered to the sidewalk and picked his teeth while we spent the best part of half-an-hour unsnarling ourselves without causing serious collateral damage.

So, with my WBCs turning tail, I had only me to defend myself. And I did it with spirit. Visitors were denied entry, doors and windows were shut tight to keep out germs, bacteria, viruses and all suchlike pests. I covered myself with a shawl and lay absolutely still, resisting all forms of exercise that might lead to the dreaded FEVER. And yet, who knows through what crack or cranny, it came. It came right in and made itself comfortable in my defenceless body.

The doctor said, get her to the hospital. NOW.

My first ever visit to the aseptic confines of a large hospital. The WBCs and the FEVER were now monitored round the clock. While nurses stuck a thermometer under my arm, took syringefuls of my blood and checked my pressure every few hours, I was busy wolfing down magnificent south Indian breakfasts and comparatively indifferent lunches and dinners. During the long afternoons, Girish read Wodehouse to me. With the merest flick of the eyebrows, an occasional sideways glance, minimal hand gestures and subtle vocal inflections, he ushered the entire Wooster gang into my hospital room in all their endearing eccentricities.

On the second day in hospital the FEVER sank to normal, and the WBCs, treated to booster injections, began to revive and return to duty. By the third day, the men in white were swarming into the bloodstream again, all charged up and raring to go

The climb up from the great WBC fall was magical. And mysterious too. For suddenly I was seeing chicken. As I lay in bed on the morning of my discharge, this vision of a sublimely browned leg of chicken flanked by a hot buttered potato filled my imagination, leaving no place for any other thought. I called Jabeen urgently and said, I want chicken for lunch. She said you want chicken? I said yes, I want chicken. But, she said, you've gone vegetarian. You don't eat chicken. So I said just you watch me do it now.

Back home, the vision turned into delicious reality. I looked on hungrily as Jabeen pulled a succulent chicken leg out of the oven and set it before me complete with a steaming potato as ordered. I don't think I've ever enjoyed a meal more.

I'm not asking myself how or why a mind that had for the last 12 years dwelt exclusively on things that grow above and below the ground, had suddenly been seduced by chicken. The human body has its own compulsions, I told myself. Therefore, ours is not to question why. Ours is but to say Aye Aye and go to it!

My second chemo dose happens tomorrow. We're going to make damned sure that both the drugs, the pink and the white, treat me with due respect. That means no sequel to "Funny side up"!

At the end of two rounds of chemo, I was bald and looking a lot like my father who had balded somewhat prematurely. Girish ordered me a magnificent grey-haired wig from America. I got my hairdresser Shobha Raut to trim its luxuriance to approximate the scanty growth I had lost. I was wearing this wig when I went for post-surgery radiation at Hinduja Hospital supervised by Dr V. Kannan. So full of admiration was he for this piece of artistry that I am certain, even today, twelve years down the line, I could say to him, 'Good evening Dr Kannan. This is the woman with the wig,' and he would know who I mean.

At the end of four rounds of chemo, the lump had shrunk only 30 per cent and would shrink no more. Dr Smruti sent me back to Dr Jagannath. 'Ask him to operate.' Dr Jagannath set the date for 25 February 2005.

The surgery had its own moments of drama. On the morning of the event, after the nurse had finished shaving every bit of me, including thighs in case a skin graft was required to close the gash in my breast, two doctors walked in briskly, members of Dr Jagannath's team. They stood on either side of my bed eyeing my left breast with great concentration. One doctor said maybe we could do a vertical cut. The other said that would be problematic. We'll do a horizontal cut. They jiggled the breast then, shook their heads despondently and left. Dr Jagannath didn't come. He was in the OT, gowned and masked, ready to receive me with his usual warm smile. It was cold in there so I said can't you guys give me a warm covering. Dr Jagannath said, wait and see. This is nothing. We will soon show you some snow. Meanwhile the anaesthetist was circling me like a bird of prey waiting to pounce on its toothsome morsel. I smiled to myself and hummed 'Dhundo dhundo re sajana dhundo more kan ka bala'. I amuse myself with this jaunty ditty each time an anaesthetist or phlebotomist goes on a hunt for a vein to inject into or draw blood from. Since chemotherapy, my veins which used to offer themselves generously to phlebotomists at the first tap of their fingers, had buried themselves somewhere deep.

The anaesthetist finally found a vein in my ankle and soon I was seeing the promised snow. The first question I asked Dr Jagannath when I came to was, 'Which way did you make the cut? Vertical or horizontal?' He said, 'Neither. I went diagonal. But we had a difficult time getting enough skin flap to cover the wound for suturing.'

The next morning one of Dr Jagannath's team came on his round and told me I should start physiotherapy exercises right away. I was to stand against the wall and raise my left arm to touch the wall over my head. No problem. Here goes. Later, as I was having a large tray of breakfast, Dr Jagannath walked in. 'What? Eating already?' he said. I chirped, 'Not just eating. Started physio exercises too.' Dr Jagannath went pale in the face, summoned his assistant, the one who had ordered exercises and said, 'You were at the operation. You saw how delicate the sutures are. You want them to rip open?' The assistant smiled sheepishly. Dr Jagannath wagged his finger at me, 'No exercises till I say so.'

When my wound stopped requiring dressing, Dr Smruti said, 'Time for radiation.' At the Hinduja Hospital oncology department headed by Dr Asha Kapadia, Dr Kannan explained the procedure and made markings on my chest. When I, accompanied by Girish, arrived for the first day's radiation—there were going to be thirty such—I was surprised to see people who had gone in before me, come out smiling broadly. Was there a Mad Hatter's tea party going on in there I wondered. My dose lasted a minute and I think I too came out smiling. I realized then that this was simply a sign of the sense of fellowship we shared. Also of the sudden flash in which you thought more intensely than ever before that life was beautiful.

Cancer confirmed my implicit belief in the random theory. I had carried a cancer in my body for twelve years or at least ten. It was difficult to tell. Dr Jagannath had said to me, 'How did an educated lady like you not see what this was?' There was no point telling him that my gynaec had assured me I had fibroids, if I wanted to convince him that I was not a stark, raving idiot. The random thing here was that my criminal negligence of what was happening in my body had not been punished. As evidence of the randomness with which people go down or stay up, my cancer was slow-growing. By the time the radical mastectomy was done, it had affected only one of the ten lymph nodes that were taken out and there were no secondaries. Had I been a believer, I'd have attributed this to the grace of god. But why then was similar grace not shown to the young boy who was with us in the radiation ante-chamber for two weeks and then not?

I received almost 80 per cent of my hospital costs from my mediclaim policy, so I called Ruby Dharamsey, my ex-colleague from Glaxo, to thank her profusely. After I left Glaxo she had reminded me that I was no longer covered by the company's health scheme and I should immediately invest in a mediclaim policy. Ruby knew one reminder was not enough for me to act. So she had kept calling me once every few weeks. Problem was that I hated forms. I still do. They bring me out in hives. And applying for anything in India calls for forms in triplicate.

Chance entered as a player exactly when it was needed. It came in the shape of the tall and elegant Anuya Purohit. She was one of the walkers in Shivaji Park with whom I exchanged a smile and a wave every morning. She had stopped me once and asked if she could drop in to see me. It turned out she was an insurance agent and wanted to sell me a policy. I almost flew out of my chair to hug her. Do you do mediclaim, I asked. Yes of course, she said. You fill all the forms, I asked. Yes, of course, she said. You will enter the Yogakshema building and deal with the clerks there? Yes of course she said. I gave her tea and biscuits, and bought a mediclaim policy. That was ten years before the cancer. The policy had grown fat on my annual premiums in the interim. Now it was pay time.

Another chance took care of the cancer drug bills that followed and had to be paid through the nose. Renuka and Girish laugh at what had once been my idea of a comfortable cushion in the bank. Five thousand rupees. Life had not been quite hand-to-mouth later. I breathed easy with a sum fluctuating between twenty-five and thirty thousand in my savings account. Renuka and Girish were always there as back-up support, but they respected my need to be independent. On thirty thousand as a cushion for cancer drugs?

Bachi Karkaria was my saviour. When she was with the Times, she had asked me to write for the *Sunday Review*. When she moved to *Mid-Day* she said you can't write for a paper I have left. Come to *Mid-Day*. So I moved my column to *Mid-Day*. She left *Mid-Day* around the time of my cancer. I had no income while I was going through cancer therapy. Now I needed a fixed income to pay my drug bills. Meenal Baghel had been Bachi's colleague in *Mid-Day*. She was appointed editor of *Mumbai Mirror*, the new tabloid in the TOI stable. She, urged by Bachi no doubt, asked me to write a column for the paper. I agreed with the greatest alacrity. I started as soon as cancer therapy was over and I am still there, eleven years on, holding up culture at the back of the paper.

But before the column, during the months that I was protecting myself from infections, I wrote my second novel, *Tya Varshi*. Shri Pu Bhagwat, founder of the prestigious Mouj Prakashan, was one of those rare editors who scouted for and persuaded writers to write. When I wrote my first novel *Rita Welinkar*, I had sent the manuscript to Granthali, a publisher's collective full of our friends supposedly on the lookout for new writers. For two years there had been no word from them, neither a yes nor a no. Shri Pu Bhagwat called me one day and said, 'I hear you've written a novel.'

'Yes I have.'

'So where is it?'

'Granthali is sitting on it.'

'Are they publishing it?'

'I don't know.'

'Would you mind letting me have a look at it?'

'Of course. I mean most certainly. I mean gosh.' I was falling over myself to show how honoured I felt at the request. I sent him a copy of the manuscript. Within a week he called to say, 'We would like to publish this.'

Five years later he decided a decent amount of time had elapsed for me to start thinking of my next novel. He called. 'I hope you're working on your next novel.'

'No.'

'You should be.'

'Yes, I should be.'

'So let me know when it's ready.'

A novel was indeed taking shape in my head. But a publisher needs something more substantial than an idea in the head. Over the next few years, the novel was completed. In my head. It had to spill on to paper now. But where was the time? The question worked like Ali Baba's open sesame command. Suddenly I had time, although not quite as expected. I was about to spend nine months doing nothing other than recovering from cancer. There was time enough and more for writing my novel. I wrote like a fiend. At the end of nine months, I delivered. I had done it. I had written my second novel. Shri Pu Bhagwat proofread it personally, twice over, to bring it to Mouj's zero-error standards although he was not at all well. As it happened, *Tya Varshi* was the last work he looked at. He died in August 2007. The novel came out in March 2008.

Vijay Tendulkar was keen to read it. Arun and I had once run into him near Shivaji Park and he had asked what I was writing. I mentioned the script I was working on for Arun. He shook his head and said pointedly, 'I'm asking about what you are writing for yourself.' Every time I ran into him after that, he would ask, 'What's happening to that novel of yours?' And I would say, 'It's happening.' And he would say, 'I want to read it.' And I would say, 'I'll bring you the first copy hot from the oven.'

He came over during my cancer therapy and I told him the novel was finally underway. He had come, not for a chat, but to give me a cheque for twenty-five thousand rupees. He said it was my share as translator of the royalty he was paid for the successful run of *Sakharam Binder* in New York. Knowing Tendulkar, I think that was also a way of contributing to my cure.

When *Tya Varshi* came out, Tendulkar was in hospital with myasthenia gravis. He was in no state even to hold the copy I sent him, leave alone read it. He died in May of that year.

Cancer therapy over, I was back to normal life. The only

changes in my daily routine were the very expensive six-monthly injections I had to take to counteract the adverse effect on bone mass of Arimidex, the drug I had been prescribed; and the six-monthly tests I underwent to make sure my cancer which had been quelled, remained quelled. The injections stopped after five years when the drug was changed for another. The tests stopped after ten. I was now officially a survivor. By I, I mean my body. Although there's a strong rumour that a positive attitude helps recovery, I have seen many with indomitable spirits go down. When death comes, newspapers love to say 'she succumbed after a long fight against cancer' but that's because nobody wants to admit that the human will is powerless against the human body. Dr P. Jagannath once said to me, the body is a mystery and a miracle. It was this mystery, this miracle that fascinated me as I went through those years of understanding my body in every way possible. I got to know its bones, its abdominal and pelvic region, its liver function, the beat of its heart and the sounds of its digestive system. Then I read Siddhartha Mukherjee's *The Emperor of All Maladies* which told me how the drugs that helped kill the cancer in me had been evolved over centuries of speculation, experiment, failure, more questions, more speculation, more experiment, a small success here or there and so on. The history is long, the fight has been unequal. But it is this human spirit, courageous and unconquerable in its quest for knowledge, working over centuries, and not some nebulous positive attitude, that has aided my body to come through.

27. Cataracts

Dr Nisheeta Agarwala had told me before I was diagnosed with cancer that I had cataracts in both eyes and they called for early removal. In the old days doctors waited for cataracts to 'ripen' before taking them out. But now the procedure was different. It involved using a high-frequency ultrasound device to pulverize the cloudy lens causing dimmed vision and removing the small pieces by suction. Dr Agarwala used the analogy of raw and ripe mangoes to explain the procedure. The analogy was bang on. I saw instantly that a raw mango would lend itself perfectly to pulverizing while a ripe mango would turn into a mess.

When the cancer was detected, what one part of the body, viz eyes, required, was contraindicated by what another part of the body, viz the breast needed. The month already decided for my cataracts to come out had been February 2005. But with chemotherapy on, Dr Agarwala decided at least the one in my good eye had to come out right away. I told her Dr Smruti had advised against it. Dr Agarwala called her. 'I understand you are worried about infections,' she began. It was going to be interesting hearing two doctors negotiate a treaty over my body. 'But let me assure you, we will take the greatest care of the patient. We will make sure she remains free of infections while she is with us. But she has to have at least one cataract out. Now.' Dr Smruti gave in.

Usha had had her cataracts removed just before I did and she had told me it was a breeze. With me, it was more like a storm. This was the report I emailed to friends describing my experience.

30th December 2004: New Year, New Eye

The two chemo drugs I am being administered appear to be made for me. One causes water retention that does no good for my glaucoma. The other contains steroids, which aggravate cataracts. My cataracts were due out next February anyway. That was the plan before the unplanned cancer happened. Now, with my friendly chemo drugs, the cataract operation became truly urgent. My wonderful surgeon Dr Nisheeta Agarwala, decided to do the left eye first because that's my good eye. The right lost half its vision five years ago thanks to my then opthalmologist, who had merrily allowed the glaucoma to go undetected.

Everybody who had ever had a cataract operation had told me it's hardly an operation at all—just a 15-minute diversion in your regular life. All that the doctor does is benumb your eyes, incise, pulverise, insert lens, cover with pad and send you home, all roadblocks in your vision removed for ever. Cool.

But not so cool, as it happened, in my case. If you have glaucoma, your pupils don't dilate sufficiently to allow the surgeon free entry into the eye. Or at least mine didn't. So before I knew what was happening, oxygen tubes were shoved into my nose, I was hooked up to a drip, attached to a heart monitor—the kind that goes ee-oo-ee-oo when all is well and falls silent (visual: flat line) when all is over—and a blood pressure belt. All this because my recalcitrant pupils had left no choice for the surgeon but to use what are called iris hooks. I'm going to look this up on the net, but I have a vague notion that the hooks hold the iris back and give the surgeon a clear view of what she's doing.

The next 45 minutes were full of strange images and sounds. Up above me, two iridiscent halves of an oblong kept forming and dissolving, sometimes acquiring halos of orange and violet. Gently nudging them out once in a while was a dome of the finest lace which then gave place to white light till we were back again to the oblong halves engaged in their floating pas de deux. The visuals were accompanied by sound effects that came from the incessant ee-oo-ee-oo of the heart machine, the whooshing of air rushing in and out of the blood pressure belt and the quiet murmur of human voices—my surgeon explaining to her assistants what she was doing to my eye.

Then suddenly there was a series of crunching sounds with a talking machine commenting on the proceedings in a curt code language. When it comes to the crunch, the cataract is done for. The doctor declared the operation completely successful.

They sent me home four hours later. I felt fine—no pain, just a slight discomfort in the left eye. But the world looked at me askance. Even amongst the weird appearances one observes in hospitals, mine was a spectacular presence. My scarf-covered head (hair chemoed out of existence!), green-patched eye and masked nose and mouth (to deflect infections), declared me a major war victim at the least, if not an alien.

As I stepped out of the lift and advanced towards an empty seat in the lobby to wait for papers to be processed, a nine-year-old boy sitting in the seat next to mine, scampered away in dread, casting alarmed backward glances at me all the way to his mother's lap. His younger brother did exactly the opposite. Obviously endowed with an enquiring mind, he left his mother's lap to clamber into the seat his brother had vacated, and proceeded to examine me from top to toe with unblinking interest. Where had this creature sprung from? Was I an earthling at all? This was clearly the question he was seeking an answer to. I am not entirely certain what conclusion he arrived at; but he must have decided I was more harmless than I looked. For, after a few minutes of intense inspection, he lost interest in me and ran off to beat up his older brother.

It feels good to look at the world with at least one new eye. No longer are distant objects accompanied by ghost images. Clarity has replaced confusion. This is the first gift 2005 has brought me. How can I not feel gratitude towards my highly skilled surgeon and the wonders of modern medicine?

28. Time, Space, Work

Cancer is a home-grown disease. You can hold neither germ nor virus responsible for it. You may be as disciplined and moderate in your habits as a yogi, but eating spinach every day doesn't stop your cells from deciding one day to start misbehaving. When I was diagnosed with cancer, a childhood friend of Shantaram's, V.B. Kulkarni, said it's a lifestyle disease. He ticked off all the wrong things he presumed I had been, but shouldn't have been doing if I hadn't wanted to have cancer. I listened to his list of don'ts patiently because he was obviously concerned about me. Then I assured him I hadn't been doing any of them. I hadn't been an eater of red meat or junk food, my diet had been moderate, full of vegetables, salads, fruit and nuts and I had walked every morning for an hour. Stumped, he said, 'Then why did you get cancer?'

Believers in random theory don't ask 'Why?' They ask 'Why not?'

The freedom I had won in 2000 after Arun moved out had given a boost to my writing. Cancer did not interrupt it. The years following 2000 told me how important it was for a woman writer to have a room of her own and time to herself if she was to be productive. Let me correct that. Let me say a woman writer like me who is not driven enough and has not fought for her rights as hard as a committed feminist should against intractable husbands. I know writers who have had much less space and fewer privileges than me and done large amounts of writing of amazing quality. But there are inadequacies of the spirit as there are of the body. Before Arun moved out I did as much as my spirit would allow. Even after he left, I continued to work with him but as an independent script-writer. I loved writing scripts and he paid me for my work as he had always done. In 2001, I scripted *Hathi ka Anda*, a children's film for him. In 2002, I scripted *Narayan Gangaram Surve*. It is a script I am particularly proud of for its unusual form. In the same year I translated the Marathi classic *Dhag* by Uddhav Shelke for Mini Krishnan who was working with Macmillans at the time. It came out in 2002, but for reasons beyond my control, did not make it to the bookshops. It went straight into the publisher's godown. Three years later I rescued hundred copies of it for myself, buying them at half price, before the entire print run got pulped. It had a miraculous rebirth as *Kautik on Embers* with Speaking Tiger in 2017. In 2003, I translated Durga Khote's autobiography *Mi Durga Khote* (*I, Durga Khote*) also for Mini Krishnan who had moved from Macmillans to Oxford University Press (OUP). It came out in 2006. In 2005, the year of my cancer, I wrote *Tya Varshi*. In 2007, I began translating Prabhakar Barwe's essays, *Kora Canvas* for Jesal Thacker's Bodhana. I completed the job, one of the most difficult I have ever undertaken, in 2008. The translation was published five years later as *The Blank Canvas*. In 2009, Anuradha Parikh, director of the Mohile Parikh Centre for Visual Arts, said she would like to host a reading and discussion of *Tya Varshi* and could I find a discussant. I knew of only one person who could fill the bill for such an event. This person had to read the book in Marathi, know something about Mumbai's visual arts scene which was central to it, be able to look at the book critically as a piece of fiction and be able to discuss it with me in English. That person was Jerry Pinto. I felt I knew him well enough to make a claim on his time. He obliged and the evening was a success.

After that, Jerry entered my life as a zealous missionary, seeding ideas for books and midwifing them. This autobiography (of sorts) comes from his persistent persuasion that I have a story to tell. I was translating Makarand Sathe's remarkable novel *Achyut Athavale Ani Athavan* at the time. As consultant to Penguin, Jerry took over the completed translation, edited it and sent it off to the publisher with a strong recommendation. Meanwhile, like Shri Pu Bhagwat had done with the writing of the original novel, he nagged me to translate *Tya Varshi*. I did, and it was published in 2013 as *Crowfall* (Jerry's title). A year earlier Penguin had published Makarand's novel as *The Man Who Tried to Remember*. In 2011, Niyogi Books published the book I had edited on Satyadev Dubey's fifty years in theatre. In 2014, OUP published my book *The Theatre of Veenapani Chawla: Theory, Practice, Performance*. They also published Priya Adarkar's and my joint translation of *Majha Pravas: Adventures of a Brahmin Priest* in the same year. In 2014, I translated from English into Marathi, one of the most challenging novels I had ever dared to engage with—Jerry Pinto's harrowing but heartbreakingly funny award-winning novel *Em and the Big Hoom*. Popular Prakashan published the translation in 2015. I spent all of 2015 editing *The Scenes We Made: An Oral History of Experimental Theatre in Mumbai*. Speaking Tiger published it the same year.

My new year's resolution for 2015 had been to translate Lakshmibai Tilak's classic 1934 autobiography *Smritichitre*

(Pictures from Memory). I had vowed to do this decades ago but had not found the time for it. It was a 458-page book that would demand many months of concentrated work. I began translating it on 30 January and completed the first draft in October. It was published by Speaking Tiger in 2017.

Time flew. For ten years after cancer surgery and therapy, I had done my six-monthly tests regularly—lung X-Ray, mammogram, ultrasound of abdomen and pelvic region and bone density. I had seen Dr Smruti with all-clear reports after each round of tests. But meanwhile other things had been happening to the body. In 2008 I had developed a tremor in the voice which made me sound like Nani, the old woman that Vijaya Mehta, the doyenne of Marathi theatre, had created in Jaywant Dalvi's *Sandhya Chhaya* (Evening Shadows). After that, every actor who played a woman of sixty-plus had quivered and quavered through her lines. My problem was not only a quaking voice, but of a voice that came and went within a single sentence. It was like the tali and khali in tabla, the first beat stressed and indicated by a clap, the second unstressed and indicated by a wave of the hand.

I found it unacceptable to live with a bodily impairment without trying to discover its cause. I had had enough of doctors. So I satisfied myself with my own explanation. My condition was the result of a malfunctioning epiglottis. The epiglottis is a traffic policeman which functions in two ways. It stands up to direct food into the windpipe and lies down to allow breath to flow into the windpipe. It was doing well for food; but when it came to breath it was stubbornly refusing to lie down properly with the result that the flow of air was allowed or blocked erratically. Happy with this explanation I had been croaking and glugging my way through speech for seven years.

In 2011, my right hand sprang a tremor. The tremor would come on when I wrote, brushed my teeth and served myself from a saucepan. I told myself it was time I saw Dr Medhekar. I told myself I should also see Dr Smruti. Perhaps eleven years after surgery and ten-and-a-half after the last day of radiation, she might want to take me off Tamoxifen, the standard cancer drug she had put me on after Arimidex was stopped. In short, I had to let doctors into my life again.

29. And Now the Brain

When we were growing up there were only three kinds of brain. There was the bright brain, the dull brain and the off-kilter brain. You could tell the three brains apart without Magnetic Resonance Imaging. The bright brain occupied the top half of the class grades. The topmost got called a genius or bookworm depending on the speaker's perspective. The dull brain occupied the lower half of the class grades, the lowest being called a dunce and often made to wear a conical cap and sent around the school to announce the fact to the world. The off-kilter brain caused you to talk to yourself or stare into space or throw things around. You were then called mad. Now things are not so clear. The brain has come into its own. It has thrown up a variety of interesting conditions that cannot be labelled with single instantly digestible words.

At school I was a bright brain. It got me into the top five ranks in class. My memory was shaky but my native intelligence made up for it. Things worked pretty well for me because examination questions at school required shortish answers. The fact that I was a slow writer did not matter too much then. It did at university where answers to examination questions were long, complexly argued essays and I could never complete a paper. My grades slipped. I became a middling performer. Mr Nicol knew why I was a slow eater and he set the problem right. But who knew why I was a slow writer? There was no Mr Nicol to help my hand along. I now wonder, did I have, do I still have, borderline disgraphia? Of the hundred-odd issues listed as manifestations of the condition, at least one seems to apply to me: has trouble getting ideas down on paper quickly. What I am saying is, the brain is not what it used to be.

When my voice and hand began to tremble I had assumed I would have to live with it. Sindhu Maushi's hand used to tremble. Her doctor had called it 'essential tremor'. She had lived with it till she was eighty, and when she died it was not on account of a trembling hand. But citing aunts does not convince friends who care for you. Bachi insisted on taking me to an ENT specialist who had diagnosed her son's problem accurately when no amount of poking and prodding had helped others to arrive at the answer. This wizard of a doctor made me say ahhh and ooh into his machine and informed me there was nothing wrong with my vocal chords. Then why was I croaking? Perhaps it had to do with other parts of the vocal mechanism? The larynx for example? I had gathered from the net that essential tremors affected the larynx too. But the doctor said nothing about the larynx which lay squarely within his field of specialization. Instead he charged into a field leagues away, pronouncing the tremor in my voice as an early sign of Parkinsons. He obliged me further by suggesting the name of a busy, super-duper neurologist whom I should see promptly and also recommended a speech therapist in Opera House who would help me speak properly again.

Bachi was thoroughly dismayed by the doctor's diagnosis. What will you do now she asked. Ignore him I said, confident that my tremors were not connected with any stage of Parkinsons, early or late. I had seen Parkinsons at close quarters.

Usha's mother had suffered from it. I had looked after her when Usha was away on one of Shantaram's foreign postings. Later, Usha herself was diagnosed with it. I had watched its progress in her till the day she went. It was not a pretty condition.

My condition was easy to deal with. Voice shakes? Stop accepting invitations to seminars. What a relief it was to have a valid excuse not to attend them. I had rarely gained anything of value from the ones I had attended. Putting my two bits into the machine had never appealed to me. For somebody who loves language, it is painful to hear academics binge on words like negotiate, problematize, navigate, inscribe, predicate, hegemonize, subaltern and site. Worthy words all, but without any resonance of sound or sense. Does that make me anti-intellectual? No. It makes me anti a certain stripe of academic. I believe that those who speak and write this turgid jargon use it as easy currency for an exchange of ready-made positions. If intellectual means thinking independently, struggling to find words to express thought and coming up with fresh formulations to stimulate further thinking, then the people I had heard in seminars weren't it. Excuse me if I don't listen I would say and doze off, dreaming of resonant words like crepuscular, chiaroscuro, ephemeral, gambol, diaphanous, gossamer, insouciance, mellifluous, palimpsest… One could go on forever. The riches of the English tongue are infinite.

The Sokal affair had also confirmed that jargon provided easy cover for charlatans. What Alan Sokal had submitted to *Social Text* was, in his own words, 'a pastiche of left-wing cant, fawning references, grandiose quotations, and outright nonsense'. The grand old men of postmodernism presiding over the prestigious *Social Text*, had failed to see through it.

But I have strayed. Give me one of my bugbears and I stray.

Let me return then to my voice from whose tremors I took off. I would have gone on living with them as I had done for seven years had a little pain and swelling on my right foot not taken me, at Jabeen's urging, to see Dr Medhekar. He looked at the foot and knew what it was. Within a week of his medication, the pain, swelling and redness had vanished. But while I was there, I mentioned my tremors. He ordered a battery of blood and urine tests, a chest X-Ray, ultrasound of the abdomen and pelvic region and one last test that I had never been through before—an MRI.

The blood test first. After chemotherapy, every episode of bloodletting had become a novel experience. This is how it went this time. I am in the chair in Dr Phadke's Pathological Laboratory, five minutes' walk away from my house. My right arm is extended. 'The other one please,' says the phlebotomist, grabbing my left arm. 'No. That's my operated side. No pricks allowed there.'

The phlebotomist nods sympathetically. She brings out her equipment.

'You'll need a finer needle. My veins are difficult to get at.'

The phlebotomist nods—she is humouring the elderly woman who thinks she knows her veins—and proceeds with her normal equipment. I sigh and wait for the inevitable. 'Dhundo dhundo re saajana dhundo' begins in my head. The phlebotomist calls for assistance. Now there are two of them, both tapping the crook of my arm turn by turn. I tell them the crook of the arm is the wrong place to look. It's the back of the hand they want. But the girls are optimistic. They slip the needle in. Turn it around. Remove it. Slip it in again. 'Oh dear,' says the senior girl. 'Can't find the vein.' With remarkable restraint I don't say I told you so. She doesn't need to tell me to turn my hand palm down to offer her more promising ground.

'Ah, got it,' she enthuses. She pulls the plunger which is attached to the collecting vial. 'Is it coming?' she asks. Her companion who stands behind her says no. The girl pulls out the needle and plunges it elsewhere. Now her assistant is squatting on the floor with the vial to let gravity aid blood flow.

'Is it coming?'

'Not a drop,' says the squatting girl dispiritedly. A third colleague, an experienced older woman, steps up. She holds my wrist tight and begins to squeeze and unsqueeze it like the bulb horn of an old truck.

'Now?'

'It's coming. Don't stop,' the girl on the floor shouts. Pump pump pump goes the bulb squeezer with enhanced brio.

'It's rushing. Go on,' cheers the floor squatter.

Moments later, she springs up, all excitement. She holds up the vial for all to see. 'That's enough,' says the experienced woman, weary with effort. Triumph all round.

'Did it hurt?' asks the first girl while the third sticks little plaster squares on four spots, two in the crook of my arm and two on the back of the hand. One of these spots is already swollen and blue. 'Put ice on it when you get home,' says the senior woman, looking genuinely contrite. I pat her on the shoulder comfortingly and walk out. After all, the recalcitrant veins are mine. She needs sympathy for having had to deal with them.

A couple of days later, I am at Lilavati Hospital for the ultrasound. Renuka is with me. Normally Girish is, but he's out of the country. Renuka is a celebrity. People want to talk to her, sit beside her, have pictures taken with her. I walk into the sonography room. The technician enters, all smiles.

'Is that your daughter?'

'Yes.'

'I love her work.'

'Thank you.'

And while this exchange is going on, the young woman has slipped the probe up my rectum.

'I think you're in the wrong place,' I say.

'No no, don't worry. It's okay.'

'Actually it's not okay. Because, quite honestly, you are in my rectum. You'll see for yourself if you look under the sheet.' She lifts the sheet, peers in and apologizes. Not too profusely. It's just a question of one orifice in place of another.

The MRI is a totally new experience. Here the doctor in charge looks very grave. He goes through my blood reports with a furrowed brow. He does not bill us before the procedure. 'We might have to inject a dye. That'll cost more than a simple MRI.'

I change. I am led into the room dominated by a giant machine. I am given outsize earmuffs and strapped down on the moving plate that transports me into the innards of the machine. There's nothing to see there so I close my eyes. Soon sounds of infinite variety pierce through my earmuffs. There's a hammering and a thudding, a screeching and a clackety-clack, a foghorn, a siren, a whooshing and a hooting. When the sounds stop, you think it is over. But it is not. Another round begins and then another, all set to the same hypnotic rhythm.

I come out of the tunnel laughing. I say appreciatively to the assistant technician who is standing beside the machine, 'That's quite an orchestra you have there.' The man is deeply offended. 'Go anywhere in Bombay madam,' he scolds me, 'and you'll find MRI machines making the same sounds.' Thus chastised, I wipe the laughter off my face and return soberly to my clothes.

The MRI report when it comes says, 'Non specific white matter lesions in the pons most likely chronic ischaemic lesions.' Does that worry me? No. Chronic is a reassuring term. It means it's been there a long time. I've lived with it. Acute is the chap to fear. This is probably not anywhere near the way Dr Medhekar sees the problem. But he too doesn't appear unduly worried. In any case, he doesn't say these are early signs of Parkinsons. SO I WAS RIGHT, MR ENT SPECIALIST!

I had thought naively that Dr Smruti would say, 'Is it ten years already? Stop Tamoxifen. You don't need it now.' She did say that, but she also said, have a CA 25 blood test, a mammogram and an ultrasound of the abdomen and pelvic region done. I had already had the last one done for Dr Medhekar. So now it was just the mammogram, my eleventh. And this is how it went.

I have an appointment at a well-known hospital practically within walking distance from my home. I will not take its name because of what followed. After a wait of fifteen minutes, which is nothing by hospital standards, I am ushered into the room where the formidable mammography unit stands. Hello friend I say mentally. It is not a friend. There is no give-and-take between this machine and breasts. Your breasts must accommodate themselves to it. Your breasts are curved, as they are meant to be. The machine wants them to be flat. It is built to achieve what it wants. The technician shoves you right up against it to get your breast to sit on a cold plate. Then an upper plate, seemingly forged from some ten tonnes of pig iron, descends like a guillotine on it, simultaneously squeezing it and producing a traumatized yell out of you. When the upper plate is lifted you look down at yourself expecting to see carpaccio of breast. But that's not the end of it. Other angled views of the distressed body part are required, for which the machine's demand is for a front-looking breast to be twisted into a sideways glancing one. This involves your standing on tiptoe while your right shoulder blade is thrust forward and the left shoulder blade is wrenched back, giving the machine an uninterrupted view of your breast in profile. When you have achieved perfection in this position, you are ordered to freeze. The technician takes a picture, isn't satisfied, twists-shoves-pulls again, clicks, sighs, grunts and lets you go. I stumble out, smiling weakly for the benefit of the line of patients waiting in the hall. They should not think I have come out of a torture chamber. No sir. See, I am alive!

The breast, it would seem, is so complex a collection of tissues, that one assault on it doesn't make it yield its secrets. There has to be a second—the digital mammogram. An assistant technician prepares me for it. Topless now with my single breast gelled, I wait for the doctor to arrive. The assistant does her own little bit of practice on me, then sits in the corner. The door will swing open any minute now and a white-coated doctor will walk in. There will be stroking of the breast this way and that with a cold thingy, peering into the monitor, this way and that again, then across and up and down. And you're done. Twenty minutes. Maybe twenty-two-and-a-half max and you are home for lunch.

The room is small. There is a computer in the corner and the digital recorder of my breast beside me. Up above is an electric bulb enclosed in a semi-circular frosted glass shell. And there is a clock. Or is there? Is there not a clock? Then what is this ticking I hear in the silence of the room? The clock in my head? This clock, whether on the wall or in the head, says fifteen minutes have passed since I lay down splayed on this table which, under the sheet, is undoubtedly covered in brown rexine. My right arm is raised over my head to give the still absent doctor free play over my breast. Garbled lines from the 'Love Song of J. Alfred Prufrock' begin to run around in my head in harmony with the ticking of the clock: 'When the evening is spread out against the sky / Under a crisp white sheet I lie / Like a patient etherised upon a table.'

The clock says it is twenty minutes. There is, of this I am now certain, a clock on the wall. No doctor has thus far entered. Should I get up and walk out? Or close my eyes to the clock and think twenty minutes is nothing in the eternity of time? No that's dangerous. I must keep awake and let my anger grow so it comes to a point where I simply get up and go without second thought.

I lie awake, my eyes fixed on the only thing within direct sight, the frosted light on the ceiling. I begin to feel like Rip Van Winkle. My upstretched arm, which I cannot lower because my breast is covered in gel, has gone numb. Am I growing a long beard? No. I am a woman. If I am a woman and can't be Rip Van Winkle, who am I? What am I? Kohum? I am that most pathetic creature, Gregor Samsa, lying on my back, turned into a beetle. Less pathetically, more usefully, I am a cabbage that's gone dead in its bed. 'The time has come the Walrus said to talk of many things: / Of shoes—and ships—and sealing-wax— / Of cabbages—and kings—' That is not me. Bracketed with kings? You must be joking. I am neither Rip Van Winkle nor a cabbage. I insist I am a human. Maybe old. Decidedly old. Growing older by the minute. 'I grow old ...I grow old / Dare I tell the clock to hold? / Can I hope the doctor will come and go / Talking of Michaelangelo? / Will I say shut up, attend? / Or will I dare and will I dare /

To turn my back, descend the stair / With this bald patch in the middle of my hair?'

It is the first time I have experienced solitary confinement. I twist my head on the pillow and say to the assistant sitting in the corner, I'm leaving. I'm going to put on my clothes and leave. The waiting room is where we are supposed to wait. I'll wait there. Call me when the doctor decides to come. Just a minute says the assistant and disappears. The problem with law-abiding citizens, among whom I count myself, is that they submit to the system, even when the system is an absence of a system. The student said just a minute. She's only twenty or thereabouts. I am fifty-six years older. Yet I stay pinned to the couch waiting for that promised minute to pass. It does, then turns into more minutes which turn into…

When the doctor finally does appear, I have waited forty-five minutes in all, on my back with my arm stretched above my head. Is she saying sorry? Is she looking apologetic? No. She is only looking brusquely professional. In her hands I am finally convinced I am a cabbage, but one which must have enough understanding of the human language to obey when told curtly to turn this way and that. Cabbages shouldn't expect niceties.

Outside, the first lot of waiting patients has given way to the next. As I leave the room, my stomach growling for lunch, the first technician of the mammogram machine grabs me and whispers in my ear, 'Please wait. The doctor isn't happy with the X-ray mammogram.'

I want to scream. Instead I whimper. Half an hour later a technician rebeckons me into the mammography room. The first technician is with her. The second goes through all the earlier motions, explaining each to the first who, it turns out, is a trainee. Why was she let loose on me? There's not much difference between the mauling methods of the second technician and the trainee. But apparently the second one gets it right. The doctor is satisfied. I leave the hospital three hours after I entered, a severely reduced human being. The report, when it comes, says inter alia, 'Distortion at nine and ten o'clock in the right breast.' That is what they have done. They have distorted the only breast I have of the two I came into the world with.

30. Today

Today my voice has suddenly decided to do my bidding. The epiglottis is behaving itself. I am back in the early eighties when Renuka, then in junior college at St Xaviers, and I on my Saturday stint at *Femina* putting Literatti to bed, would meet at end of day, eat somewhere and take the train from Churchgate to Andheri for an hour of music under the tutelage of the gentle, sweet-voiced Pandit Jal Balaporia of the Gwalior gharana. My voice was fine then, shallow, but tuneful; Renuka's more robust. It was a joy to blend mine with hers as we sang brilliantly composed Gwalior bandishes, ending with hot snacks that Jalsaab's wife, Roshantai, hospitably pressed upon us.

That voice has miraculously returned to me today, perhaps only for a brief while. I am overjoyed. I am bemusedly humming a song that haunts me. It is a Tukaram abhang sung by Pandit Kumar Gandharva. Kumarji sings it very softly in a voice that is almost childlike, accompanied by nothing more than a minimalistic beat on the mridanga and an occasional clink of cymbals. Tukaram says : 'Lord give me the gift of smallness / The ant is small, happy to eat grains of sugar. / Airavat the divine elephant is great / But must bear the prick of the spur / Floods uproot large trees / But the bulrush bends and lives / He who is big / Suffers agonies / Tuka says know then / To be smaller than small is best.'

The abhang sounds anachronistic in a world in which greatness is the goal. My beloved country wants to become the jagadguru, the spiritual leader of the world. Our prime minister's chest measures 56 inches, something that his devotees think indicates greatness. The proposed statue of Shivaji in the Arabian Sea off the coast of Mumbai is going to be taller than the Statue of Liberty. Our richest man lives in a twenty-six-storey house. A Pune builder has a fleet of twenty-five cars. Bigger, louder, better, more. Produce more. Sell more. Produce even more. Sell even more. You out there. Consume. Keep consuming. Throw out the old. Buy the new. Later, we can crash together if we must. But we'll recover. And with redoubled motivation produce, sell, consume, produce, sell, consume…

A man lay on the sands of a beach in Goa looking up at the sky. Another came by and said what are you doing? The man said, nothing. The other said why do you do nothing when you can do something? You have a boat. Go out and fish. Sell. Sell. Sell. Get a bigger boat. Then get a trawler. Out in the deep sea you can catch lobsters and king prawns. Export. First world countries pay millions of dollars for king prawns.

And then? asked the man still gazing at the sky.

Then? Then you can lie back and enjoy life.

The man turned his eyes briefly away from the sky to the questioner. So what am I doing now?

What does Tukaram's abhang mean in the context of our aspirations? Does the poet mean people should not achieve anything at all that is extraordinary or else they will suffer agonies? Or is he merely warning human beings against hubris, and recommending the virtue of humility?

Dada Sabnis of the dark, round, gentle face, forehead adorned with black ash, the mark of the Warkari, sang a Haripath abhang of Sant Dnyaneshwar to mark my father's untimely death from a massive heart attack barely eighteen months after he had moved bag and baggage from Bombay to his retirement home in Talegaon. Father had named his home Abhang in memory of Tukaram. The saint-poet had composed many abhangs sitting on Bhandara Hill which was visible in the distance from the picture window of Abhang's master bedroom. It was in this spacious room, with the westering sun bathing the stone-flagged floor in lemony light, that Dada Sabnis and his group had sung, 'Kunache he ghar / ha deha kunacha'. (To whom does this house belong? / And to whom this body?) The answer was self-evident to him. The human body or the house of the soul belonged to its creator. Neither body nor house were ours to claim. Dada Sabnis's faith was deep and uncomplicated. But the man whose death the abhang marked had been an atheist. He would have appreciated the poetry and the melody of Dnyaneshwar's abhang, but would have rejected outright the answer that its question implied. If pressed to answer, he would have said, 'The house belongs to my wife and me. The body belongs to me alone. When I am gone my wife will live in the house. My body will turn to ashes. No soul will rise from the ashes to join its maker. For there is no soul and there is no maker.'

I have inherited my materialism from Father, along with much else, including my love for literature and the arts. For me too, the human body when alive, houses all the intangibles that spell what is human—emotions, desires, passions, aspirations, ideas, creativity. But once it dies, they die with it. There is no such thing as a soul. This is not a depressing thought for me.

It is how it is. But the other is not a thought one can simply toss off either. Many fine minds have argued in favour of the soul and its continued existence after death. I have tested my beliefs against theirs and found that, at some stage, the word faith creeps into the argument. It is the concept of faith that I have a quarrel with. Faith does not strike me as a given without which you cannot live. Faith is a choice. The one who needs it, lives by it and for it. The one who doesn't gets by pretty well without. There is no reason why you cannot live in and for the here and now in the best way you know and be prepared to be done with it once life ends.

'Death be not proud, though some have called thee / Mighty and dreadfull, for, thou art not soe.' Donne is one of my favourite poets. I take him seriously. By personifying death, he turns it into an adversary, endowing it with the human sin of pride. Defeating death then becomes a moral mission. So how do you kill it? By comparing it to sleep which is a temporary shut-eye. 'One short sleepe past, wee wake eternally, / And death shall be no more; death, thou shalt die.' Donne was a poet of conceits. To me this too is a conceit, no different metaphysically than the flea which sucks the blood of two lovers, 'And pampered, swells with one blood made of two'. But I am moved by Donne, because I know faith has not come to him easily. He has had to struggle against stubborn reason and equally stubborn skepticism. He has had to plead, 'Batter my heart, three-person'd God, for you / As yet but knock, breathe, shine, and seek to mend; / That I may rise and stand, o'erthrow me, and bend / Your force to break, blow, burn, and make me new.' He is asking for a violent takeover. He must be forced to submit. Donne was after all the Dean of St Paul's.

I do not owe it to my profession to ask faith to thrust itself violently upon me. I do not wish to be ravished in order to believe what I do not need to believe. I do not wish to believe that I shall awake eternally in the Christian way, or be reborn in the Buddhist way or escape from multiple rebirths in the Hindu way. Reason, which has served me well enough all these years, faced its severest test when my father lay on his tragically premature deathbed. If there was ever a time in my life when I might have needed to seek god, this was it. Father was only fifty-six. He deserved the retired life he had worked so hard to earn. I clasped his hand in mine but did not clasp my two together. I looked down at him with profound grief but not once up at the sky where god supposedly lives. His hospital was near the railway station. The bell clanged, signalling the arrival of a train. '…it tolls for me,' he murmured with his lopsided smile. When he breathed his last, I howled. But I did not ask, 'God, why did you take him from us?' I knew. His heart gave way. He died. That was it.

'Do not go gentle into that good night,' says Dylan Thomas. 'Old age should burn and rave at close of day; / Rage, rage against the dying of the light.'

I am old but I would feel silly to rage against the dying of the light, against the natural order of things. I believe the law that applies to all things applies to human beings too—utpatti (creation), sthiti (maintenance), laya (dissolution). Beyond that, there is only one thing. A neat, clean, elegant full stop.

But before that, there is a life to be lived. How do I propose to live it? For as long as I can exercise my brain and limbs, for as long as they are under my control, I will walk, solve crosswords, read, listen to music, see plays, films and art shows. And I will write. Writing has been and is my life. At the moment there are three pots bubbling on the fire. Each has been shoved ruthlessly on to the back burner when a duty, social obligation or professional work has called. One pot holds a full-length play half-done, another holds a short play just begun, the third holds the fourth start of my third novel. The latter has changed during the last five years like the Ship of Theseus. Only one thing has remained constant so far in all versions. The form. It is a picaresque novel with shades of Moll Flanders. My heroine is low-caste but not a rogue. I know how it will begin. I also know how it will proceed. But I do not know how it will end. Novels, like life, must come to their ends organically. The only certainty that governs them is that they must end, one way or the other. Will my heroine live? Maybe. Will my heroine die? Maybe. Will the novel change form in the writing? Maybe.

My one regret about my own end is the one that Samuel Beckett has expressed so well: 'If I was dead, I wouldn't know I was dead. That's the only thing I have against death. I want to enjoy my death.' I am told that when the famed architect Charles Correa was dying, his doctor asked him, 'How do you feel?' And Charles said, 'Curious.' I too am curious about death. But how can curiosity be served if I am not present at my death? That's an insoluble conundrum.

Meanwhile I will continue to love life which is now acquiring new meanings as seen through my grandsons' eyes. I will also continue to demand from it as much as it can give. Comfortable shoes for instance.

31. Boots for My Bunions

I am at the local Bata shop. I am carrying with me a paper bag. In this bag lie a pair of old walking shoes. I've walked through their once tough soles. There is now only a layer of sock between my sole and the road. Walking is good for my glaucoma, good for my ischaemia, good for my brain and good, I am certain, for any cells that might be waiting to proliferate. I have chosen an hour of the day when the shop will be empty. Office workers will have returned to their desks after lunch and homemakers will have lain down for a brief snooze before hurrying to the kitchen to make hot snacks for the family's tea.

There is indeed nobody in the shop besides two sleepy assistants, one sleepy cashier and one alert boss. One assistant, urged on by a sharp look from the boss, stands before me asking if he can do something for me. *Do you think I'm here for a chinwag then?* I say that to myself. To him I say, 'I'm looking for walking shoes.' It is a clean, simple, direct statement. I allow it to sink in before adding, 'Like these.' I lift my old pair out of the paper bag and place it carefully on the floor between us. He looks down with what I suspect is incipient disdain. Before the look ripens, I nip it in the bud. 'These were bought from your shop two years ago. I don't suppose you'll have trouble finding me a new pair, same style, same size.'

I should know better. Business does not work that way; not

even a down-to-earth business like shoes. Not even Bata, which has been for all my lived life, the generic name for sensible shoes. In business, what was once made is never made again.

The shop assistant lifts the left-foot shoe gingerly and looks it up and down. 'I don't think we have anything like this,' he purrs and drops the shoe carelessly. It falls on its side. *You disrespecter of low things. You elitist. You ageist.* I bend down to straighten the shoe, giving him a look which I hope he interprets as disgust. 'But I'll show you what we do have,' he hastens to add and makes a move to go. I need him to understand that I'm not a dawdling shopper. I know what I want and that is all I want.

'Don't bother to show me all the shoes you have. Just the broad-toed ones.' He turns around looking puzzled. 'Shoes that are broad across the front? As in not narrow?' I say helpfully.

'Oh, you want broad-toed shoes?' I nod encouragingly. He goes away.

The boss is eyeing me curiously. 'I've seen you somewhere.'

'I come here once every two years for walking shoes.'

'No no. I mean somewhere else. Not here.'

'Do you see plays?'

'Plays? My father used to take me to Bhangwadi when I was a boy.'

'Do you go for classical music concerts?'

'You mean that ooh-aah stuff? I've heard…I don't remember his name. He sang bhajans. Not Anup Jalota. Old man. Gone.'

'Bharat Ratna Bhimsen Joshi?'

'That's the one. How did you know?'

I let that pass.

'Got it. I think I've seen your picture. Small one. It comes in some newspaper. Wait. I saw it this morning.' He whips out from under his counter two crumpled pages of *Mumbai Mirror*. He turns them over and slaps his hand triumphantly on one.

'There you are. That's you. Don't say it isn't.'

'I won't.'

'I knew I had seen you somewhere. What do you write? Sorry I don't read. I do the crossword on the next page.'

I do not have to answer that one. The assistant has returned with three boxes of shoes. My heart plummets. His is obviously jumping.

'Here madam. Latest. Best design.'

I can see almost without looking that every shoe he whips out of its box with a flourish is elegantly narrow at the toes.

'See,' I say, extending my left foot like Cinderella before the Prince's footmen. I point to the bunion. 'I need a shoe that accommodates that, without causing me excruciating pain.'

He looks at my foot with great sympathy and rises with a sigh. 'I think I have something for you.'

His look reminds me of the one I was given twenty years ago in Matheran. There is an unwritten rule. If you go to Matheran you must buy a pair of locally cobbled slippers and/or a walking stick. I followed rule number one. On our first day there, I asked around for a good cobbler. One came along whom I did not trust. He was cross-eyed. But I reproached myself for being ungenerous towards physically challenged people. I put my feet out one by one to be traced on sheets of paper. A day before we left, the cobbler returned with a pair of oversize, oddly shaped chappals in which you couldn't tell right from left. I was livid. 'Where's that paper on which you traced my feet?'

'Didn't bring,' he said, looking away.

'Look at my feet then. Look. Are they like those chappals?'

He continued to look away into the sunset, delicately refusing to look at my feet.

I pointed at the chappals and yelled again, 'Are my feet like that?' He turned then and murmured apologetically, 'Some people have them.' I nearly burst a vein. 'Don't tell me about some people. Do I have them? Here. Look.' He looked at my feet reluctantly and I saw his eyes fill with sympathy. I stared at him; then at the chappals. Then I cracked into helpless laughter. It is a story Arun loves to tell.

The shoe-shop assistant is away for a long time by which I mean a very long time. I get up and look at the shoes on show. There is a row on the top rack that is exactly what I am looking for. I beckon the other assistant who is doing nothing more useful than staring into the middle distance with open mouth. It takes a while to catch his attention. Finally I stand in front of him, cutting off his sight line. 'Those. I want any one of those shoes.'

'He's getting.' Apparently they don't tread on each other's turf.

'But can't you just take one down for me to see?'

'Men's.'

'You mean women can't wear them?'

'He's getting.' Having said that he wanders off and pretends to get busy opening and closing shoe boxes.

My assistant returns with another narrow-toed pair of shoes.

'I've found what I want. I want one of those.'

'Not for ladies.'

'Do they bite ladies?'

'Not like that madam. Not ladies' fashion.'

'I'm looking particularly for unfashionable shoes.'

'We don't have them in your size.'

I sigh and get up. Ta-ta Bata. It was nice knowing you. But the assistant springs up from his haunches faster than me. The boss has seen my empty hands and has given him another look.

'I'll see in our old stock.'

'That's where you'll find them. Old shoes is what I want.'

He trots off and soon returns with a pair that I recognize instantly as one made for bunions. And they aren't pink either. A sober navy blue. I slip my feet into them. Yes, slip, not squeeze. I lean back for a moment in my chair to savour the exquisite pleasure of a shoe that fits.

My morning walk the next day is a radically altered experience. I spring. I stride. I smile. Back home I unshoe and unsock my feet and wriggle my toes. They are happy toes, crooked though they may be. I observe them fondly. What are feet for anyway? They are for walking. Bearing human weight. These ones have been doing that for seventy-seven of my seventy-eight years. I began walking at one year old and haven't stopped at seventy-eight. Heaven's Gate...Seventy-eight...Bingo!

ALSO IN SPEAKING TIGER

THE ENGAGED OBSERVER
THE SELECTED WRITINGS OF SHANTA GOKHALE

Edited and with an Introduction by Jerry Pinto

'Gokhale's writing is informative and stimulating, and provides extensive glimpses of facets of life in modern India, that in turn is sustained by a multiplicity of traditions and cross fertilisations...More such writings are needed in order to set up conversations essential for the qualitative progress of humankind.' —*Tribune India*

For over four decades, Shanta Gokhale, one of contemporary India's finest minds, has entertained, informed and challenged us with her insightful, witty and forthright writing in both English and Marathi. With rare objectivity and consistency, Gokhale has tried to decode our unique social etiquette while subtly exposing our hypocrisies, and celebrated tradition-defying women while forcefully criticizing the patriarchal and misogynistic structures of society. Her essays on theatre not only illustrate its evolution in India, but also provide arresting portraits of theatre personalities such as Satyadev Dubey, Vijay Tendulkar and Veenapani Chawla. And her detailed yet accessible articles on Indian classical music are a delight to read.

In her short stories, she shapeshifts effortlessly from old men to teenage boys and college students. And finally, her two takes on Shakespeare show us how the Bard's ideas continue to remain relevant and, more importantly, how little attention he paid to his women characters.

Candid, intense and often humorous, *The Engaged Observer* is also an invaluable record of the social, political and cultural changes that have taken place in Bombay, Mumbai and beyond.

ALSO IN SPEAKING TIGER

SMRITICHITRE
THE MEMOIRS OF A SPIRITED WIFE

Lakshmibai Tilak

Translated by Shanta Gokhale

'Without any exaggeration, I can say that the kind of frankness and fearlessness displayed by Mahatma Gandhi in *My Experiments with Truth* is also the kind that can be found in Lakshmibai's writing.' —Acharya P.K. Atre, renowned playwright and poet

'Shanta Gokhale's translation of the book by Lakshmibai Tilak is the gold standard of autobiographical writing in India.' —Jerry Pinto

Lakshmibai Tilak was born in 1868 into a strict Maharashtrian Brahmin family in a village near Nashik. And at the age of eleven, she was married off to poet Narayan Waman Tilak, a man much older than her.

In *Smritichitre*, Lakshmibai candidly describes her complex relationship with her husband—their constant bickering over his disregard for material possessions, which quite often left them penniless, and his bouts of intense rage in these moments. But at the core of their relationship was their concern for society and the well-being of every human being, irrespective of caste, class or gender, and their unwavering devotion to each other. Equally touching is her recounting of his conversion to Christianity which led to a separation of five long years. After their reunion, she, too, was gradually disillusioned with orthodox Hindu customs and caste divisions, and converted to Christianity. After Narayan Tilak's death in 1919, she came into her own as a matron in a girls' hostel in Mumbai and later gathered enough courage to move to Karachi with her family.

When first published in Marathi in 1934, *Smritichitre* became an instant classic. Lakshmibai's honesty and her recounting of every difficulty she faced with unfailing humour make *Smritichitre* a memorable read. Shanta Gokhale's masterly translation of this classic is the only complete one available in English.